The Hands of Pianists

A Novel

Stephen Downes

Fomite
Burlington, VT

ISBN-13: 978-1-947917-73-6
Library of Congress Control Number: 2020945521
Fomite
58 Peru Street
Burlington, VT 05401
www.fomitepress.com

4/7/2021

About the Author

Stephen Downes is a Franco-Australian writer whose food-themed non-fiction has won international and national awards. *Last Meal*, one of his short stories, won the 2020 UK Fiction Factory's competition, and others have been longlisted and shortlisted in prestigious British contests.

Also by Stephen Downes

Wild Whores, Golden Soup and a Great Red's Farewell

Top Fifty Restaurants in Australia

Advanced Australian Fare

Paris on a Plate

Adagio for a Simple Clarinet

Blackie

Gut Reaction

A Lasting Record

I detest audiences — not in their individual
components, but *en masse* I detest audiences. I
think they're a force of evil. It seems to me rule
of mob law.

— Glenn Gould, pianist

AS I FEARED, I eventually succumbed to the photograph of Dinu Lipatti above my workbench. In black and white and shades of grey, it does me no good to look at it, no good at all.

Taken at his last concert, it shows the pianist side-on. Audience members in the background listen to his playing with such intensity, such concentration, that they might be waiting to hear wrong notes. (Lipatti never played them.) Some cock their heads a little to the right, others to the left. Their eyes, I always think, are focused beyond the pianist. At me! They pierce the glass and say I caused Anna's suicide. I'm guilty, they say, and I agree. And I feel acute remorse because of it. This is the problem. I'd like to take the picture down but I can't.

I imagine that many of the rapt music-lovers in the image are desperately hoping that Lipatti will recover his health. Fat chance, as they say. A woman in the second row appears to be downcast … on the verge of tears. She might even be shaking her lowered head in despair.

As for Lipatti himself, his back is straight and his perfectly arched fingers command the keyboard. Unlike the grim-set mouths of the concertgoers, his is slightly open, and he gazes upwards. Is he beseeching, imploring a higher power to inter-vene? A small glass beaker half-filled with a clear liquid is on the piano, and a pale handkerchief — probably of silk to match his glossy Croatian tie — blooms in the top pocket of his jacket. And as the shutter of the camera opens and closes, his body is rotting.

I CAN'T SAY precisely why his story hijacks my thoughts when a cool change is due, when Melbourne's temperature climbs beyond forty Celsius before sudden gusts from the south drop the mercury in a matter of minutes by twenty or more degrees. On the day in question, the thermometer outside my window read forty-three. Through the glass I could hear a corrugated-iron roof screaming under the sun's torture, and I wore sunglasses over my reading spectacles to reduce the glare. It's at times like these, too, that images, many from memories and dreams, bound into my thoughts, and I ask myself who puts them there. I saw the recurrent image of myself wearing spikes on my feet that get stuck in unidentified rough timber planks, rendering me incapable of moving. In a clip from a dream, I worry that I am unable to find my room in an enormous hotel, having spent hours, it seems, looking for it, alighting from the elevator at constantly wrong levels. And I saw the lid of a piano slammed on my childhood hands, failing to injure them. Who thrusts these images day-by-day into my thoughts? Is there a second consciousness — or perhaps unconsciousness — in all our minds? I'd like to know its ethics. Its motives. Why it's there. Is it sinister? Does it sometimes direct what people do? And we have no control over it.

The air conditioner had failed again. (It declines to work, striking in temperatures of more than twenty-seven Celsius.) I sweated copiously, and I gave up the page I had been editing to return yet again to Lipatti, whose last days I can reconstruct from easily obtained facts, as they do on true-crime television.

On the morning of the 16th of September 1950 — a Saturday — the pianist woke feeling better than he had in a long time. Perhaps the experimental injections and cortisone were working again. On certain days in recent weeks he had experienced extraordinary vitality. Only the day before he had written to Florica Musicescu, the renowned coach who had guided him throughout his career, to tell her he felt fine. Perhaps he would be in top form at the Salle du Parliament tonight. But the piano would decide, he told himself. It always had, always did.

He dressed slowly, knotting a silk tie striped in autumnal colours. I like to think that his wife Madeleine had bought it for him in Split, the Croatian city that is the home of neckties. She must have been pleased that he was feeling so well, of course, but she would have also tried to encourage him, to top up what strength he had left. She was his rock. In the photograph, the knot of his tie is just the right fullness, the fall perfect. I picture Madeleine adjusting it before they leave for the concert hall and a final rehearsal.

When he reached the Salle du Parliament, the Gaveau piano was probably being tuned. And because he was the kind of man he was — countless sources will tell you that he was modest and polite — I suspect that he chose not to interrupt the tuner. I like to think that he waited perhaps half an hour — we don't know — his illness beginning to prowl, before he could begin rehearsing.

His warm-up went without incident. He ran through a Bach partita, Mozart sonata, two Schubert impromptus and a few of Chopin's more challenging waltzes. When it was over, he returned to the hotel and had a light lunch — nowhere is it recorded exactly what he ate. Then at some time during the afternoon he developed a high fever, which worsened as the hours passed.

Madeleine would have summoned his long-time doctor, who had followed him from Geneva to ensure that he had the best possible treatment for the Hodgkin's lymphoma that had infected him for the past three years. Records show that the doctor urged him to cancel the concert. And Lipatti would have said, I like to think, that he could never consider such a thing. And with his next breath, which was probably taken with great difficulty, he might have conceded that he was in no state to perform. I see Madeleine sighing in relief.

In my reconstructions, though, Lipatti and the doctor discuss sacrifice for the sake of art, Madeleine submitting her own thoughts on the subject. The doctor suggests that no one so ill should kill himself for a piano, grand or upright. And being the gentle and understanding soul he is, Lipatti agrees. The piano would decide, though, he tells the doctor. It always has, always will, always does. And late that afternoon, it decided that he should play.

The doctor injected him with several drugs — probably including morphine and more cortisone — and he walked robotically to the car. At the hall, he shuffled to the green room, where musicians relax — or try to — before concerts and during intervals. He told the Salle du Parliament's manager that he would remain seated at the keyboard during the recital. He would just turn to the audience and nod, smiling in return for applause between pieces instead of bowing and exiting and re-entering, as was the custom.

The critic of *La Voix du Doubs*, who signed himself 'Le Soupir', a crotchet rest in music but also a French sigh, wrote that extra seating was needed to accommodate an overflow of concertgoers. Lipatti had always attracted full houses, but this time he was dying. Were they ghouls? Were they wondering how well someone so critically ill might perform? Would his playing fall apart on the stage in front of them? Would he collapse in time with the music? More importantly for me, was the audience convinced that Lipatti had sacrificed his life for his art? Could they infer from his gestures and facial expressions that the piano was goring him to death, so to speak? As he played?

At the scheduled moment he made his way to the Gaveau and began the concert. His Bach was crystalline, his Mozart, as one source has it, brimmed with the drama and pathos that had marked the lives of both the composer and the player.

I search the photograph for smiles on the concertgoers' faces but see none. During the Schubert impromptus, I picture Lipatti reflecting on — if only for a split-second — the composer's death at the age of thirty-one, even younger than he was. I see — and believe Lipatti saw — Schubert laying down his spectacles and their curiously small oval lenses on sheets of manuscript paper on which he has sketched short motifs to develop into major compositions.

'Le Soupir' wrote that by the time the pianist got to Chopin's set of waltzes, he was battling exhaustion. He fumbled opus 64 number 3, as another scarcely sympathetic critic put it, but performed the *Grande Valse Brillante* as if his life depended on it. (A ghoul might say it did.) Then came the final piece, opus 34 number 1. 'Le Soupir' reported that the pianist began it, but after the first four notes he stopped, stood up, stooped — head bent forward, probing for an escape route, as terrified as anyone stumbling in the dark and smoke to find a stairway in the World Trade Center's conflagrated towers — and shuffled off the stage. Audience members, who had applauded enthusiastically throughout the recital, now began to grieve in advance, knowing the terminal nature of Lipatti's condition. Their silence rolled in like a heavy fog, filling the hall. I imagine that those who had come with macabre intent were embarrassed into silence. His most loyal fans would have been shocked into a kind of stupor. Stunned, I suspect. They were witnessing the worst.

Minutes passed — 'Le Soupir' fails to say exactly how many. The critic noted, though, that some in the audience began to shuffle their feet, and others folded their jackets over the crooks of their arms, preparing to leave. Then Lipatti re-appeared — looking frailer, the critic observed — to resume his position on the slat-backed timber dining chair in front of the instrument. At that moment, I like to think, all might have become clear: Lipatti must surely have been struck by the cost of the sacrifice he had made for his art. The scores of thousands of hours he had spent all alone with pianos to the exclusion of a normal existence. And how much of himself — his being — he had expended doing it. It seems that giving in to the daemon that had stalked him from the age of three was no longer an option. The piano had ruled his life, had always decided for him, but this time, perhaps for the first time, he would have a say in what happened next.

He lifted his hands above the keyboard and brought down

the left to sound with the greatest delicacy the G-major octave that begins Bach's *Jesu, Joy of Man's Desiring*, that most spiritual of waltzes, a devotion in three-four time, the lilting and lovely piece with which Lipatti had launched his professional career fifteen years before. In the following three-and-a-half minutes, the pianist negotiated a truce with the piano. I have heard the result, an elegiac and melancholic yielding, a pact. You may corroborate my view.

He was never to perform in public again, cancelling concerts later in September and again in October. He is said to have played for the last time on the 20th of November, performing at home for Madeleine a Chopin prelude and the sublime slow movement from Bach's F-major *Pastorale*. In the afternoon of the 2nd of December, which was a Saturday precisely eleven weeks after the Salle du Parliament recital, an abscess in his good lung burst and he died soon after. He was thirty-three.

I OPENED the bottom drawer of the filing cabinet beside my table and took out a small sharp vegetable knife, its handle wound with thin wire, that I use to whittle pencils. I examined the backs of my hands, the extent to which I've punished them, their cross-hatchings of scars, the rails and sidings on my forearms, especially the one that resembles an eighth-note and its flag. And I waited, grasping the little blade so tightly that my fingers began to sweat. I feared, paradoxically, that I might make a mess on the floor if I cut myself. (Perhaps I might be at last managing my condition, I thought.) Out the window, clouds the colour of old bruises were rolling in from the south. The cool change was on its way, and I needed relief from Lipatti and the concertgoers. An image leapt into my mind of some sheets of music that I was incapable of placing right way up on the stand of a Steinway concert grand, an island in an auditorium as big as an ocean from which I was unable to escape. An audience of several thousand behind me were waiting for me to play. Some exchanged whispers. Even upside-down, the music looked like Beethoven's. I knew I couldn't execute it.

Perhaps half a minute passed, and, to my credit — and a certain amazement — I willed myself to replace the knife. I closed the drawer, and promised myself not to re-open it. Leaving the room now became essential, of course, and I surprised myself by standing, turning my back on Lipatti's photograph, and walking out into the street.

I had the intention of drinking a double-strength espresso — arguably the worst refreshment for my condition — at a small café in High Street not a hundred metres from my apartment.

The cool change blew my plans to bits. It arrived like a collision. A first blast of wind propelled a young woman in shorts and runners against a brick wall, from which she rebounded as if she were a rubber ball. A second gust demolished the wall, and she stopped and stared at the strewn bricks, askance, eyes wide. The wind thrust an old white-haired gentleman with a bent spine along the pavement as if he were being frog-marched to a police station. At one point, his raincoat flew up his back and over his head, blinding him, and he thrust out his hands, feeling for something — anything — to grab, a cast-iron Victorian verandah-post finally arresting him. A cattle dog barked incessantly at the force of the gale, nearly pulling its owner between parked cars and under a passing tram.

My café was in sight, though, a refuge, and I was about to take the single marble step up to its front door when a devastating blast propelled me forwards into the plate glass and I passed out.

PERHAPS THREE or four hours must have elapsed before I felt a pillow beneath my head and heard someone humming in a barely audible baritone Beethoven's Eroica symphony … the funeral march, *Dum, de daaa, de daa, de daa, de daaaa, dum.* A strange young man stood in a doorway perhaps three metres away. At least, that's what I saw. He bit a fingernail and hummed on.

I sat up, plumping the pillows behind me, and looked around. Institutional cream walls, stainless steel bedside cabinet, crucifix behind my wicket-style bedhead. *Dum, de daaa, de daa, de daa, de daaaa, dum.* Unmistakable. I was back in St Sebastian House, where I have been admitted — and admitted myself — several times. And I felt sure that I was alive, even if the strange young man in the doorway might have existed in another way. (I have several times willed myself towards death, knowing it can be done by withdrawing into my mind with what's left of me. I am convinced that — once there, there completely — I shall meet whoever puts up the mysterious images that interrupt my thoughts. And perhaps be dead.)

The chap in the doorway stopped humming and grinned. So thin was he that khaki cargo shorts flapped around his spindly thighs like luffing sails. The shorts appeared ready to tumble around his ankles, and he tugged at them to keep them up. His calves were sticks, and tufts of hair in many shades — purple was notable — sprouted above a face of knife-blade thinness. A Hawaiian shirt printed with scarlet hibiscus flowers and sway-ing coconut palms hung off his shoulders. A breeze got up that set the palms to trembling, and a coconut dropped, bounced on a shirt button, and rolled away like a marble, disappearing under my cot.

I'm Lee, he said, approaching.

Wasn't it a lovely coincidence?

What? I said.

That he *also* loved classical music, he said.

Dum, de daaa, de daa, de daa, de daaaa, dum, he hummed. Funeral march, he said, tapping his skull. Eroica. Beethoven.

I nodded.

He looked around my room, which was small, then began tracing a wide U around my bed, appearing to glide — as if on rails — to arrive back where he had started. He reminded me of a shunting locomotive. His shorts flapped. The palm trees swayed more vigorously. I expected more coconuts to fall.

My problem could be approached from several directions, he said. He could not guarantee that any would work — he was not a pro. But his experience was long, and he and I both loved great music, a lovely coincidence. His own problem was simple, he said. He was unable to rid his head of the funeral march. *Dum, de daaa, de daa, de daa, de daaaa, dum.* It played on a loop, trapped inside his skull, and had done so for more than thirteen years. But at least the conductors and orchestras changed, his favourite at the moment being Georg Solti and the Chicago boys.

And girls, I added. Do you see the musicians, the conductor, I asked, as you listen to the music? Are the images still or moving?

He failed to answer, and I reached in his direction, trying to brush against his forearm but felt nothing.

Did I keep a journal? he said.

I'd tried to in the past.

I should resume writing one on a daily basis, he suggested. What went through my head, my activities. Put the date on top. For patients like us, writing out thoughts is paramount. He grinned. Is it water in the beaker on Lipatti's piano, for instance? Or some other liquid? Did Madeleine knot his tie? What was he injected with before the concert?

Of course it's water, I snorted. When I'd written notes before, I said, it had made me even more anxious. I was afraid of what might happen if doctors read my most intimate musings. (As I said these words, an image of graduated blues becoming black interfered. I was sinking into an ocean trench several kilometres deep. Falling, slowly falling, getting colder and gloomier as I went.)

Lee hoisted his shorts and harrumphed.

I asked him why no one had come to talk me through my cool-change trauma. Dr M, for instance, who knew my story.

Holding his shorts in one hand, he shrugged and looked at his watch. It was Sunday and past five o'clock, and I should know what that meant. He began to hum but stopped. He said that we must understand ourselves through unconscious thoughts that occasionally bubbled — he bubbled the fingers of his free hand like a pantomime dame — to the surface.

Sneezing violently, he glared at the crowns of mature English plane trees outside my window. First-floor with a view over the garden, I realized. The nicest of St Sebastian's rooms. He spied a box of tissues on the bedside cabinet and reached for it. Honking loudly as he blew his nose, he shrugged, hitched up his shorts, and sat at the end of my narrow cot.

Once you get out again, he said, you might like to take a holiday, to visit somewhere in the world where the landscape, the people, their needs and pleasures might displace your obsessive thoughts about pianists, at least for a time. Might distract you.

I'd taken holidays before, I said. In fact, I added, one of the specialists here had suggested some time ago — half in jest, I suppose — that I should journey to the mountainous jungles of Papua where pianos had never been heard of. I told her that, on the contrary, my father, who had been in New Guinea during the war, had once taught me the pidgin for piano, the mellifluous expression so long and involving a big-song-no-words-chief-him-black-and-white-big-smiley-teeths that I had completely forgotten it. I shouldn't have, I said, because the phrase had been luscious.

Lee's face went blank, my frivolity failing to register, but he was much younger than I am, and I sometimes notice that young people — and even some who are old — seem to make fewer demands on humour these days.

Does the actual idea of the hand make you anxious? he asked, frowning, his pointed nose stabbing the air. Just the hand as such, or only hands that can play a piano at elite levels? It's a wondrous thing the hand, he added. (Yes, I thought, until it gets mangled. There is Anna, holding up her right hand, wiggling its little finger, the only digit intact, the others twitching on the pavers where they fell. And she giggles like a little girl. The blood begins to make rivulets down her forearm, and my mutilating her hand has changed both our lives forever.)

Lee got up and began retracing his U around the bed, constantly arriving back where he had been, gliding like a camera on a dolly. He tapped his fingertips together, creating a scarcely audible beat whose echo was surprisingly loud. We are the senior species only because of our minds and hands. A bony finger pointed at the lopsided crucifix above the bedhead. The index, he said, is capable of telling stories without resorting to words. His finger drifted from the crucifix to the open window and flicked, as if he were dispatching the cross into the garden below. The gesture shocked me enough that I felt obliged to check that it was still attached to the wall. It was, but by some miracle, it was no longer askew.

He said that I needed to continue to confront the truth. It was inescapable, and I would have to live with my sister's demise for as long as I breathed. Yes, he said, you were holding the saw, but we must *reinforce* your lack of intent. She was trying to help, and there was an accident. That was all. An accident. How long ago? Thirty years?

Thirty-one, I said. I could tell you the exact date, I added, even the day and the time. Ten-thirteen in the morning.

You confront this memory constantly, a truly awful situation.

Daily, I said. Several times. It shapes my life, confuses my thoughts, puts me in here. I ask myself if the accident occurred out of indignation, revenge? Was it a purposeful act to relieve her misery? That I have been unable to answer these questions feeds my guilt. Makes eliminating it impossible. Or so it seems.

He sneezed. And you have so far failed to find atonement for something that — *all* the doctors must have told you — you should *feel no guilt over whatsoever*. And, from time to time, you believe that the only answer to your melancholy is to follow your sister's leap into the abyss? Is that correct?

I nodded.

Then you should try something new, he said.

I frowned, but was prepared to hear him out.

There might be value in intensifying your obsession with pianists' fates, he said, if only to understand that your sister was not alone. Tragedy intervenes in many of their lives, he said. Few live without it. You might begin to think that her death was not at all uncommon. You might gain by exercising your madness.

But, I began …

He held up a hand so bony that the phalanges appeared as if they had been x-rayed. (I saw myself being slid into an enormous scanning doughnut, which clattered loudly. Perhaps to investigate my dreams.)

We ought to begin this evening, he said. The great Freud put his patients through the wringer to unearth what troubled them. It just might work with you.

It had never been tried before, I replied. Not with me. No professional had ever advised it.

Lee waved dismissively and tugged his shorts higher. It might help, he said. There was even a chance that I might enjoy it. That I might revel in the detective work. We will compile lists of pianists, he said, and try to measure the degree to which fate afflicted each of them. Then we will see where your sister fits in. Perhaps she was not so unlucky as you think.

Perhaps, I thought, this man is mad. Not all there. But, then, who isn't crazy?

Looking malevolently through the window at the plane trees, he sneezed so violently that I thought he might shake his head off. He blew his nose, and for several seconds his knife-blade face was expressionless. He resumed the Eroica's funeral march at bar six: *Daaa, da dee da dee daaa-aa-a*, he hummed. Smiling, he tapped his skull. Melbourne symphony, he said.

His candor had surprised me, and for an instant I invested great confidence in him. I shouldn't have. I usually trust no one, not even St Sebastian's doctors. And he wasn't one of *them*. So I can't explain why his words seemed not just soothing but worth considering. On the face of it, his idea seemed to have ballast.

I already knew most of the musicians who would make our list, I said.

We should do it anyway, he said, because he was about to astound me. I am, like you, a rare beast in what some have called the unaesthetic era, a time when music aims merely to bring on the jitters, he said, smiling.

He had last year helped to bury a maiden aunt who had died from breast cancer at the age of fifty-nine. As a boy and youth he had become very fond of her, and she had loved him and his brothers with utter devotion. She had introduced them to recordings of many of the great Beethoven works, he said, beginning with easy things such as the concerto for violin, cello and piano, the famous triple concerto, which she called a C-major romp.

Next was the violin concerto. Lee remembered hearing it for the first time while his aunt smashed ginger root in a mortar and pestle made of a strange green stone that was at times as luminous as jade and at others quite dull, appearing in this latter guise to be fit only for road metal. The crushed ginger roots would go into what she called her famous ginger beer, Lee remembered her saying as she pumped away. Those four haunting beats on the kettledrum that begin the concerto were in time with the persistent way in which his aunt had crushed the ginger. *Phlump, phlumph, phlump, phlump.* It intrigued him so much that he had asked her if he could begin the recording again. She agreed, and he replaced the needle of her ancient gramophone at the start of the LP. But this time the drumbeats and his aunt's pounding were syncopated — eight instead of four, an equally arresting effect despite its weird rebounds. *Phlu-lump, phlu-lump, phlu-lump, phlu-lump.*

Coming from the back of an orchestra, Lee continued, the beats are soft and muffled for a listener in the audience of a big hall, a portent of something indescribably mysterious and compelling. Perhaps even ominous. That very first hearing of Beethoven's violin concerto, he told me, made him wonder if the performance of music necessarily catalysed the intervention of fate in our lives. Music released all manner of demons, it appeared, he said. Devils. It was what made a list of unlucky pianists so interesting.

In a matter of minutes, Lee and his flapping shorts, purple tufts of hair and coconut palms had become empathetic, an accomplice. To this day I cannot work out precisely how it happened. Was it his fond recollection of his aunt's smashing ginger? My confidence in him, at any rate, had grown.

As the sun descended, we began volleying names *viva voce* between us, listing keyboard artists, as their managers like to call them, for whom life had been scarcely generous. After a few minutes, he left and returned with a laptop and several blank St Sebastian notepads normally used for clinical observations. (I have watched the shrinks use them. The institute's logo, a thatch of arrows, is in the top left-hand corner.) He winked and gave me one. A brace of St Sebastian ballpoints flourished in his top pocket, making an ersatz hibiscus bloom, and he offered me one. He hitched up his shorts, sat on the bed, opened his laptop and a notepad, took a ballpoint from his pocket and said he was ready.

NO BETTER person to begin with was Dinu Lipatti, he said.

I flung up my arms in protest. We may dispense with him, I said. Recalling his last recital was what got me in here this time, I added.

He died of Hodgkin's lymphoma, Lee said. Was I aware?

Of course I was, I said. Let's not dwell on him.

He was supposed to have dripped blood onto the keys, said Lee, rubbing a finger under his nostrils. Whether the blood fell from his nose or ears or mouth or frayed fingertips I have never been able to find out, he said.

We looked at photographs of Lipatti in the digital cloud. Handsome, he had the pallid physiognomy of many great pianists who died young — indeed, said Lee, it was uncanny that they all looked alike, people of the whitest skin, probably because they spent their entire lives, day after day, year after year, indoors at the keyboard, and thin because they almost never ate. Thin like he was, he smiled.

But why did he play when he was so ill? Lee asked. Play to the last? For the sake of music? Was it a rational decision? Give me some plausible answers, he demanded, sniffing.

It seemed to me, I replied, that Lipatti felt he had an obligation to make the most of his gifts. All great performers probably feel the same, I said, a huge burden to carry.

Our second name was Julius Katchen, an American who excelled in the works of Brahms and who had studied with Nadia Boulanger in Paris — as had Lipatti, of course. He died of cancer in 1969 at forty-two. I saw him play in the Melbourne Town Hall when I was younger than even you are now, I said. He performed the Brahms first concerto, handling the first movement's treacherous descent of octave chords from high up on the keyboard with elan and contemptuous ease.

Lee said he knew it well, mugging its first few notes with his bony hands and humming, *Da dim, da dim, da dim dim dim dim dim dim dim* … his voice trailing away. A descent as tricky as the most malevolent of downhill runs in World Cup skiing, he said, a passage that had undone many of the finest players, most famously the phenomenal Artur Schnabel, who muffed it during a recording session.

No easy repeats then, I said. Wire recorders and all.

I remember Katchen's performance as if it were yesterday, I said, even what the pianist wore — he dressed in a white tuxedo, a red flower in the buttonhole, probably a carnation, which was unusual for that era of starched, coal-black tailcoats and white bow ties. He sauntered to the piano grinning, suggesting an affable character, just an all-American guy, you might say, doing his job. People who knew him said he was a charming and friendly man, as most great pianists appear to be.

Why do you think it was a carnation? asked Lee, his forehead creasing. Because it looked like one, I said, and he scribbled a note.

Lee and I discovered that Katchen's last performance in public was of Ravel's concerto for the left hand, bringing to mind the hapless Paul Wittgenstein, for whom it was written. Lee mentioned Paul's brother Ludwig, who famously constrained human activity within logical boundaries. He wondered whether the force of Ludwig's logic and his philosophy, which limited both the thinkable and the unthinkable, had been able to ponder its way through, penetrate the psychical barrier surrounding the amputation of Paul's right arm after his elbow had been shot to bits in the Great War, and if the magnitude of such a loss for a pianist was thinkable or unthinkable when most piano music emphasises treble melodies played by the right hand.

Paul had pushed on, you see, said Lee, which was admirable, commissioning concertos for the left hand from notable composers.

He was not a nice man, though, I said. He argued with creators over the merits of their works, falling out with Ravel especially, and he often changed the music to suit himself. He hated it when critics said he was a good pianist for someone with only one arm, I said. He seemed to have been as unbending as his brother.

For all that, said Lee, Paul's dedication and persistence should be especially comforting for you, bearing in mind your sister's accident. Hers was a right hand, too? he asked.

I nodded. But Anna showed no interest in the left-handed repertoire. After the accident she was empty, I said.

Lee began to hum the funeral march, his eyes searching high and low, as if he might have thought that his larynx was no longer the source of the sound. That it was coming from the walls or through the open window.

Solomon Cutner, who was born in the ragged East End of London, suffered a cataclysmic stroke in his fifties that *paralysed* his right arm. He never again played professionally. Lee grinned, and asked how Solomon — the only name by which the world of music knew him — managed to endure the remaining thirty-six years of his life, contemplating what might have been, the heights to which he might have risen but for a blood clot inside his skull.

I was tempted to compare his plight with Wittgenstein's, to wonder why he didn't learn the pieces for the left hand and continue his career, but kept the thoughts to myself. We all die differently, I thought, and at different speeds and sometimes, but only sometimes, the luckiest of us, in the manner of our own choosing. It's an idea I see merit in, especially since Anna's accident.

Glenn Gould, the Canadian Bach genius, died at fifty of a stroke after years of hypochondria, prescription drugs, all-night practice sessions, midnight phone calls, overcoats and gloves in summer's heat and what might be labelled a general eccentricity, said Lee. His father took him off life-support. Alexei Sultanov had a fatal stroke at thirty-five, Mischa Levitzki had a heart attack at forty-two, and Dino Ciani died in a Roman road accident at thirty-two. Natan Brand, a phenomenal Israeli pianist, died at forty-six of lymphoma, and Joseph Villa, an American, died of AIDS at the same age. Yuri Egorov is also believed to have died of AIDS, said Lee, peering at the screen of his laptop … At thirty-three. The brilliant Australian Aaron McMillan died of brain cancer at thirty, and Mozart, as we all know, who was superlative at the keyboard as well as composition, had his life ended at thirty-five by a mystery illness.

Lee began another bout of violent sneezing, and he glanced again at the plane trees, their pollen clouding the air so intensely now that I began to think I was talking to myself, that he had disappeared into the ambience and I was alone. Because of the pollen, his khaki shorts had turned a dark yet cinematic lime-green, his hibiscus flowers were wilting, and the coconut palms began to tremble again, as if they were fearing a typhoon. A coconut fell.

SEVERAL fine pianists have suicided, I said, a subject dear to me … Died of their own will perhaps because they could no longer endure the pain of being tortured by pianos. They had surrendered to the implacable enemy, as Alfred Brendel, one of the piano giants, has described the instrument.

We looked up the brilliant Bolesław Kon, whom some experts say was the greatest pianist ever, a youth who extinguished his life at twenty-nine but was never able to leave behind proof of his brilliance in the form of recordings. Christopher Falzone jumped only recently from the tenth floor of a Geneva hospital at the same age. The distinguished winner of many of the top piano prizes, an American who had played with the best orchestras, he decided to die after having been admitted to hospital against his own will, reports said. His wife and parents appeared to have been on opposite sides when it came to advising him on decisions about his life and career.

A vortex seems to swirl around many of the finest artists, I said, ineluctably drawing those who love them into its blackest depths. Falzone feared that his parents were trying to remove him from his wife Lily, whom he could not live without. He fled their house. An obituary in the *Richmond Times-Dispatch* said the pianist was a gentle soul with a sensitive heart, and the true story of his death will no doubt be revealed in time. (How long before Anna's true story emerges?)

Could Falzone's parents have in fact stood in for the piano? Represented it? After all, they would have forced him to practise when he was very young.

Lee failed to answer my stupid question, instead sneezing volcanically. We decided to continue chatting in the gardens below, away from the trees' malevolence.

WE STROLLED in the twilight along a path of crushed Lilydale toppings that appeared to be short but at every turn continued farther and farther, curving and recurving between rows of dense bottlebrushes — their cylinders of buds keen to explode into scarlet — as if we were taking a long bushwalk and would neither arrive at its end nor return to where we had started, that the path might eventually push on beyond the high walls of concrete blocks enclosing St Sebastian's grounds all the way to Uluru, providing we were facing away from the coast. The hike would free us, I felt. We trudged on in silence, the stones beneath our feet drumming softly, reminding me of the kettledrum's beginning of Beethoven's violin concerto and its syncopation with Lee's aunt's ginger-crushing.

Lee stopped, hitched up his shorts and said that at just that instant he had had an a-ha moment. A week or so before his aunt died, she had recommended a book about the tragic life of William Kapell, the phenomenal American pianist. She had revelled in its many layers, including a love story, Kapell's tours of Australia, the New Yorker's neurotic temperament, the recent discovery of a priceless amateur recording of his last concert, the air crash that had killed him, and a legal stoush — the words he used — over compensation in New York courts that the airline Qantas and the Australian government ought to be ashamed of. And they're not, added Lee.

Moreover, for reasons that escaped him now, he continued, he believed that the book's author lived in the suburbs of Melbourne, if not quite close to the city. As a task, he suggested, it might be a good idea to listen to words from the horse's mouth about Kapell's life, to visit the biographer and glean the details of the pianist's tragedy.

Might it help me to move on? I asked, a useful expression I hate.

Well, to come to terms with your fixation, he said, nodding. Exercise it. Aspects of Kapell's character worked against his success, he supposed. He might have been dying of lung cancer anyway, my aunt said. He chain-smoked. Many critics disliked him, and he was a real Manhattan Jewish boy, among other things.

There must be many types of real Manhattan Jewish boys, I thought, but I was too tired to debate the question. My cot beckoned.

Kapell had pressed on? I asked.

Until a DC-6 aircraft and a mountain abruptly ended his career, Lee said.

He cocked an eyebrow, grinned, and listened for several seconds before beginning to hum. *Dum, de daaa, de daa, de daa, de daaaa, dum.* The Berlin Philharmonic had just begun its version, he said. He smiled. He preferred the Chicago band, he said, but he'd listen to the Germans. Hear them out. Sir Simon Rattle conducting.

Despite his help and suggestions, I never saw Lee again.

A FEW DAYS after being admitted to St Sebastian's I felt well enough to ask for a discharge, which Drs M and P, who knew my file, endorsed. They introduced me to a much younger man called Dr K who stood sullenly behind them, a talented resident, said Dr M. He was learning the ropes of mental turmoil and had a special interest in my illness, he added. He didn't say why.

Wearing a scorching white lab coat, the young medico forced a smile. A clipboard was wedged under an armpit, and so immaculately turned out was he, so precisely tonsured his beard, so uniform in height the stubble of his skull, so unblemished his pallid skin — almost a pianist's — so black his eyes, that he became less real — increasingly spurious — the more I studied him. He rubbed the tar-black bristle on his scalp. My hair was once so dark, I realized, and it suddenly struck me like an uppercut that Dr K resembled me as a young man. Very closely, in fact. A mirror image. I stared at him, mute, perhaps open-mouthed.

Because Dr K had taken a special interest in your case, said Dr M, he would like to contact you occasionally, on Skype and by email, just to see how you're getting along. The new healing, he added with a grin. Cyber. Would that be OK?

Yes, I said, mesmerized by my doppelgänger. Glued to the spot, spikes stuck in timber.

Dr M frowned. Are you sure you want to leave St Sebastian's? he asked. I turned and headed for the door.

ON RETURNING home, I fitted a padlock to the knife drawer, invented three of the most random odd and even numbers I could think of as its combination and tried to forget them. I Googled intensively, within an hour or so tracking down an email address for the author of the book about Kapell to which Lee had drawn my attention. I sent off a courteous message asking for an interview, and two days later — on the anniversary of the pianist's death, as it happened — I received a reply from JL to say that he would be delighted to give me an hour or two of his time. He lived a hundred kilometres north-west of Melbourne on a small holding that was not far off the freeway, easy to find.

And then I panicked, challenging the worth of talking to anyone about a dead pianist. How could it help me? What possible value was the advice of a man with a funeral march playing inside his skull? Lee and his swaying palms! Who heard things! How would investigating the unlucky life of a neurotic New Yorker help me to get over Anna? A pod of five dolphins — I counted them — in a sea as metallic and flat as mercury surfaced near where I stood on a narrow timber jetty. They arched their backs so uniformly, moved with such grace, submerging and emerging in pairs and trios, their flukes surprisingly small, dorsal fins large, their blowholes emitting wet flatulence at every surfacing. I could see why people wanted to ride them. One of the pod — he or she must have had a name — came within a metre of where I was standing and beckoned me, but I was spiked to the jetty, incapable of leaping on to its back.

JL and I arranged to meet the next day.

PASTURES either side of the four-lane highway were already desiccated, and within weeks the heat of the sun would turn the long stalks of ryegrass and oats into a yellow brighter than a traffic sign. The Calder freeway meanders to the north and west, mounting slowly what appear to be treeless and perfectly rounded foothills that signal the intention of higher altitudes, of mountains even, but are in fact the last vestiges, the last decaying mounds, of the Great Dividing Range, one of the oldest geological formations on Earth, running for thousands of kilometres, a reversed L that on other continents might be grander, sharper, and called a spine. And as I drove, I was overcome by the feeling that I should be somewhere other than where I was, that I was heading in the wrong direction, that I should be returning to the city, not leaving it. At one point, my misgiving felt so acute that I looked for a place to U-turn. But the median strip was very wide and grassy, and none was offered. Indeed, as I drove on, the separation between carriageways widened until I could no longer see vehicles going in the other direction. There seemed to be only one direction to take, and I committed myself to pressing on. The long vast sweeps of the highway induced a resolve to continue, against my better judgement, perhaps, bringing on a kind of torpor that propelled me towards whatever new things I might learn.

Perhaps forty minutes from the city, Mt Macedon and its plain white cross on the summit came into view. The cross and the hill's abrupt western face appear to leap out above the tarmac, menacing vehicles that pass, as if the crucifix's purpose is to repel vampires. At any rate, mountain and emblem appear dangerously close. The cross commemorates the dead of wars, of course, and is a place where snow sometimes falls on the coldest winter days, which probably still delights picture editors in the big city, where snow never falls. Accumulating on the cross's horizontal, snow at Mt Macedon is among their favourite images, and photographers race up the freeway to capture it before it melts, which happens quickly.

Farther on, I passed Hanging Rock, an enormous tor of granite boulders that rises a hundred metres or so above a skirt of surrounding scrub. So mysterious is this pile of grey stones, many of them perfect ovoids, so beguiling the narrow tracks that mount and descend within the dark shadows that the stones cast, parabolas of sunlight sometimes interrupting turn on turn, that many who have entered Hanging Rock are said never to have exited.

On St Valentine's Day in 1900, a group of genteel schoolgirls picnicked near the boulders before exploring the labyrinths that were created when, millions of years ago, the stones were flung, scorching hot and glowing red, from the centre of the Earth. All but one girl was lost forever. So goes the myth, which was based on an obscure newspaper cutting that was converted in 1967 into Joan Lindsay's magical novel, which in turn became two movies. The idea that a group of well-bred schoolgirls in frilly Victorian dresses and lace collars, starched, pressed and of blinding whiteness, could simply disappear within the stones, save for one, captivated imaginations to the extent that truth and fiction — what might have actually happened and what one permits oneself to imagine happened — became so blurred, so merged, that in the end no one could tell them apart.

Although professing desires to solve the riddle, readers and others captivated by the story would never have wanted it unravelled, I believe. Uncertainty titillates even the most jaded of us. Several attempts to get Lady Lindsay to throw light on her story

— on how much she knew was true and how much she had made up — faltered in almost two decades between the publication of her book and her death, and the mystery is not just sustained but affectionately reinvigorated with every mention of the Rock, as locals call it.

I ENTERED JL's drive off an unmade road, navigating initially between high red-brick pillars then along a dirt track either side of which were rudimentary strand-wire fences demarcating paddocks cleared of vegetation but for low yellowing grass. To the horizon, the landscape was deserted and beige, the colour turning paler with distance. A few metres off the track, a quartet of galahs foraged in the grass, their slow swagger and the extreme softness of their pinks and greys moving me deeply, much as dolphins do. Brought almost to tears, I stopped to watch them for a few seconds.

Three hundred metres farther on, I arrived at JL's house, a small weatherboard chalet, its two-storey A-shape seeming quite out of place in the middle of brown, undulating Australian pastures. It would have been best suited to a perch on the side of a lushly green Swiss mountain.

After swinging a heavy brass knocker several times against a front door of bevelled hardwood, I waited, getting no response. I listened at the keyhole but heard only a chortling of magpies that strutted down the drive behind me, as if they were guardians keen to know my business and, in the meantime, mock my attempt to rouse someone. Quite a small house, the cottage was surrounded on all sides by a wide verandah against the sun, its roof of corrugated iron the colour of dried blood. I peered through windows, seeing only unidentifiable shapes in the gloom, none of them moving, as if the dwelling had been uninhabited for some time, reminding me of the ancient jails perversely on display throughout the world in which one forces oneself inside dank claustrophobic cells, walls still inscribed with graffiti, to imagine the experience of confinement, what the ghosts who walk the bleak corridors nowadays must have felt during their years of imprisonment as sensate beings. The air smelled of dust and a sterile aridity.

At the rear of the dwelling, I noticed several paths of large bluestone cobbles leading to copses of various species, including an orchard of twenty or so fruit trees, among them lemons and peaches, and a long alley that headed under a steel-framed archway of climbing roses towards outbuildings of old tanned timber. Coarse bluestone blocks the size of shoeboxes contrived man-made structures, mainly walls, which, it seemed to me, were attempting to defy inevitable decay.

I took a path between enormous thickets of roses smothered at their summits high above me in pale pink blooms. Their scent was dizzying, so sweet and pervasive that I feared it might disturb my balance and I might collapse in a faint, fall into the bushes, no one knowing. The blooms floated on a forest of thorny, wrist-thick stems that I urgently wanted to put behind me. Caught among the barbs were scraps of what appeared to be parched, paper-thin skin, tufts of pale-grey fur here and there lifting in a breeze so light it could not be felt.

The path arrived eventually at an enormous octagonal vegetable garden fenced with knee-high stone walls, galvanised chicken-wire on a frame of thin tubular steel rising from the ground to cover it completely. Bird-strikes, I thought. Tomato seedlings flourished in many of the wedge-shaped beds, but also oak-leaf lettuces and rambling vines that in a few months might bear cucumbers, I supposed. Zucchini plants already sprouted orange flowers, and beans and snow peas flowered. More alleyways led to the centre of the garden, and along one of them a man in white overalls blotched with paint stains of many colours, as if they had been applied intentionally, a fraying straw fedora on his head, bent over a garden bed and tore at weeds, throwing them into a barrow alongside him, often missing. Perhaps more weeds were outside the barrow than in it. JL (I presumed) failed to notice me, so intent was he on his work, and I had to say hello quite loudly before he looked up and brightly volleyed my greeting.

He stood up, creaking a little and revealing chipped lips and deep crevasses that radiated from the corners of each eye. He swept off his hat, arcing it below his waist and bowing as if he were a musketeer in an old movie. The gesture revealed thick dark hair but white sideburns, and, although he was far from young, the ensemble of his features signalled youthfulness. Showing beneath the short sleeves of his white shirt, for instance, were tanned muscular arms, yet his uncertain shuffle as he approached me to shake hands suggested a certain dodderiness.

JL told me that he had bought the property only recently, and it was a lot of work for someone of his years. His wife was often away, sitting on various company boards and making the pocket-money, as he called it, from which they lived quite well. Few writers make any money at all from books, he added. The blue-stone paths, garden beds and the Nook, the small stone house

I must have already seen — Did you visit it? — were all built by hand over some twenty years. Not by him, he added, but by one man, the former owner, who was a stonemason. And JL couldn't help thinking, he said, that in a few hundred years, if they prove more fortuitous than the world's daily events suggest, and human beings persist that long, the paths and the walls and the Nook and the stonemason's other fantasies — there were fountains I hadn't yet seen, he said, waving an arm — would remain, the mortar crumbling, turning to dust between the stones, the stones themselves, even in their hewn states, settling back onto the plain from which their parent rocks had been expelled millions of years before. He was reminded, he said, of Claude Lévi-Strauss's remark that Man was absent when the universe began and would be absent long before it ended. Long, long before, he repeated.

JL: writer, vegetable grower, philosopher, I thought. Also pompous. But I was here to listen.

He wanted to show me a comfortable place to chat, and he began plodding along an alley behind the vegetable garden that skirted more fruit trees, rampant strawberry runners and raspberry canes on elevated beds, arriving at a large lily pond behind a circular stone wall. Enormous orange goldfish sheltered from the sun under dish-sized glossy-green leaves of various water plants. The dolphins returned, but I laughed to myself and managed to repress them. Opposite the pond was another nook — what JL had dubbed the Cranny, if the tiny cubic building was the Nook, he said. It amounted to a spacious U-shaped basalt bench, its own arched roof obviously designed — the precise edges of the keystone signalling the fact — not to collapse on anyone sitting beneath. He gestured towards it, and we sat and began to talk. I hoped I'd get him on to Kapell and keep him there. He showed signs of being a conversational wanderer.

I HAD ordered his book about the American, I said, but it had not yet been delivered.

He wanted to know exactly how he could help, he said, and I told him that … I paused momentarily, wondering whether it would be unkind and unnecessary to burden him with my problems and knowing, anyway, that my circumstances and the real reasons for my wanting to understand more about pianists' unhappy fates would probably be of little interest to him. So I told him that I had been for a while a music journalist who wrote columns for a magazine he was unlikely ever to have heard of — all of which was true — but that I was thinking now, because of the strange ways that many of the world's finest pianists had died, of writing a book about their ill luck.

No one would publish it, he laughed. What are you calling it?

I thought again, coming up in an instant with *The Hands of Pianists*. (I have no idea why I didn't say *The Fates of Pianists*, for instance, which would have been a better suit. Perhaps my unconscious thought that the rhythm of the words in *Fates* was somehow wrong, the *F* and *P* unmusical in sequence. Or that *fate* was unmarketable. The things writers have to think about.) JL rubbed the back of one of his own tanned hands and I sat on mine, hoping he hadn't noticed the scars.

Jósef Gát's famous volume about piano technique has many photographs of pianists' hands, he said. He had drawn on it for the Kapell tome. He had turned Dr Gát's pages slowly, fascinated

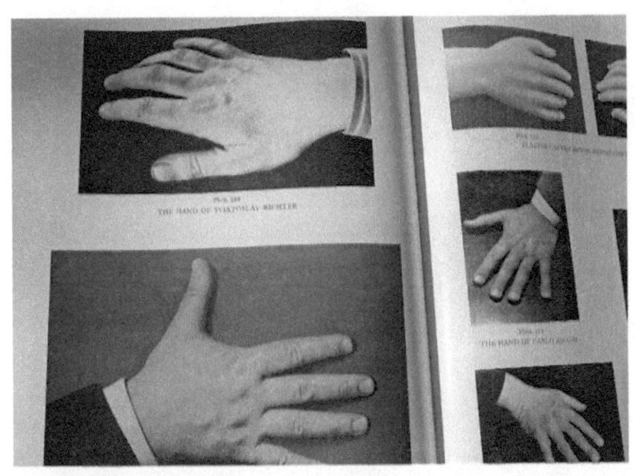

by the morphologies. Here were the hands of Sviatoslav Richter, Emil Gilels, Anton Rubinstein, Lev Oborin, Vladimir Horowitz, Arthur Rubinstein, Annie Fischer and Wilhelm Backhaus, great pianists all. There were also photos of plaster casts of Chopin's left hand, Mendelssohn's right, and both of Liszt's. Most striking were the lengths of the pianists' little fingers, he said. In practically all cases they seemed to be extraordinarily long, so much so that when the fingers were splayed, their tips formed a shallow arc. Most people, he continued, have quite a step down from ring to little fingers and another, not quite so pronounced, from middle to index. Perhaps even more remarkable, he said, was the general meatiness of great pianists' hands. Thick through. Powerful. He smiled. They were the implements of labourers, he said. Pianists are not the effete and delicate artists many people think. He wagged a finger. Their hands are made for hard work. He had never checked, he added, but he believed a fair number of today's best players, of which there were many, must go to gyms and *pump iron*, the expression he used. The hands in Dr Gát's book could dig graves and chop wood, mend fences or hold stallions on a tight rein. They were the hands of peasants and tradesmen,

33

Annie Fischer's perhaps the ideal. One could scarcely imagine their being appropriate for the long, delicate and very soft *pianissimo* passages that abound in piano literature. Only Chopin's

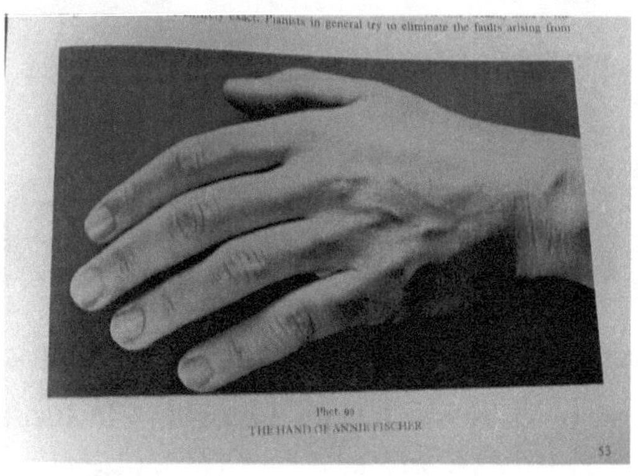

left hand shows any variation: the ring and little finger are fine and seem somewhat fragile. But it could have been a fault of the cast. Richter, a pianistic giant, was very defensive about the size of his hands. They hung from his sides — like spades, a critic once remarked — when he strode to the keyboard. But Richter was no baboon. JL himself had seen the pianist's hands from a fair distance at the Festival Hall in London a long time ago. They looked huge. If a music writer told Richter his hands were shovel-blades dangled with salamis, which once happened, he took offence. He thought they were not especially large. Richter's father was a German piano teacher in a Russian conservatory — the irredeemably glum-faced artist had no tradesmen or farmers among his most recent forebears. His mother was in fact a *landowner's daughter*. In many pictures of Richter's hands, JL went on, the nails of the right thumb and middle finger are dirty — as if the pianist had come in from heavy work in the fields. But he hadn't, and his wrists are strangler's.

JL inspected his own hands, which I noticed were small, fingers relatively thin, but very strong across the palms, the abductor muscles on the side nearest the little fingers bulging considerably.

Do you play? I asked.

I have a Bechstein, he said, but not enough. Do you? he asked.

The teaching I got, I said, took me no further than a few easier Chopin and Haydn pieces and a slow movement or two from Beethoven sonatas. My sister was phenomenally talented, I added. But when *I* sat at those eighty-eight white and black keys I often wanted to escape, to be free of the chains that shackle pianists to their practice. I needed to be released from repeating the same three bars of music over and over again to try to perfect them, an impossible task. Pianists are enslaved to an endless cycle from which there is no escape, I added, adopting JL's pomposity.

He nodded. There *are* ways of escape, though, he said. Twice, years apart, I experienced the happy phenomenon of leaving my own body, hovering above it as I played. I seemed to float in an armchair of nothingness a metre or so above the keyboard. Looking down upon my hands, I watched my fingers in wonder. I found it hard to believe that I was making the music; the perpetrator of the trick, yet had to own it. There was no question that the arms and hands and fingers were mine, and I remember clearly how the brass block capitals of the piano-maker's name RÖNISCH glowed, how the glossy French-polished timber veneer in which they were embedded shone. I was very close yet far away, enjoying my performance as if I were in the dress circle of a concert hall.

I wonder, I said, interrupting, if the best pianists stick to their work to enjoy rare moments such as those.

JL shrugged. Possibly because of that experience, playing the piano was what I wanted to do, said JL — play professionally, I mean — but my parents were against it. The gorgeous English language and the magic of writing saved me, he said, and I became a journalist, like you I suppose, and I have survived despite low fees.

He stopped for perhaps half a minute, studying his boots and scratching at a clot of Brunswick green on his overalls.

Anyway, my hands were too small, he said, turning them in front of his face. He looked up, eyebrows raised, and said that it thrilled him to recall the first time language really excited him. A peculiar shock accompanies the memory, he said, and he had just that instant felt it. Every single cell in his body quivered the moment he pictured the day in third grade when we, the children, began to use nibbed pens for the first time, dipping them into small cylindrical inkwells fired from the finest of white porcelain — too good for us. And that holes had been especially routered to contain the inkwells in the ledges of our wooden desks seemed preposterous, amazing. Why bother for kids? And to be able to write in ink on paper, dipping nibs into these precious receptacles, was magical after having used pencils and crayons in earlier grades. It seemed to me a tremendous indulgence, said JL, an enormous demonstration of belief in the value of children and filling them with knowledge — he made a pouring gesture — and inspiring them, and it aroused me to fever pitch. To put down in ink, permanently, so to speak, your own compositions, whole series of sentences of your very own — they must have been fairly puerile, of course — but to do that as a kind of hallowed toil, to follow in the footsteps of real writers, of Dickens and Flaubert, say, using real pens and real ink was intensely exciting.

And one day our teacher, Miss Fortune, who seemed very old to us, ancient really, was demonstrating on the blackboard the calligraphic nuances of copperplate, very slowly curling the entry into a capital *M* for the word Miss in green chalk — we were to write our names in our exercise books, dipping our pens, linking the letters and copying the models that she had chalked across the top of the blackboard — and she continued on, astonishing us, her eight-year-old charges, by writing at snail's pace *Miss Eileen Fortune*. Now, in those days no schoolteacher was known as anything other than Miss Fortune or strap-happy Mr Nankervis — Pop Nankervis makes me nervous, we used to chant … out of his earshot of course — or Miss Fisher or Mr Stone, and as Miss Fortune wrote her name, she spoke it loudly, articulating every syllable as she went. When I think today about that image I have of her writing slowly and pronouncing her given name as she went it shocks me. It was as if she had removed all her clothes and had stood there naked before her pupils, an unimaginable vision for a Methodist boy.

If Miss Fortune had taught me to love pen and ink, she also forced me to fall in love with stories, JL went on. At lunchtimes certain students and teachers organised events for what used to be called social service. And you paid your threepence, I think it was, to hear the school's recorder band or listen to a short talk by an old-boy or old-girl who had become more or less famous, and the money went to charities.

Miss Fortune put on readings, the school's most successful social-service events. In her fifties or early sixties perhaps, she would mount rather unsteadily — a student on each side helping her up because the crook of one arm would be filled with books — a chair and then a desk and then a chair on top of the desk, rising to perhaps a couple of metres above the throng around her. And once up there, standing quite still on the chair to counter tumbling off it, a summiteer, her head grazing the ceiling, she would adjust her thick-lensed spectacles and begin to read for an hour in a slow, deliberate, perfectly articulated manner, the stories of Henry Lawson — *The Drover's Wife* and so on — the poems of Banjo Paterson — *Clancy of the Overflow* — and other selections, in a voice that was not at all theatrical but was so clear, clear, and nuanced that it captured the children, us, utterly and completely. We heard perfectly well even at the back of the biggest classroom, which had to be set aside for Miss Fortune's readings because of the size of the crowds she drew, a well-lit room that, curiously, always had Wanderer butterflies fluttering outside its windows, beating their wings on the glass in desperation, it seemed, asking us to explain the senselessness of their brief lives, desperate to know why they existed, I used to think. Perhaps they were keen to hear Miss Fortune. At every one of her performances the butterflies seemed to have been present — as if they were among her biggest fans, trying to listen from outside the panes. We pupils, at any rate, would swallow her stories whole, embed ourselves in the narratives, start to own them. You could have heard a feather land, and during the pauses I used to try to hear the butterflies' beating wings.

One day the last item of her recital was O. Henry's *The Last Leaf,* and that was it for me. You know the tale of course: a last leaf hangs on a vine climbing up a wall, and when it falls the girl who is dying of pneumonia and sees it through her window will pass away too. During a storm the leaf actually does fall, except that the elderly painter who lives in the apartment below the girl paints a replacement on the wall, a false leaf, which saves the girl's life. Because of the weather he had been out in to do it, the painter forfeits his own life to the same disease. It is a wonderful story, so passionate, and with faultless circularity. When Miss Fortune read so slowly and with such deliberation those last words — *he painted it there the night that the last leaf fell* — there was complete and utter silence, and I heard for the first time quite clearly — clearly — the deafening beats like rolls of thunder of the butterflies' wings against the glass, and eons seemed to pass between the word *fell* and the children's applause, our manic clapping, the slightest of smiles spreading on Miss Fortune's face, eyes behind her thick lenses watering, I noticed, because the story must have moved her too, and she slowly closed the book, took the hand of a student who had reached up for her, and climbed down with the utmost care from her precipitous perch. I had to hide tears in my snotty handkerchief as we left the room for fear that my classmates would see my sobbing. I was gone to words and their power to move, and I had to be a writer no matter how badly I would do it.

JL paused again and tapped on a cinnabar blob on his overalls. We took turns at being ink monitor, of course, filling the wells each morning, a job we loved because we could spend the whole day grubby, our hands stained blue.

He got up, ambled to the edge of the pond, pulled a weed from a crack between stones and returned to where he had been sitting.

I said that all this was intensely interesting, but I wanted to know about William Kapell and his fate. I understand that he was especially unlucky, I said.

Yes, said JL, if you consider — as we all must — that being a passenger in an aircraft that collides with a mountain at speed is unlucky. But let me tell you about the miracles that great pianists conjure night after night. I have counted the notes in the manic last movement of Prokofiev's seventh sonata …

Is what you are about to tell me in your book? I interrupted.

Yes, he said.

Then I shall take great pleasure in reading it. But what about Kapell? I said. I'd like to drive back to Melbourne before dark, I added, probably impertinently.

JL swept his straw hat in a low arc, apologized and began a summary.

Kapell was a New Yorker born of parents of no evident musical gifts but enormous appreciation of music. Brought up in several bits and pieces of territory that are these days parts of mother Russia, Edith and Hymie — called Harry once he had landed in America — made sure their two sons, Willy and Bob, listened to fine music all day on the radio, went to concerts and learned to play instruments. Bob, who became my friend, said JL, adored his big brother, who took him to concerts, the boys entering Carnegie Hall illegally. Once, an usher threw them out.

Willy took up playing the piano seriously at about the age of ten after seeing a little girl his own age performing sublimely at the kind of Sunday or perhaps Saturday afternoon concerts people used to put on in those days before capitalism commodified amusements. You can picture, said JL, the little tot in her

Sunday best, perched on a mahogany three-legged piano stool with ball-and-claw feet, the balls of crystal, legs dangling, gliding through *Für Elise*. And this restless Jewish boy, all big hands and twitches, already neurotic, watching her and thinking he could do better. She was a challenge to Willy, Bob once told me, and from then on mastering the piano became Willy's obsession. He was lucky enough to get excellent teachers for free or almost free, despite the Depression, the downturn in Harry's stationery business and his eventual filing for bankruptcy after his bookstore on Lexington Avenue failed. Such was the New World's symphony of generosity towards the wide-eyed hordes passing through Ellis Island and its amazing main building, which has the grandeur of a European train station, I always think, its vertiginous ceilings and broad arched windows signalling hope, but was, I think, more a kind of sorting house of nationalities, health status and drive to succeed. That building made America.

I worried immediately that JL had switched to a branch line and was about to head up it.

Willy became famous very quickly? I asked.

Yes, replied JL, making connections with New York's finest musicians, winning prizes and concert bookings and signing on with Arthur Judson, America's biggest agent. Willy was only nineteen, handsome, intense, and striving to be a great pianist to the exclusion of pretty much everything else, even though he married in his twenties a wonderful woman, a nice Presbyterian girl whose family detested Jews, herself a considerable pianist, a woman I spent two short periods with at her nursing home in the last weeks of her life and who paid me perhaps the greatest compliment of my writing career. Anna Lou and Willy had a son and a daughter. But, reading between the lines, JL continued, a decline in his physical and psychological health accompanied the flowering of his genius.

He stood up, stretched, and tottered to the edge of the gold-fish pond, lifting a lily leaf, leaning his face near the water and peering through the blackness beneath. He replaced the leaf, saying that the pond's water plants were parasols for the koi, using the Japanese name, which I suspect amused him because he possibly expected me not to know the word. He stopped and gestured, palms upturned, as if he were waiting for my applause, before sitting.

Fiddling with the brim of his hat, he studied a bluestone cobble near his left toe, scuffing its surface with the sole of his boot. Minutes passed, and I wondered if I should break into this weird stoppage. It almost appeared as if JL was trying to exert control over the passage of time. Slow it. Stop it so that his story had more room. He looked up, swallowed, and fixed me with a stern gaze.

I hope my readers understand, he said — I did not want to spell it out in the book — that Willy's obsession with the piano led to his hollowing out as a man. By all accounts, even Anna Lou's dying words, he was a loving father when he was at home between concert tours and performances. And he loved her. But music came first, and as his doubts increased about whether he could ever play perfectly, precisely as he believed the composer wanted the music to sound, his instability increased. You can see it in the last letters he wrote to his wife, the last long one from Melbourne beginning, Dearest treasurelet. He was near the end of fourteen weeks criss-crossing Straya during which he had played thirty-seven concerts.

Straya? I said.

Australia, he said, laughing softly. Love the word Straya. Strayan vernacular, he added.

Anyway, he was beat, as the saying goes. The Sydney critics, especially Lindsey Browne of the *Sydney Morning Herald*, who was better at devising crosswords than criticising musicians — he was the paper's crossword maker … you know, three down, piano key but not allowing access to vault of ivory or some such, as well as its music critic — had conspired to cut him down, the scything of tall poppies being a great Strayan pastime. JL grinned.

In that last letter to Anna Lou, who waited in New York for his return in a matter of a week or two, he divulged that people were noticing his depression. The conductor Bernard Heinze had told him, said the letter, that he appeared to be down in the dumps a bit, my boy. He told Anna Lou he had been sick to his stomach before one concert and dreaded walking out onto the platform where the big black Steinway awaited, the instrument that had given him a life whose richness was beyond all imaginings but was also slowly eviscerating him.

One of JL's small hands scooped the air in unison with the word eviscerating then scratched at a turquoise smudge. But he had played well, he told her, so that he could sleep without remorse and guilt, the exact words he used. (Words that unsettle me, I admit, as soon as I hear them. I saw my sister's fingers twitching on the pavers, the wounded hand, the wiggling pinky and her giggling.) He could no longer practise, and even looking at a piano filled him with unwillingness, the word he used. During an afternoon nap before a concert, he dreamed that the great John Sinclair, an excellent critic for the *Melbourne Herald*, had written a rave notice about wee William Kapell playing Brahms. I have seen the letter, held it in my hands, felt the frailty of the ink-blue airmail paper, and it shows that Willy wrote the name John Sinclair in bold capitals — JOHN SINCLAIR— and wee William Kapell playing Brahms in minute copperplate. Tiny. Yet he was world famous. Later, he wrote that he was being picked up for a concert in a hearse. He was cracking up is my view, said JL.

The last recital arrived, and you probably know the strange things that prevailed.

I don't, I said.

The black cat? he said.

Know nothing about it.

It was in Geelong, in the bluestone Plaza Theatre, which was pulled down and replaced with a performing arts centre. A freezing decrepit fleapit built during the goldrush, it would host at that last performance some of the finest piano-playing the world had heard, executed on an aged and dying grand that the fine player Paul Badura-Skoda had himself tuned during the intermission at his own recital the year before. Such eerie things happened the night of Kapell's concert, though, that you might have thought the pianist's daemon had emerged and was manipulating the performer and the audience. The Plaza's black cat, for instance, padded out from the wings after intermission and sat by Willy as he was about to play. It composed itself, licked its fur — Willy blinking at it — before sauntering off-stage. The night was also unseasonably chilly, and some of the concertgoers had brought rugs to put across their knees, thermoses to drink hot soup from.

While Willy opened with Mozart, the second piece, the last before interval, was Chopin's sublime *Funeral March* sonata, and he played it as he had never played it before. Some unknowable entity had got into him to elevate his performance beyond the superlative. Or was he projecting some mysticism all his own over which he had no control? Who governed him that night? That's the question. (As JL said these words, I wondered who projected my own mental images.) Was he above the keys as he played? Did he leave his body? Let the musical genie inside him emerge and take over? In that single performance, anyway, he paid his dues to the keyboard and he knew it. The Australian Broadcasting Commission recorded the performance and relayed it to its radio stations across the length and breadth of the country. It went to air at ten o'clock Melbourne time — after the concert was over. Willy *knew* how well he had played. I have listened to a recording of Sinclair's saying the exact words that follow: Willy burst into the ABC's offices in Melbourne the next day shouting, The tape, the tape, I've never played it like that before. Meaning he had never played it better. The ABC asked him to read the fine print of his contract, because a clause in there — probably in six-point type — said that recordings made for broadcast were erased immediately after use. Willy wanted a receipt, is my view. Can you imagine that when you have repaid with a single performance the debt you owe your art, relieved yourself of a creditor called music after having gone without and lost your way, shall we say, in the process — exhausted your last joule of energy — the least you would expect in return was proof that the cost had been worth it, that it had resulted in the creation of something priceless, immortal? A recording of that single performance of the Chopin *Funeral March* would have done the job just nicely.

But I understand a recording of it *was* found, I said.

JL jumped up, turned to face me and jammed on his hat, as if he were about to leave.

Decades later, he said in a raised voice. When Willy was long dead.

He sat down, swept off the fedora and turned to me sternly.

Moreover, it was a recording made from *the radio broadcast.* By an amateur, too. At home. On domestic equipment.

When Willy heard that the tapes were erased, he was devastated, and in the week before he left Australia — JL jabbed the air — his depression deepened. The night before he left Melbourne, he and Sinclair visited Jascha Spivakovsky at his mansion in Toorak and Willy and Jascha played pianos all night. Probably to lessen Willy's distress. JL paused. He seemed to be pondering something he'd said.

Spivakovsky, he burst out … now *there's* a story. Cossack Imperial Guards hunt him out of his home in Russia, he flees to Berlin then England, where critics call him the new Anton Rubinstein, a *wunderkind,* the king of the keyboard. He gets imprisoned in Germany as a Russian alien, but on his release he becomes one of the world's greatest pianists, upsets the Nazis, who put him on a list of artists who are to be dealt with in a certain fashion, as their paperwork used to say, and was urged to flee Germany, warned by none other than Richard Strauss, the great composer himself, in a cryptic message written in music. *In music!* Days before Hitler ascends to power Spivakovsky takes off for Australia. Now *there's* a story, JL repeated, and one could easily say that fate had dealt him a *poor* hand, if these are the kinds of things that interest you.

But not so bad as Kapell's, I said, attempting to switch him back to the New Yorker.

Yes, he said, poor hands, if you mean playing cards. Willy's was a two-seven off-suit.

Two-seven off-suit?

Texas hold-'em, said JL. Worst hand.

In the days before he left to go to Sydney to catch his flight home, he held up the palm of his hand to several Melbourne friends — JL re-enacted the scene — and told them to witness the shortness of his life line, pointing to it. I should not be here, he said, the very words he used. I am convinced that he saw a fatal denouement on the way. Absolutely convinced. He had obeyed his muse, performed to the nth degree for his art and had rendered up his soul in return, a hollow man, is my view.

DC-6s hopped across Pacific Ocean islands in those days, and when the plane landed at Honolulu he rang Anna Lou. She had been on part of the tour with him and she knew how exhausted he was. Also how transcendentally he had been playing. She urged him to stay in Honolulu. Wind down, charge his batteries, relax. She had even gone to the trouble of booking him a hotel room, she said down the long-distance line.

I can picture Willy now at a public telephone booth inside the Honolulu Airport concourse, anxious, gesticulating his big Jewish hands about, a diametric opposite to the Polynesian girls in grass skirts just beyond the glass, hula dancing to lilting ukuleles, their arms laden with leis of pastel-coloured orchids freshly picked to give to arriving passengers. The piano had consumed Willy, I believe, had eaten up any of the common sense that might have led him to make a rational decision. He couldn't see the danger, couldn't see that pianos fight a war of attrition. Chaining himself to a keyboard was the only way he could live his sort of life, and there were no pianos on board DC-6s of British Commonwealth Pacific Airlines. He needed to get home.

JL paused and shook his head.

Willy told Anna Lou he was getting back on the plane.

The next morning, just before nine o'clock, the DC-6 crossed the coast of California in an approach to San Francisco airport but was, it transpired, badly off course. BCPA pilots had the despicable habit of taking a shortcut across mountaintops higher than those beneath the official flight path. The plane's left wing hit a redwood growing at an altitude of more than two thousand feet, shearing off more than four metres. Disabled, the aircraft hurtled on through the branches of what are said to be the world's tallest trees, crossing a ravine, probably upside-down, before smashing — JL punched his palm — into a steep mountainside. An inferno broke out, consuming all nineteen on board. Rescuers who saw the wreckage from the air reported clouds of toxic gases billowing from ponds of boiling aluminium.

He sat down and looked at the toes of his boots, waiting several seconds, perhaps half a minute or more, before continuing.

I have hiked to the site of the crash, he said, along a trail for mountain-bikers through a forest of total unimaginable silence, where you can hear the cyclists' tyres in the dirt from hundreds of metres away, where turns in the path obscure further turns, where one is unsure where one is going, where one will end up, tall trees on either side, and where there remains still, to this day, once you arrive at the site of the accident, quite a lot of debris. Bits of fuselage can be seen, appearing to slide down the steep hill below the point of impact, as if these pieces of evidence are ashamed of the pilots' behaviour and want to disown it. Parts of

undercarriage, wires and tubes of various sorts are there for all the world to witness.

To my utter shame, I got on my knees and ran my fingers through the dirt, finding irresistible the morsels of wreckage embedded in it. I souvenired a sturdy press-stud that probably held in place the tartan fabric with which the seats were covered, possibly even from the very seat where Willy had sat, I sometimes think, an alloy fragment of what might have been a window frame, and the metal coupling that might have restrained the pressure at the end of some kind of tube or hose. I am ashamed of my thefts, but when I hold these bits and pieces and turn them between my fingers many questions arise that I am incapable of answering. We can only report, JL said, and you may make what you like of the playing cards that were held and the ones that were played, even those that Kapell had lain on the green baize of life and that coincided with his early demise. May I put a ridiculous thought to you? he asked. Did a piano and an aircraft collude to put an end to Kapell's misery?

A long silence followed. He was thirsty, he said, and it was time for a cuppa.

RETURNING to the house, we passed the rose thicket and its scraps of skin and fur caught among the thorns. JL pointed, saying that he had come out one morning to find one of the local kangaroos, a young one, flailing among the barbs. The sight distressed him, he said, because the more the poor wretch kicked the more inextricable his situation became. I don't have a gun, he said, so I rang my neighbour Kevin, a slaughterman who breaks horses, shoots rabbits, runs a few Berkshire pigs and acts part-time as an Aboriginal parole officer. And he came over and put the poor beast out of its misery. But getting the body out of the rose stems was a challenge, and it was only through Kevin's sharp knives — the two of us working together for a couple of hours — that the job got done. I had to hose blood off the thorns.

I HAD EXPECTED that JL's house would contain a lot of books, but its interior walls surprised me. They were wall-papered in volumes, if the metaphor sits not too uncomfortably. I failed to see a Bechstein, grand or upright. Collecting books was his only hobby, he said, and he far preferred to own books he loved and could write marginalia in and dog-ear rather than to try to borrow them from a disorganised library in the nearest town. I would need to order them, he said, and sometimes they arrive and sometimes they don't, for reasons that are beyond me and the staff.

I cast my eyes along the shelves while he put on the kettle. There were biographies of writers, shelves about music and musicians, including numerous books on the piano and pianists, many philosophical tracts, including Freud's *The Uncanny* and an introduction to Wittgenstein's *Tractatus*, a book on the technicalities of melancholia, which I was beginning to think suited JL's cast of mind (and definitely mine), volumes of military history, many on the Second World War, Kershaw's *Hitler* and Ellmann's *Joyce*, books by Australians and on Australian topics, among them Dunstan's *Wowsers* and the heavy fifth edition of *Australian Native Plants*, a metre or so of lurid hardcovers and paperbacks that dealt with bull-fighting, including two biographies of American matadors, one from Brooklyn, metre upon metre of fiction in hardback and paperback, two complete translations of Proust and a pocket edition in a microscopic font of *Du côté de chez Swann*, old Pelicans on number theory and ants, among other subjects, and strong representations of JL's own books, ranks of identical, pristine titles, indistinguishable one from the other, their spines perfectly aligned like royal guards in dress uniforms waiting to parade. Dust had accumulated on several of the volumes and the shelves in which they sat, and I noticed very faint — fading to illegibility — block capitals written in marker pen here and there denoting topics such as ETHICS, ANTHROPOPHAGY, SEBALD, and RUINS.

JL entered with a tray holding cups and a teapot and said he had given away many boxes of books to a local charity — these were what was left of his library.

What crossed my mind was the sheer concentration of knowledge and wisdom that the books represented and whether there would come a time in the not too distant future when children might be digitally injected with the collective intellect of centuries and a means of using it for the common good. They would no longer need to read texts at all, which even today they find onerous. I reckoned that JL would have strong views on the topic so I declined to open it. But I also wondered what would happen if the injections didn't work and that books failed to get read. *If, eventually, no one reads books at all.* Or if the intellectual digital injection was developed but failed to function properly without some initial reading of real books printed on real paper, which might — I am no scientist — calibrate the brain's electrical circuits so that what was injected could be used.

On a shelf in the Australiana section my eye fell upon — it was shelved beside bird books — the title *Picnic at Hanging Rock.* I opened it to discover a French translation.

Lady Lindsay gave it to me, said JL. The first French edition, Flammarion 1977. I was editing education pages at the time, he added, and had published a long interview with her because *Picnic* was a set text for Victorian students, and Joan — as she insisted on being called — had agreed to be revelatory about the schoolgirls' disappearance.

Was she? I asked.

No, cagey, he said, but what she said about writing *Picnic* was intriguing. I went to her gorgeous old home — an elegant, weatherboard turn-of-the-century mansion on the Mornington Peninsula only a fortnight after her husband, Sir Daryl, her partner for more than half a century, had died on Christmas Day. His paintings hung around walls of dark-stained hardwood panels, and, before they talked, said JL, Joan had taken him from picture to picture, lovingly, like a gushing gallery guide. Several of the canvases were of elegant Russian ballerinas — backstage — strongly reminiscent of Degas's paintings, and Joan was especially fond of some of the landscapes Daryl had painted in Europe.

He'd heard that Sir Daryl had been a medical artist during the First World War, and had had to paint distressing images of soldiers who had lost parts of their faces. Lady Lindsay nodded, adding that she hung none of those. They were painted for technical reasons, not for aesthetic ones, and had no place in the home, didn't I think? I decided that it was not a subject to dwell on, but I did add that it was remarkable how the loss of a nose or a chin or both, say, organic bits and pieces, seemed to detract from the personalities of the men who lost them, as if a part of their intellect, their ability to reason, part of whom they had *been* even, had disappeared with the flesh. What did someone with such a wound think when he looked in the mirror? Did he notice a diminution of his self in the glass — the sum of all the bits that had made him — because his flesh and blood were incomplete? I have given away a book, JL continued, about the facial wounds of First World War veterans, the men whom Sir Daryl had painted, called *Gueules cassées*, and in it a French historian described their grotesque and gruesome appearances as *sites of memory*. But the craters left by their wounds are strangely revolting and not actual sites but *voids* of memory, and, perhaps because they create an uncanny repulsion, a certain humanity weirdly disappears along with the skin and the bone, and the mutilated end up lacking advocates for their very existence. We prefer that they absent themselves from us who are whole. No poets plead their causes, their contributions, the effects of the wounds on their bodies and minds.

I interrupted. Perhaps, I said, the piano devastates great players as effectively as shrapnel, even if it fails to disfigure them physically. We don't notice the excavation of what the faithful might call their souls.

JL nodded. Yes, he said, their losses are invisible. The loss of flesh and bone is a visible invisible, of course. We imagine the intact faces and are appalled.

Joan just wished, he went on, that people could see that her book was written straight from her heart or mind or whatever I wanted to call it. She didn't analyse her writing but just wrote as the words came and cleaned up her work the next day, as writers did. As we were both flagging, I asked her if *Picnic* was factual or fictional, perhaps my most banal yet important question. She said that, in her mind, fact and fiction were almost indistinguishable and the older she got the more she doubted what many people called facts. A thousand years hence, she said, or in another state of time, what we call fiction today might be fact, and she was being quite truthful about it, she told me.

HAVING started to list unlucky pianists with Lee and learned from JL the facts of William Kapell's life, my balloon had begun to soar, only to have it burst by an elderly widow and her insistence that truth and untruth were inextricably mixed, as if in a kitchen blender, perhaps indistinguishable, and that I would have less luck than any of the fated pianists on my list when it came to mining their stories to understand what *really* happened to them and the psychological balm that I had hoped would flow from my discoveries.

JL jumped up and turned to one of his walls of books, outstretched fingers settling on the spine of a volume, which he snatched from the shelf.

Filling its cover was a black-and-white photograph in azure shades of a pianist playing a Steinway — William Kapell looking at his hands, his little fingers long, a glistening mop of well-coiffed black hair rising above his thin forehead and breaking back over his skull. The expression on his face is as brooding and rebellious as — and quite indistinguishable from — the visage of the Hollywood actor John Garfield, who mostly played tough guys.

JL tapped the book's cover. Now here's a story, he said. You know about Noel Mewton-Wood and Richard Farrell? I searched my memory, hearing only faint echoes. Yes, I said, vaguely. Pianists? Farrell was a New Zealander who studied in Sydney, said JL, and Mewton-Wood was a Melbourne boy who studied in London. They were of similar age to Kapell, all three of them dark and — as they *failed to say* in those days — hunky. All three of them stupendous keyboard artists. The ABC toured Mewton-Wood the same year as Kapell and tried to keep them apart … a publicity strategy, hoping that each on his own would draw more column-inches in the papers than if the boys appeared together. Farrell was in the wings in case Kappell or Mewton-Wood fell over. But you know the strangest thing about all this? said JL, wagging the paperback.

I shook my head.

They all died violently at thirty-one.

I have never been shot, but this revelation struck me with the impact of a bullet (or perhaps three), simultaneously exciting me — thrilling me — and striking me dead. Anna had also died at thirty-one (a fourth bullet), I remembered, and it crossed my mind that perhaps the early thirties was an age when a player gives in to the piano. He — or she — raises Lipatti's white flag, surrenders, and is quietly removed by undertakers or people in white coats, a life cancelled by some kind of invisible keyboard treachery. Three great pianists all dead at thirty-one, not to mention my sister. Farrell and Mewton-Wood were two more unlucky players, and the manner of their deaths and the reasons behind them I would need to investigate.

Having noted my open-mouthed reaction to his revelation, JL looked rather pleased — smug even. He handed me his book, saying that he had wanted to include a photograph of the three pianists together but had failed to find one. Several photographs were taken of Kapell and the Australian in earnest pianistic poses.

I began leafing through the pages until he tugged the paperback out of my hands and began a monologue on the difficulties of getting anything published these days. No one reads books any more so there was no point in writing for ink and paper and the stitching and the binding and gluing that make real books. *Real*, he shouted. The disappearance of literature was so distressing, that some days when his wife was away, a day like today, for instance, he sometimes wished he *owned a gun*.

The remark arrested our conversation, and I soon after excused myself, thanked him for his invaluable help and the cuppa and drove back to Melbourne.

JL'S STRANGE admission that sometimes he felt he should own a gun had shocked me more than I had at first realised. It had reminded me of the frailty of humans — all animals, I suppose — in the face of fate's interventions. We care deeply about the cards we are dealt, and we are affronted when our hands are poor. Instead, we might marvel at why humanity — why we — should take such trouble to continue to populate plains and prairies, wind-blown savannahs, remote, sinking islands and jagged frozen slopes, humid forests and parched deserts if our destiny is ultimately out of our hands, left to chance. Why try so hard? Take such trouble to hang on? Why persist if whatever we construct, the music we make, the pictures we paint, and the poems we write are, in the flow of eons, of no consequence, will surely turn to ash and dust and silence?

Only the past looks forward, I thought, indicating how best to live the next second, minute, hours of our lives and invest the present with value. The rest is out of our hands. If you need to know what *might* happen, look backwards at humanity's long history of despair. Leave to fantasists, I thought, our aspirations over Mars and Venus and the billions of habitable planets, some of which are bound to harbor life, the astronomers say, the closest only several million light-years away, a long, long journey, perhaps farther. I'm no astronomer.

And I lapsed into a despondency that lasted throughout a summer (in which I was slow-roasted; air-conditioning engineers make only empty promises) and several weeks into autumn. My depression provoked a recurring image I have of a rat on an exercise wheel. He spins it desperately. The rat is me, of course, and the image emerges unbidden, like the spiked shoes that fix me to a timber floor, when I am most vulnerable. Within an instant, it is accompanied by a second image — Anna's detached fingers twitching, dying on the pavers. Confusing questions follow. Just who might have been the principal culprit that day mystifies me. She did murmur once as she lay in her hospital bed, for instance, that she was pleased with the accident; separation from her fingers was the only way out, I thought she said. But I might be twisting the truth.

All I know is I was there and held the saw. Getting anything else straight is beyond me. Obviously. Anna could have planned the accident, for instance. She was so bright. She knew what lay ahead if she were to become an elite pianist. The anxiety. The terror. Losing her fingers, she realised, was a means of escape. But, I thought, if I were able to block my obsession with the accident, a compulsion to investigate the lives of unlucky pianists might be a saviour. If I could just keep the rat hard at work spinning the wheel, I might never again be tempted to do what she did. I had already endured decades of mental turmoil, a man alone, toes over the brink, ready to jump, so obsessed as to preclude finding someone with whom I could share my anguish, not that I could allow myself to foist it on others.

I felt a strange confidence: if I applied myself this time, I might never again endanger my life. I saw a train driver in a cabin holding a dead-man's handle. (The driver's death-defying grasp was a powerful recurring vision in my childhood.) If the driver dies and his grip loosens, the handle, which must be on a spring, automatically adjusts to zero and the train slows and stops. In the cabins of the world's fastest trains these days I'm sure that dead-man's handles are absent. But the thought intrigued me as a child; if I didn't keep control of where I was going, what I was thinking, how I was reacting to events, grasp the dead-man's handle firmly, my life might become useless. In a way, unlucky pianists would become — had already become — a kind of dead-man's handle for me, a failsafe device. As long as I researched them, gripped the handle, I might feel relatively well. If I let go, the engine propelling my own being might come to a screeching halt. The thought terrified me.

With these ideas uppermost, I set to work immediately, redoubling my efforts to find out more about the unluckiest pianists. I should try just to sit back, I told myself, and enjoy the ride, as they say, hoping fateful stories might continue to distract me. Lee was possibly right. Perhaps other pianists' lives would be sadder — much more — than Anna's and mine. *Schadenfreude?* Not a bit, but I suddenly understood that I had already valued what I had discovered about these blighted folk and was thrilled with the thought that more was to come. I was beginning to perceive my project as less of a manic quest for some kind of relief, an absolution from my involvement in Anna's accident — an impossible idea — and more of a *vocation*. I would need to persist with it — relentlessly, ceaselessly — and not let morbidity overtake me. In Farrell and Mewton-Wood I had new targets. They offered me a fresh challenge, and their brotherhood with Kapell was eerie.

RICHARD FARRELL merited only a single biography, said the etherous electronic cloud that envelops the Earth; I sometimes wonder if it contributes to global warming. And it occurred to me, as I searched in vain for versions of his life, that our knowledge, despite the knowledge explosion, remains limited these days by digital protocols written by experts who decide what we need to know and how we should learn about it. What we understand, it seems to me, is both *ordered* and ordained by young men of unimaginable wealth who pull the levers of the binary system. We are being discouraged from searching in dusty files, old newspapers and crumbling tomes for information. If we are unable to click knowledge onto a screen, it is apparently not worth knowing.

A few national libraries carried *Farrell*, the biography, but it was absent from the shelves of several esteemed universities and music conservatories, for instance, that one would think should normally shelve and lend a work about such a considerable musician. Two second-hand copies were for sale in New Zealand, and from Shakespeare's Plume in Dunedin I secured one of them, a slight paperback of around 170 pages that arrived a week or so later.

David Jillett, its author and another virtual absentee in the digital ether, was a soldier in the Second World War, finishing his military career with New Zealand's 14th intelligence brigade. The more I read about him the more improbable seemed his life, which ended in 2006. Post-war, he became a journalist who wrote military histories while also composing prolific amounts of art music, much of it sacred and for voice and keyboard. He studied in Rome in the 1970s and had cycles of his own German and Italian songs published there in 1980. The following year he wrote the beatification music for Saint Jeanne Juggan, Sister Mary of the Cross, whose lifetime devotion to the neediest, the poorest and the elderly led to the establishment of the Little Sisters of the Poor. He had worked with the choir of the Sistine Chapel and the Melbourne Conservatorium, the *Farrell*'s blurb noted, the latter having commissioned him to compose the first English mass sung in Australia.

Then — suddenly — this summary of Jillett's life dislocates, as if something Damascene, a fulguration of immense force, had intervened. At thirty-three, two years older than Kapell, Mewton-Wood and Farrell when they died, Jillett began a second

life, entering holy orders, studying philosophy with the Jesuits and theology with the Vincentians. Of the many journalists I know, none would have done such a thing, preferring to keep on drinking and exaggerating their war stories. Settling on psychiatric counselling — for want of better terminology — Father Jillett was for a quarter of a century a chaplain in hospitals for the mentally unstable while undertaking various ecumenical activities. (He would have seen me as a suitable case for treatment, I'm sure.) A saint, the blurb borders on suggesting, he was in 1996 made a member of the New Zealand Order of Merit for his services to music and the community.

He begins his book on Farrell by calling it, modestly and perhaps too dismissively, a casual biography. Yet he opens the narrative with a nightmare that Farrell dreamt in Milan in 1949. A small boy who lives in an alpine village befriends a fox. In winter, they climb to a mountain cave for shelter, a falcon soaring above them, presumably protectively, as they ascend. The fog thickens, and when the boy and the fox reach the cave, they find the falcon dead, its wings outstretched but severed from its body. (At this moment, you may guess the image that emerged. One of Anna's fingers has the habit of curling all by itself into a hook.) I shuddered, and forced myself back to Farrell's nightmare — from one nightmare to another, you might say. During a long winter, the boy sheltered the fox inside his jacket until one day, when the fox was strong enough, he ate the boy. Nothing was left except blood on the snow and bones on a jacket. Father Jillett writes that the nightmare mirrors Farrell's life. I had to read on.

The scene shifts to a Carnegie Hall concert almost two years later during which, according to the *New York Times*, the twenty-four-year-old Farrell had exhibited mastery, massive volume and fine tone. He possessed the necessary poise and authority to work with New York's best orchestra. (The NY Philharmonic, I presume.)

JL's biography of Kapell had arrived, and in it I discovered that, as a 1945 Australian tour ended, Willy Kapell had cabled his teacher at Juilliard to beg her to take on one of the most talented pianists — Farrell — he had ever heard. The New Yorker and the Kiwi sailed together from Melbourne's South Wharf on the Empire Haigh. Hearing the day before that the steamer had no piano and carried sand, not cargo, for ballast — not that its freight was relevant, I reminded myself to tell JL if ever I saw him again — Kapell bought a piano for £25 and had a dockside crane load it on board, keeping the short dummy keyboard that he took with him on overseas tours in reserve. Through a chain-wire fence, he allegedly told gathered newspapermen that some of his dearest friends had wanted to throw coloured streamers, as was the habit in those days when ships left port, and see him off properly, but aggressive officials had kept them behind barricades hundreds of yards from the vessel.

In New York at Juilliard, Farrell needed to perform only once for Olga Samaroff, who had taught Kapell and whose students always called her Madame, before being admitted to her class of classes, which numbered ten of the world's best young players selected from thousands of applicants.

Born Lucy Hickenlooper in San Antonio, Texas, Madame was the daughter of a businessman destroyed by the Galveston hurricane of 1900 and the floods that followed. She was the first American woman to study piano in Paris, and also the first woman to debut in Carnegie Hall after having hired both the hall and an orchestra. She made famous her second husband, the conductor Leopold Stokowski, but divorced him because of his womanising. Stokowski, of the flourishing white hair and demonic demeanour, the conductor as cliché, the ether notes, later became world-renowned when he teamed up with Walt Disney to create the film *Fantasia*. Olga fell in her New York apartment in 1925, injuring a shoulder. Forced to relinquish her concert career, she turned to teaching, producing prodigious pianists such as Kapell, Rosalyn Tureck and Alexis Weissenberg. And, of course, Farrell. He was her most talented student, she would tell anyone who listened. Among her friends were George Gershwin, Irving Berlin and the movie actor Cary Grant.

While Father Jillett excuses the lack of facts and fullness in his account of Farrell's life, which covers really only its last thirteen years, he claims that many of the conversations he transcribes come from Farrell himself. The book is otherwise inflated with inconsequential chattering and Farrell's letters home, the banter mostly among Juilliard students. In a conversation on a California beach, for example, a fellow student wrings out of Farrell how he makes his special tone in return for a pickle sandwich. Good tone, says Farrell, comes from the depths of one's being; it's mind over matter, or rather intellect *through* matter. I had no idea what that meant and hoped that, at the very least, Father Jillett did. We learn that Richard knew every detail of the van Gogh reproductions hanging around the walls of Vincent's, a Manhattan café Juilliard students frequented. We are told that — tall, slightly built but with matinee-idol looks, as was said in those days — he enjoyed running and would do it at Bondi beach in the years when he studied in Sydney and on the dry side of Fiji, north of Nandi, even earlier. As a boy in New Zealand he had won the sprinting championship, writes Father Jillett, other details of the competition, even its name, left unsaid.

The whimsy in Father Jillett's text extended to the chapters themselves, which were — curiously — in chronological disarray, chapter four, for example, being set on a beach in La Jolla, California, in 1946, chapter five at San Francisco airport four years later, chapter six at the Juilliard School in 1946, chapter seven a few months after that, and chapter eight half a year earlier. I wondered what to make of what was for all the world a hagiographic and erratic account of the pianist's life. What was Father Jillett thinking as he sat at his typewriter? Was he attempting a kind of complimentary poetics based loosely on a few incidents in Farrell's admittedly short life? In its tenderness, was his book meant to emulate a soaringly melodic musical romance, which he might have composed for piano and violin, say? And my key question — did playing the piano harm the pianist? — went unanswered.

The reader learns that William Kapell and his family were loyal to Farrell, to use Father Jillett's word, right from his arrival in Manhattan, getting him admitted to one of New York's best hospitals after he had blacked out with double pneumonia. Willy paid his medical bills. Willy bought him an overcoat, bought him lunch. (I wondered if the boys drank beer and wine. And who paid for it if they did? I suspect that most top pianists don't use alcohol, can't afford to jeopardise their fine motor skills.) Father Jillett handles delicately what few shocks Farrell felt in the last years of his life, but without indication of how they affected him in any other than a superficial way.

For instance, Father Jillett writes that the New Zealander and another Juilliard student crashed a Cadillac into a tree near Central Park. In a letter to his mother Ella, Farrell says that his friend Clive broke an ankle and cut his chin in the smash, and that his own face and ear had hit the windscreen. Doctors suspected that he had burst an eardrum, but neither hearing nor auditory nerves had been damaged, and a cut inside his mouth was fixed with several stitches, he writes. The borrowed Cadillac, a rare and beautiful vehicle, was a wreck, a complete write-off, and, the letter goes on, Clive and I were amazed that we had escaped life-threatening injuries. And there was another amazing thing about it, mother, a great mystery. Flo Fitzgerald, who from my earliest days sitting on a piano stool always taught me to sit with my belly button facing middle C, straight back, hands rested, wrists high, always a very practical and down-to-earth woman who never believed anything other than the here and now, by some kind of second sight or spiritual hunch seemed to have known about the smash before it happened. You ask me if our family is accident-prone. Let's not forget that the Bechams were all drowned, the Pattersons hired an aircraft that disintegrated in freak weather in a pine forest — I suspect a tree might have helped in the disintegration, mother — and fewer than half of my classmates from school are still alive. Fewer than half, mother.

Farrell's brand of nonchalance — as reported by Father Jillett — unsettled me; his contentions were scarcely believable. Here was a pianist who, if we are to believe the Jillett testament, nothing could unnerve — assuming its author had transcribed the letters and conversations accurately, which I suspected was the case. Farrell seemed to be, as they say these days, bullet-proof, the perfect man, the perfect musician, and a match for any piano. How could the keyboard demons that had snared and gouged the souls of so many pianists have affected Richard Farrell? They failed to lay a glove on him.

Farrell must have discussed with Kapell his nightmare about the boy and the fox and the falcon soon after experiencing it, because they were to talk about it at least once more on the telephone. Farrell asked Kapell what he thought about the dream and Willy called it pretty grim. Farrell was talking from the parlour of a mansion on the New England coast where he was having a short break with Madame, the anthropologist Margaret Mead, and other friends. In response to Kapell's gloomy assessment, Farrell told him that the day before, he had opened sitting-room French doors onto a sea fog. In the mist, he made out an eagle-thing, as he put it, perched on top of a balustrade, presumably surrounding a terrace. It stared at him, so grey and still that, at first, he took it to be a sculpted ornament. But as soon as the bird moved the pianist began talking to it just as he used to talk to his horse in New Zealand years before. Farrell declined to tell Willy exactly what he said to the eagle-thing, whether he introduced himself, first-name basis, told it that he liked the cut of its feathers, that he himself tickled ivories for a living and so on, but whatever words he chose to use left the winged one unmoved. It failed even to blink. Madame got out her box Brownie and took a photograph of it, and Willy suggested back from Manhattan that the raptor had probably got lost in the fog because of faulty magnetic-variation equipment. (Kapell the physicist, now.)

Whatever the reason, the appearance of the bird, which was a falcon, Kapell told Farrell, signified flight and hope, higher altitudes, better things, and souls soaring to new endeavours.

A few days later, Farrell, Madame and Margaret Mead, whom they all called Doctor, were walking along an upstairs corridor when Madame disappeared through the floorboards, crashing to a landing below. Farrell reports that they all thought she was dead, but when Doctor checked her over, she had suffered only a shock and severe bruising in what he calls a terrifying incident.

Reporting on Farrell's performances, Father Jillett suggests that they were all brilliant, and that the curve of his success and musicianship constantly ascended. His friendship with Kapell deepened to the point where the younger man, Farrell, could chide his older counterpart, Kapell, about the portable keyboard the New Yorker took with him between engagements. Father Jillett writes that Kapell liked bagpipes and that Farrell referred to the keyboard as overgrown bagpipes, even if it made no sound. On one flight, teenage girls with artificial eyelashes asked Willy if he could play them a few tunes on his accordion. He fails to record if their eyelashes batted. And even though a betting man would stake his house on the New Zealander's talent bringing him wealth and security, when he was short of cash, Kapell lent him money. Willy bought Farrell a compulsory morning suit needed to attend a concert in Memphis, and when Willy married Anna Lou, he sent enough champagne to the Juilliard students at Vincent's to flood the café and drown them to the last pianist.

On page 113, Father Jillett reproduces a publicity poster in landscape orientation that has as its topmost line in big bold capitals RICHARD FARRELL. Beneath, we read that the Sun never sets on the successful career of the brilliant twenty-four-year-old, the sentence ending abruptly with a racy exclamation mark that seems windblown, leaning forward, perhaps tossed off the vertical by the bluster of the sub-heading, or perhaps straining to see what the future had in store for the pianist. (An image of Lee's coconut palms bent by a sea zephyr came to mind.) Farrell stares at us in the lower half of the poster, his tie Windsor-knotted, a silk kerchief sprouting from the breast pocket of his jacket, the slightest of smiles beginning to tease. Behind his portrait, the world is contained in two overlapping discs, not quite a Mercator projection but similar, each bigger than the photograph of the pianist. The continents are in white, the seas black. Dotted curves from various countries end in arrowheads at headings in italics such as 3rd American Cross-Country Tour, 2nd Tour of Great Britain, and Tour of Australia. A few details and dates are appended.

Seven pages later, my investigations struck precious metal. It both heartened and shocked me, strengthening my hypothesis that great pianists, perhaps *all* great pianists, are afflicted by daemons they are unable to quell. Father Jillett records a conversation between Farrell and a friend, Trent, who was driving the pianist through the streets of Sydney, a city Farrell loved. The pianist said he wished his touring in Australia were longer. It's a pity, he added with his next breath, that he hadn't got longer on the planet. (Bingo! I thought.) His friend was naturally astounded at a man in his twenties, already a famous artist, the musical world at his feet, talking of death. Is it a doctor's report? Trent asked. A premonition? Neither, said Farrell. A definite spiritual intuition has conveyed the news, which he described as a knowing process of the intellect, an awareness of his sudden death. Trent pressed Farrell. He knew the pianist got grumpy, but he also knew that he was never depressed, was completely sane and had a doctor friend who was a first-rate psychiatrist. I imagine that they were driving down Macquarie Street, the splendour of the botanic gardens and the quaint pink Sydney Conservatorium and its curious, crenellated façade on the right, and in a minute or so they would come upon — or it would stop them dead, as this sight has a habit of doing — an elevated view of Sydney Harbour, one of the world's most heartening and, as they say, life-affirming blends of landscape and seascape, which, as a Melburnian through and through, I am keen to endorse. In the car, we may presume, on this gorgeous day, as most days are in Sydney, Trent plied Farrell with valuable and unimpeachable reasons to revel in his being alive. Surely his fatal premonition was the result of non-stop concerts and travelling. Nothing to do with the demands of his profession, Richard replied. As a teen-ager, he knew he would be dead by thirty, if not before, and that his demise would be violent.

I stopped reading and put down Father Jillett's book, feel-ing misery and relief in equal amounts. The piano was hurting Farrell, the impregnable. Only after several minutes had passed, a period during which I roamed my small apartment, not feeling my feet or knowing where they were going, my head empty, did I return to Father Jillett's account.

Farrell told Trent of a recent dream. He was one of several small children, including Willy Kapell, at play. The New Yorker had a magnificent falcon, which got lost in the hills in fog. Trent must have taken his eyes off the road for an instant to look strangely at the New Zealander. And, Farrell added, as the dream ended, both he and Willy met violent deaths. Father Jillett details neither.

The twenty-ninth of Father Jillett's thirty-three chapters is dated the twenty-ninth day of October 1953 and carries the heading, *Death of a falcon*. After briefly recording Willy Kapell's death on that morning some twenty-five kilometres short of the San Francisco airport's landing strip — as well as what it meant for the world of music — Father Jillett reminds us that Trent knew all about Farrell's fox-and-falcon dream. At some later date, Trent remembered every word of the nightmare and was able to interpret it, so marked had been its effect on him. The young falcon is Willy, of course, who soared only because he was a passenger in a four-engine DC-6 that hurled him into a mountain in fog. (In poor visibility, as JL constantly reminds me in emails, BCPA's pilots in the weeks preceding the crash had begun to take their shortcut instead of obeying the control tower's instructions to follow the designated long, clockwise loop over San Francisco Bay before coming in to land.) The falcon lies dead at the mouth of the cave, crushed, wings outstretched but severed.

The nightmare began to haunt Trent, he says, and the bones on the coat are Farrell's. A boy befriends a fox, a falcon flies protectively above them as they climb to a mountain cave. The falcon arrives first, but is dead when the fox and the boy get there. When the fox has secured his friendship with the boy, he kills him and eats him. And it crossed my mind immediately — the question posed itself instantly, in fact — that if Willy was the falcon and Farrell the boy, who was the fox? In the material that Father Jillett relates, neither Farrell, Kapell, Trent, nor anyone else gives the slightest clue that might reveal its identity. We are to read between the lines, it seems, arrive at our own conclusions about the grand play of fatal forces that breathe life — and paradoxically death — into the story. It struck me that the fox could be only one thing: it must represent the piano, or, more accurately, the ability to play it with superlative skill.

ELLA FARRELL heard about her son's death on the radio in Sydney. She was furious, and had a mind to ring the station and complain about the ridiculous news report that they had just broadcast. She rang her other son Paul instead, who verified the bulletin and later recalled, writes Father Jillett, that Ella's auburn hair turned white over the next fortnight. A fatal car crash had occurred at Fairmile Bottom near Arundel in Sussex. Farrell was returning home with friends Richard and Margaret Bradshaw when their car left the road, hit a tree and overturned. Thrown out of the vehicle, the three occupants were said to have died in an instant. Undamaged new recordings were found in the wreckage, and Richard's rosary was in one of his jacket pockets. A crucifix was said to have survived the tragedy. (Next day, *The Times* of London ended an obituary of the pianist by saying that his musical understanding had begun to mature and deepen in a way that presaged fine things for his future. He was possessed of great charm and a sense of humour. He abhorred letter-writing, and money spent on cables and telegrams was deemed well-spent, the obituary went on.) Father Jillett failed to say who was driving, a detail that to me seemed vital; he clearly had neglected to consult a coroner's findings on the accident.

The smash killed Richard only a year after his thirtieth birth-day, by which he had said he would be dead. I found his demise too eerie to let the world — or pianos — simply own up to it, and decided that, given the chance, I would try to find out more about the crash, try to determine if the piano, or being a great pianist, or testing the limits of one's artistic endurance had affected the car's direction in the dark on an English country road where one might imagine the traffic would be slight, the trees by the road-side much more abundant.

IN THE FOLLOWING weeks I had good days and bad. There were times when I was no longer bleak and in danger of hurting myself. On the best of them, I was beginning to see my research, which I was delighting in, mainly as a tool for curiosity. Those of us who have heard great performances revere the sites in which they took place. Is there something magical about some venues? Musicians will tell you how much they love performing in certain halls and not in others. Do the feted ones provoke sublime musicianship, conspire with musicians to conjure? Is there something in their air? And, even more important, do echoes, odours, feelings, spectres linger at these sites? I itched to find out what remained of the Plaza Theatre in Geelong, where Kapell had played his last concert, stamping Chopin for eternity. Were there vestiges of it I could revere?

IF A POLL were taken, Melbourne's five million or so inhabitants would probably decide that the freeway from Melbourne to Victoria's second city is the state's least popular thoroughfare. Unless you commit yourself to the slow, erratic and ironically named Sprinter and VLocity trains that can sometimes manage the eighty or so kilometres between the municipalities in an hour, the freeway can't be avoided. Apart from taking a wide arc around the cesspools of Werribee, where Melbourne's sewage is converted by mystical means into potable water, the M1 to Geelong plies a laser-straight course for its entire length, leading drivers to wish that the road under their tyres was the route between Nuremberg and Munich, and that in their hands was a steering wheel of the latest Porsche 911, and that they could delight in speeds of more than two hundred kilometres an hour without penalty. They dream, of course, because on the Geelong Road, they are limited to one hundred kilometres an hour, and carriageways passing over the freeway are underhung with bristles of cameras that are quick to record speeds above the limit, resulting in punishing fines and the common Melburnian protest that Victoria is a nanny state. Not only is the freeway depressingly straight and slow, a route conceived, think many, as a species of water-boarding torture for drivers, a perfect south-west pointer, but to either side of it there is a narrow verge of nothing but scrubby, contorted eucalyptus trees, none of them rising to more than about three or four metres. Beyond them is tedious flatness to the west, the prehistoric volcanic plain extending for hundreds of kilometres, and to the east, only empty paddocks until saline ponds take over near Port Phillip Bay, water-birds flying in seasonally, fewer returning each year.

I was probably on or about the ponds' latitude, a battered Toyota under my hands, and heading for the site of Kapell's last concert, determined to feel what echoes remained, when I was reminded of A. D. Hope's poem, a perfect nine quatrains that neither the slightest change of word nor syllable nor even letter could improve. It begins by reminding us that for every bird there is a last migration, that the cooling year uncannily kindles her heart, that love pricks her course in lights across the chart, as Hope so exquisitely puts it. Year after year, season after season, a speck on the map beckons her, and sure and safely guided by we know not what she is going away but also coming home, a perceptive observation that in a few words defines the *unheimlich Heimliche*, the unsettling home, a confusing place where what might once have been kindly has become alien. But she ages, the bird, the invisible thread that guides her journey one day snapping in flight, and, as Hope so sympathetically puts it, without warning or reason, the guiding spark of instinct winks and dies. The trackless world beneath her delivers no way, the wilderness of light no sign, the immense and complex map of hills and rivers mocks her small wisdom with its vast design, he writes. He ends the poem with, in my view, some of the most sublimely Romantic lyricism in the English language: Speaking of the bird, now fatally endangered, engulfed in a dark that rises from the valleys, of winds that buffet her with their hungry breath, the great Earth, he writes, with neither grief nor malice, receives the tiny burden of her death. These closing lines — *the great earth, with neither grief nor malice, receives the tiny burden of her death* — rang in my head as I drove, cautiously, at no more than a hundred kilometres an hour, and I fought to restrain, for safety's sake, the tears that my occasional recitation of them provokes.

A dozen or so kilometres north of Geelong, I passed the off-ramp to Lara, these days a small satellite community for Geelong, but on the 8th of January in 1969, when a voracious grassfire fanned by fierce westerlies swept across the road, the highway on which I was travelling became the site of a mass execution.

Although the village itself, which lies a few kilometres to the west, was razed, the road, its two-lane strips of melting bitumen separated by a wide median of scant vegetation, became an implement of tragedy. Today, any signs of death — the smell and sound of smoke and the inferno, of burning flesh — are gone, of course, and no sign commemorates the tragedy. Not here, anyway, but there is one in the town. And as one drives past the Lara turn-off it is impossible to imagine that, in the tumbling billows of grey and black tar fumes in 1969, seventeen people, including an entire family, decided to park their cars beside the road and flee with a view to outrunning the flames — only to be engulfed by them. Six who stayed with their vehicles and who, no doubt even in those more innocent days, followed the wisest practice and wound up their windows and tried to lie as flat and as low as they could, under wet blankets if they had them, survived.

Even at a hundred kilometres an hour here, one must pay attention to the traffic because of the improvisatory nature of Australian driving, but not even a sustained examination either side of the road, especially to the west, even less a glimpse, indicates the slightest potential for devastation on the scale of the Lara tragedy. In brief, it is impossible to imagine a fire's raging near the M1, or ever having been deadly, given the lack of fuel. Lara, and the seventeen folk, young and old, mothers and children, who sprinted towards their fate, as if they were embracing death, is simply an event beyond comprehension, a happening not to be understood but to be designated authentic and cruel, like, I thought, the thunderclaps of mortality in the lives of many of the greatest pianists. It happened, ordained and directed by powers that we will never understand, forces that we may do no more than acknowledge and respect. For all that, passing the spot reinforced my wish to know the unknowable, to try to get it explained, a ridiculous idea.

GREATER GEELONG, as they call it, is less than a sixteenth the size of Melbourne, so to call it a city, while officially true, is generous to say the least, bearing in mind the demotic idea the word *city* conjures. It has a nicely designed waterfront, a powerful football team that has won the AFL grand final three times in recent years, a small, low-rise, dowdy central business grid, significant unemployment, a closed Ford engine plant, no restaurants of any merit, a history of serving the wealthy squatters of the state's faraway western districts, of being the place from which their wool and wheat were shipped around the world to increase their inestimable wealth, two elite boarding schools which served the squatters' children, and, in contrast, increasing numbers of felonies. Geelong's crime rate recently doubled Victoria's average, assaults, most of them on women, increasing by more than six per cent from 2014 to 2015.

In April 2016, the government of Victoria called Geelong's municipal council dysfunctional and, with the upper house of the state's legislature, was deciding just how to go about sacking the mayor and his dozen councillors. A parliamentary inquiry had found that the council maintained a deep-seated culture of bullying and harassment, ignored complaints, and had no long-term vision. Relationships between the mayor, councillors and staff had disintegrated, and the government had decided to run the city itself, giving the people of Geelong a rest from democracy but promising to renew their mandate late the following year.

The mayor, who enjoyed being called eccentric, was once a fine war photographer and later made a fortune taking candid snaps of famous people. A man who might indeed be labelled the once and forever *capo dei paparazzi* was known mainly among Geelong inhabitants for his ownership of a nightclub that many locals viewed dimly. One of his greatest achievements, he said on the day his impending sacking was announced, was the floating Christmas tree that he had anchored near the waterfront of Corio Bay, an aesthetically unchallenging metal cone some twenty-five metres high on which had been riveted several five-pointed stars. It is alleged that he authorised spending a million dollars on it. Best-known for his sensational hairstyles and surgically-enhanced torso, he is often the subject of photographs himself, appearing to enjoy having lenses trained on him. They were there when he was tossed from a horse wearing full mayoral regalia during the filming of a promotional video. They were there again when he wore an Oktoberfest T-shirt of a naked young woman hitchhiking. He is the subject of many *clichés*, you might say, in poses that some might find outrageous. One has him doffing a silk top hat and wearing what appears to be a morning suit, a waistcoat in deep lilac, a voluminous tie in a paler shade of violet loosely knotted above it, and dark glasses. His hair is cut short but for a cockatoo's crest in dazzling pink that runs from the middle of his forehead to the back of his neck. Tinted a plum colour, a large six-pointed star stencilled on shorter hair escorts the crest.

Wearing a sky-blue jacket strewn with hundreds of small daisies, the mayor defended himself energetically the day after the announcement of his imminent political demise, saying he was one for robust debate, not bullying, that he was a tough leader, not a tyrant, and that the government's intervention was politics played out in the poorest fashion. The Minister for Local Government said that the people of Geelong deserved better, and left it at that.

I AM INDEBTED to JL's book for his quaint description of the Plaza Theatre. Made of sinister basalt blocks, it had been built during the gold-rush of the mid-nineteenth century and was razed by fire in 1926. Rebuilt with a Florentine façade and an ornate interior hinting of Spanish missions and art deco, it became a venue for all kinds of entertainments, a place in which the people of Geelong could be seen at their best, enjoying recitals, musical comedies and Gilbert and Sullivan operas.

But if there is a prevailing will in Geelong, it is towards disintegration, or at the very least decay, and by the time the Australian Broadcasting Commission had begun its praiseworthy and innovative policy of sending around to regional centres the best of the world's touring musicians, the Plaza was in disrepair. In less than three decades it had become a shabbier and grubbier cinema than many counterparts, its interior cool enough to keep local fish fresh, as JL puts it, his rhetoric striving for effect, I thought. Locals sensitive to Geelong's needs and aspirations called the Plaza every name under the sun; its horsehair seats needed respringing, whiskery cracks in them reupholstering. A local dubbed the green room a disgrace. In the 1970s, the Plaza was finally demolished to make way for the Geelong Performing Arts Centre, which opened in 1978, and it was to it that I made my way.

AN INAUSPICIOUS frontage of plate glass, steel and cement that might have been the local headquarters of a medium-sized auditing firm, say, or, but for the lack of flags, posters and slogans, the premises of a workers' union, the exterior of GPAC, as it is known, revealed nothing about its purpose.

Inside, I was immediately beset by a feeling of vertigo, of losing my way, my direction. I was somewhere alien and feared the onset of a kind of mental paralysis, of wondering what I was doing here, where I should go, and how I should think my way out of it. And when I remembered why I had made the visit I felt stupid, as if my quest was childish and idiotic. I stopped as if on a stage — my fumbling with music while an audience waited for me to play recurred in the middle of a large foyer carpeted in a dazzling cardinal plush, hoping that a dizziness that overwhelmed me would abate quickly once I had got used to the centre's cool air and optimistic, industrial odour. Was this how stage-fright felt? Painted white, large, barrel-shaped air-conditioning ducts and girders hung under a ceiling far above, and, ahead, wide ramps carpeted in more cardinal plush and bordered by balustrades of gleaming chrome and glass climbed a slope in a disorienting manner to the centre's entrance on Ryrie Street, which I could see perhaps eighty metres distant. In the course of this gradual ascent, I discerned horizontal spaces — an outdoor courtyard beyond the building's glass walls to my near right, an elevated foyer farther on to the left, a café at the same level to the right, and what appeared to be the rear of an ancient bluestone church straight ahead, beyond the glass, which took an acute diversion around it. Massive pillars of bare cement and theatrical lights overhead reinforced my feeling of being solitary and obliged to perform. Do it, they shouted. Play! I searched for lines I could remember ... To be or not to be, of course. An audience of thousands waited behind me. Faintly broadcast from somewhere overhead was — need I say? — Vivaldi's *Four Seasons*.

Apart from a handful of employees who scurried up and down the ramps at eleven o'clock on a mid-week morning, the vastness of the GPAC hosted little life. A handful of people bought tickets from three women behind a high counter to my left. How could anyone perform here? Without help? Without an audience? I couldn't. What did it say about the centre if its two theatres, which I knew were here somewhere, were hidden away, obscured by the glare of velvet, chrome balustrades and brutalist architecture? Opposite the box office, banners announced performances, titles written in appropriate type-faces. Swan Lake was in graceful copperplate, Don Quixote in a type usually used for the names above Wild West saloons. The Greats of 70s Country Music twanged. The instant I read those titles side by side, I realised that typefaces speak. (While Swan Lake, for instance, had a lilting voice, I heard frenetic hillbilly banjos when I read that country music was coming to GPAC.) The centre's theatres had to be here, I told myself, at least one of which had replaced the Plaza. But a stronger impression was that the building itself — or its interior — was trying to outper-form any other activity that it hosted, exerting every watt of its appearance in an attempt to upstage its purpose. Just what mes-sage it was trying to convey I could not discern. Acting is the art of standing still while not standing still, said a saying that had been etched across the glass wall in front of the courtyard, and it seemed to me that the interior of the GPAC was trying to resist its inanimate obligation to be stationary. Four lines of the quote beginning All the world's a stage were blocked in silver on oblongs of honeyed timber veneer, and Let wisdom and books go hang and all this endless care stand by the actor's side or sit in the jester's chair emblazoned more cladding. And the more of the GPAC's heterogeneity I took in the more confused I felt, the more its showiness swirled before my eyes, my uneasiness mounting to the extent that vertigo began to overwhelm me, and I thought I might tumble if I failed to find a chair. I closed my eyes and saw ballerinas pirouetting, cowboys strumming guitars and the Don spurring on Rocinante with his lance. Vivaldi's *Winter* engulfed me.

I had no reason to believe, however, that my unsteadiness was particularly noticeable when I was tapped on the shoulder. A woman of advanced years, her hair as white and aerated as soft meringue, her eyes watery and irises of such a pale blue that they tended to an iceberg-like frigidity, a Scottish brooch holding together at the nape of her neck the lapels of a cream-coloured blouse, told me that I looked unwell. Was I lost? she asked. Did I need to sit down? She was sometimes a volunteer here, she said, and she could help me if only she knew what I wanted. Was it tickets?

No, I said.

She had just bought some for a concert by a local choral society. You are not from Geelong, she told me, and I nodded.

I said I had come to GPAC on a ridiculous mission. I was trying to find, even to feel, the remnants of the Plaza Theatre, to listen for faint echoes of a premonition, to see if what had occurred on a particular night many years ago might have affected a young man's response to the tyranny under which one must be prepared to live one's life if one plays the piano at sublime levels of artistry. (I'm not sure now if I put it so pompously.)

She touched her brooch, a magnificent ornament of glowing red stone and silver filigree, as if to check that it was properly secured. You mean William Kapell, she said, and I nodded.

I was at the concert, she said, and I was fourteen.

I asked her if she would like to tell me about it over a mug of cappuccino or a cup of English Breakfast. If she had the time, I added. Delighted, she would be, she said, to recover memories of an event that had both frightened and pleased her, and did even to this day. She hadn't thought about the Kapell concert for a very long time. She would tell me everything.

Somewhat unsteadily and holding the balustrade, we took the ramp to the café, where empty pale-pine tables and bistro chairs were generously positioned on a floor of small, white mosaic tiles. I ordered tea for two.

SHE WAS THE daughter of an old squatting family descended from Highland Scots, not lowlanders, she insisted, that had settled in the Western District in the 1840s and had run sheep for generations. She had boarded at school from the age of eleven, a Presbyterian at Sacred Heart College, which accepted Protestants in those days, but she was constantly bullied and short-sheeted — did I know what that meant? she asked — by the Catholic girls. But when the headmistress announced at general assembly that William Kapell was visiting Geelong to play a recital in the Plaza Theatre and pinned a publicity photograph of him on the school noticeboard, we all went into a bit of a tizz. The school had managed to get several discounted tickets, announced the headmistress, but they were few, and girls studying instruments, especially the piano, would be given priority. William Kapell, whom one of the girls whose uncle was a record librarian at the ABC said liked to be called Willy, just looked so gorgeous. Sultry might be the word, if I didn't mind her using an antiquated 1950s expression, she said. Flora was her name, by the way, and I told her mine.

She was too old to mind her telling me now, she said, but when she looked at Willy's picture on the noticeboard she had blushed, in full view of the Catholic girls, and felt weak, both legs from her toes to … For a second, she paused. From my toes to my waist, really, just felt hollow and fizzy and not capable of doing anything, let alone stay standing upright, and I actually put a hand on the noticeboard to steady myself, being careful not to put even a fingertip on Willy's poster because the Catholic girls were watching. I telephoned my mother at the spread — our run was called Skye — to ask if I could go and she said yes, of course, and she would add the cost to my account.

It was a cool night and we sat in the centre of the auditorium. Some of the Catholic girls had changed into summer uniforms in October, I ask you, with bare legs and thin cotton dresses, but I was still in a winter worsted pinafore and grey tights. When Willy came on stage at 8.15 precisely in his tails and white bow tie I nearly fainted. I was so glad I was sitting down. One of my few school friends, a Catholic girl called Kathleen alongside me, clutched my arm. The funny, fizzy feeling in my legs returned, and, I suppose I shouldn't admit to this, but I began to tremble all over. He was so handsome, so determined even in the way he strode to the piano. For me, he was a living god, a protector not just of music itself but those who tried to play the piano, which I was attempting to do. And *his* playing, which began with a Mozart sonata, the second movement of which I had been learning, was out of this world. It was the first solo recital I had been to, and I had never heard anyone play the piano like that. And then he played Chopin's *Funeral March,* and the march itself was so sad I nearly cried and, look, I was convinced that I had fallen madly in love with Willy Kapell even before he had struck the sonata's last chord.

At interval we all fanned ourselves with our hands and programs even though some concertgoers had brought blankets for their knees, and it's true that as soon as Willy came out to play the second half, the Plaza's black cat padded on from the wings, stopped beside Willy, licked its fur — I was there, and I saw it — looked up at Willy, who for the first time that night appeared to be uncomfortable, lost for knowing what to do, but without his having to shoo it away, the cat obligingly left the stage and Willy began Debussy's *Suite Bergamasque.* When he got to *Clair de Lune,* I felt the strangest of sensations, as if I could fly out of my seat, above the others, soar towards the stage and sit on the piano stool beside him, resting my head on his shoulders as he played, a silly idea, but that is what I felt and feel even today — I am feeling it now as we speak — and in my mind I did just that, I flew to him. I was in love, and it's a lovely feeling to be in love, but it's also a terribly frightening, confusing, awful feeling for a young girl. He — and that recital — was why I became a piano teacher.

I was one of three girls chosen to attend the after-concert social in a large drawing room of a big Victorian house with bay windows overlooking a lovely garden, about fifty or sixty music-lovers, most of them regular patrons of the ABC's concerts, and I couldn't take my eyes off Willy. I wanted to touch him. I couldn't have opened my mouth and said anything sensible at all if I had been introduced.

Flora sat back in her seat and laughed. She smiled, her cheeks colouring, I detected.

I watched him from a distance, she said, as he met dignitaries and the mayor and Father O'Dwyer, who used to tell us to be wary of our feelings and go to confession, and he ate asparagus rolls, Willy did, held together with toothpicks, you remember, and saveloys with White Crow tomato sauce — they hadn't bothered to put the sauce in a boat and you could see the label with the crow, white, big on the bottle — and salmon mornay from ramekins using a splade, or a spork, or whatever you want to call it, and he sipped his tea or his coffee, I couldn't tell which, so delicately. I watched the way his lips felt for the teacup's edge, and I began trembling. He got a handful of photographs from his ABC chauffeur, who was going to whisk him away from us back to Melbourne, and showed them to people he was introduced to. I learned only afterwards from the girl whose uncle was a record librarian that they were photographs of his two little toddlers, a daughter and a son, back in New York. He was married, but it didn't matter to me because I dreamed of him in my bed at Sacred Heart every few nights for many months afterwards, even after he was killed in that awful plane crash.

In my dream, I was playing the piano for him and he was sitting beside me and smiling and forming my hands, shaping them, his own big hands lifting my wrists delicately and curving my fingers so that I could try to achieve the technical perfection that he possessed. His skin was so soft, apart from the tips of his fingers, where I could feel thicknesses. All professional pianists have callused fingertips. Then he would stand up and place his hands on my shoulders and gently massage my neck, and … Flora stopped. I won't say any more, she said. The dream didn't go much farther, anyway, she added, because it was so embarrassing, and I usually woke up perspiring. But I must say that those wonderful reveries, which were so exciting all those years ago — and to think that I dreamed them — shock me even today.

I asked Flora if she felt any premonition of Kapell's tragedy during the concert.

No, she said. She had been too overwhelmed by the whole experience of hearing the recital to read anything mystical into it. She had reacted to the coincidence of his startling handsomeness, she said, and his sublime artistry. It was an unusual combination, don't you think? And only one other thing crossed my mind during the concert and that was how daring it must be to play the piano at supreme levels. You would be terrified of not just making a slip, wouldn't you, inadvertently hitting a wrong note here and there, but also of not doing your best, not interpreting a piece of music as well as you know you can, because you've played it before many, many times at superlative levels. I am not referring to perfection, said Flora, but being able to play a piece as well as you know you can play it every time you step onto a stage and sit at the keyboard of a big black concert grand. And I thought at the time and still do that that must be a terrible burden to carry throughout your life. A huge weight it surely is, an enormous source of anxiety to have to cope with. I have read, she added, that great pianists are *extremely* demanding in control booths when listening to the playbacks of their recordings. Richter, in that famous recording of Schubert's *Wanderer Fantasy* produced by Peter Andry, who spent much of his childhood and youth in Melbourne — did you know? — perhaps the greatest producer of recorded music ever, classical, I mean, Richter, anyway, whom Andry asked to do another take of only a small section of the piece, which must run, the whole piece, for twenty minutes or more, and Richter turned to Andry and said that he needed to play all of it to get the artistic balance right, not a morsel of an extremely demanding and strenuous work with all its changes of mood and tempos and dynamics and massive chordal passages and delicate lyrical ones and he did. And this is what you hear when you listen to the Russian's amazing recording, as I do over and over again. I suppose I am talking about perfection, and I should clarify what I mean by it. I don't think that people like Richter believe there is an absolutely perfect way of playing a piece. But I do think that they feel under a gigantic responsibility every time they sit at a piano to give their all. It must be awful, like doing something that can be fatal if you make a mistake, like the Flying Wallendas, several of whom have been killed and maimed because they have worked without nets on wires many metres above the ground all their careers, and the matadors who face death every time they enter a bullring. The fear of failing if you are a great pianist must be like a death threat. There are some, of course, who enjoy it.

Flora's fingers were misshapen, the joints knobbly, several middle phalanges diverging from the straightness they must have had when she was a child. She spotted my downward glances and said that she had had to give up teaching in schools because her osteoarthritis had got worse with age. Pain, stiffness and swelling that had begun when she was in her forties had lessened her ability to demonstrate for students how to play particular phrases. I concentrated on teaching students at home, she said, but even that became more difficult in the end, so I gave away all my music, including a two-volume Brietkopf & Härtel set of the thirty-two Beethoven sonatas with those peculiar royal-blue sharkskin covers that I can still feel under my fingertips even today.

I refused, in the end, to sell my 1897 Bechstein grand, though, and these days its lid is closed and it looks a bit forlorn in the corner of my lounge room, gathering dust. It has become a kind of memorial, I suppose, representing piano music and what I used to love doing, and I sometimes feel that I would like to open it up and unfold the music stand into position. She stopped for several seconds. And lay a wreath on it, she said. The date of my late husband Ray's passing I could do that, for instance, because he used to sit in his favorite chair and listen to me play, just smiling hugely, even in the most poignant moments of a Beethoven slow movement, for instance, which made me a little uncomfortable, wondering if he really understood the music at all. I have no doubt that he *loved* it, and perhaps that's all that we should ask.

I wish I could do more things with my hands these days, but I am limited to peeling potatoes, which I fumble, and putting on the kettle. People used to feel a sense of worth if they could do things with their hands, I often think. It used to be so important to do needlework and the boys woodwork at school, and now young people use their hands only to tap on their mobile telephones. Have you seen how fast their thumbs fly over those tiny screens? They could be champion knitters, which I used to be, in a way. (I made sure my hands and their scars were out of Flora's sight, under the table.)

Out of a sense of courtesy, I asked Flora what had happened to her childhood property.

It had been sold about ten years ago, she said. But my question prompted her to remember her brother Norm, who, she said, was the last of her clan to have lived there. He was there even after the new owners had bought it, and he had died only three years ago after leaving the property a month before. His hands had saved his life, she said, rather than ruining it, as mine have. Our mother had German measles during pregnancy, and at the age of two Norm was diagnosed profoundly deaf. All my life it saddened me that he never heard the wonderful music that I have got enormous pleasure from. As you probably know, rubella during pregnancy can result in children who cannot see, hear and are sometimes autistic, not to mention having heart and vascular problems. And Mum took Norm into the Royal Children's Hospital twice a week for twelve years. You know, I'm reminded now, that, being the older sister and responsible and mature, sort of, I thought the hospital must have been built exclusively for royals when they visited. If, in an emergency, Princess Anne, say, who was touring Australia and needed treatment could be whisked there. A hospital just for them. Why did they bother to treat Norm? Why was he a patient there? That was when I was perhaps eight or nine and he was even younger, and Mum took him to the hospital on Victoria's very slow trains and trams and buses, which connected only sporadically, and

Norm would often misbehave, throwing himself on the foot-path in paroxysms, faking fits.

He was well-known in towns near Skye for his odd behavior. Many people believed he was possessed. I suppose in ancient times he would have been burned at the stake or drowned. (She smiled.) Even as a young boy he would run away, and at the age of six he was diagnosed as being retarded. It was such a shock to all of us, and when you hear something like that you tend to lose all hope that someone will have a worthwhile life. He was supposed to pick up lip-reading, but he couldn't look people in the face, and I often wondered what was going on in my dear brother's mind. When he was ten, experts said he should communicate using sign language, but by then it was too late for him to learn it in any coherent fashion — he should have started years before — and for the rest of his life he messaged only in single signs, unable to put together a series of them. Because he had autistic tendencies and threw tantrums, the deaf school on St Kilda Road refused to take him, and because we had the money to do it, Dad hired a specialist sign-language tutor to teach him. But just when he was making a little progress, the tutor stopped coming because, according to the regulations, as a teacher in a state school he wasn't allowed to accept other work.

He drifted away from Mum and Dad and me, a picture of loneliness. And we were faced with the problem of *how* to love him. We did all we could for him, and Mum hugged him whenever she could, whenever he wasn't too excited not to be a handful in an embrace, not to be dangerous. So we couldn't say if we were ever giving him love the right way, because he never responded to it. Perhaps he couldn't. No smiles broke over his face, his mouth mostly turned down anyway — Flora pulled a glum face — so we had no guidance, no rudder to steer our love for him.

In his teenage years, Norm became rebellious, running away from Skye — Mum would write to me at Sacred Heart with all the stories — taking his twenty-two rifle and I don't know how many boxes of *long* bullets — he never bought shorts — and disappear into the paddocks with his kelpie Angus. Often, the police and volunteers from the Country Fire Authority would have to organise searches for him, and the longest he was out for was six days. They found him in a shallow gully, Angus resting on his lap, empty cartridges all around him. By a lake nearby they found more empty casings and scores of dead shelducks, shovelers and coots, and Dad and the police had no idea what to do with him.

At school in Coleraine, they had tried him in what was then called an opportunity grade, or *oppoes*, as the boys were known — no girls were *oppoes*. Flora smiled. There was no point in trying to educate him everyone agreed, including Mum and Dad. If Mum, who told me just before she died that she had felt guilty all her life about Norm, didn't watch him constantly he would go on a rampage, tearing up books and copies of *The Country Woman*, tipping out canisters of salt and flour and tea all over the kitchen floor, and smashing crockery to the point where Mum had to have locks fitted to the nicest rooms at Skye where the antique chaises longues and a beautiful mahogany fold-up table that we were told had come from a Cobb & Co stage coach and the best Wedgwood plates and cups were kept in two Georgian display cabinets as well as sets of Waterford crystal. Luckily, Norm never got to them.

Everyone tacitly agreed that he was a lost cause, someone who would just live out his life without enrichment and wonder, in a daze, more or less, and I try to imagine to this day what dreadful turmoil, what … what *whirlpools* of incomprehension and terror turned ceaselessly in his mind and if he ever imagined how he could extricate himself from his appalling situation. Even if he believed he had the power to achieve such a task. We would never know. Perhaps his mind was a blank. I often used to think that that was probably best for him. That he was living and breathing but unconscious to the world. He was a bit like someone on life support but hyperactive, a destroyer, but not of his own will.

Flora stopped and slowly shook her head. She tugged at her collar and adjusted her brooch, running her fingertips over the glowing red stone. A smile teased the corners of her mouth.

But then one day you wouldn't believe it. We *did* know. Got all the answers. A miracle happened. We were not excessively Presbyterian, but we all thought some intervention of some magical sort, if not divine, had occurred.

Mum noticed Norm's fixation with the deputy manager's wood-chopping skills. Although we were fairly well-off, electricity didn't come to Skye until the late fifties, and our heating and cooking and hot water relied on an abundance of firewood. And it was the deputy manager's job to chop it until the day Mum gave Norm an axe, fearing for her life, I suppose, and led him to the woodpile on the man's day off. She just let him run amok on the logs. Well, you know, doing this act with his hands, chopping wood, making something, even if the something amounted to stacks of sugar gum that grew and grew and could fit in the fireplace and the stove, saved him. He appeared to understand, Mum wrote, said Flora, that he was doing something useful, contributing, and the deputy manager never had to chop another log. Of course, we were all overjoyed that he had found a way out of his wilderness. Overjoyed. Even as he developed scoliosis and a hunched back with age, Norm chopped, sometimes sitting down to do it when he was tiring.

With the help of a bit of schooling from the deputy manager, who started out terrified, I'm sure, he learned the finer points of splitting logs — that you should never have an axe that is too sharp, that you are splitting wood and not trying to imbed the axe's blade in the log, which just wastes time because the axe gets stuck on account of the tight and sinuous grains of the sugar gums, that you search for the slightest weaknesses, the smallest cracks in the log and aim for them, and that you give a quick flick of your wrists the instant the blade hits the wood. It's quite an art, and the axe-head should never get stuck. You are splitting logs, not doing surgery.

From then on, Norm chopped wood almost every day of his life, refreshing himself with tumblers brimful of lemon juice, no sugar, even eating lemons whole. He learned to smile, too, and we all thought that he was coming around. As it turned out, though, his social skills never developed much, but he did become a quieter, more stable soul.

I like to think that woodchopping not only gave him a purpose in life but enough confidence to take up painting in his forties, two or three of his watercolours of the lake where he shot the birds eventually being exhibited at the Coleraine Art Show, where they failed to win prizes but were generously received. Sometimes his skies were pale green whereas they're almost always blue over the Western District, and his improved pastures, which were watered and fertilised, came out a kind of lolly pink instead of verdant. Flora laughed. It was a change from your usual colourings. His paintings reminded me of van Gogh's, to be honest. I watched him paint a lot, and he always appeared to be listening for the right colour to use despite not hearing a thing. Head cocked, listening. Flora cocked her head to one side. And sometimes he clearly heard wrongly, we all thought, but is there ever, ever, a right answer to anything?

He could split over a ton of wood in a weekend, and eventually graziers from surrounding properties and people from the local netball and football teams and even the mayor of Hamilton backed up tip-trucks and made their own piles of sugar gum for him to split. Of course, Dad got him to charge small amounts for his services, and in no time at all he had a thriving business on his hands, the money he made going into a chainsaw and two new axes, one with a very broad blade and a handle that veered off-centre on purpose so that he could trim fence-posts without grazing his knuckles. He also bought steel feathers and wedges and a sledgehammer that he used on logs with tougher grains but also to split the straight-grained timber that would become fence-posts. So he had gone from chopping up firewood to being a businessman who made hand-hewn fence-posts, and he bought a new brace and bit, too, to drill holes in them for the eight-gauge fencing wire to run through.

Dad thought of helping him to register a business name but in the end reckoned Norm would neither understand nor appreciate it so he let the idea slip. But the president of the football club, a signwriter, obtained from somewhere, he would never say where, a beautiful plank of Queensland maple, which was perfectly smooth and had a lovely honeyed pinkness and exquisite pattern in its grain like the delta of one of the world's great rivers, the Nile, say, as viewed from a high altitude. And he painted on it the single word Norm's in a wonderful flourish in Brunswick green with gold highlights, just Norm's, nothing else, and Norm bolted it to a tree near the piles of wood and couldn't stop smiling as he chopped beneath it. His life had purpose, and he knew it.

When Skye Run was eventually sold after our parents died, the new owners always kept him on, allowing him to move out of his room in the house into the shearers' quarters, which were pretty comfortable, better than many on other runs. At any rate, he didn't seem to mind so long as he could continue splitting wood. I saw him for the last time in hospital as he lay dying of bowel cancer. He took my hands in his, and they were still very plump and callused although he hadn't been fit enough to work for many months. But have you ever held the hands of a wood-chopper or a gardener, a person who really challenges with hard labour the limits of what ten fingers can achieve?

I shook my head.

They have this strange warmth. Their hands radiate a kind of goodness and wellbeing and beneficence, I like to think. Like God's hands, the Catholic girls might say. Flora chortled at the idea. I'm reminded of a great-aunt of mine, she continued, who used to say her scones were magical — renowned in every street of Boort and at Methodist after-church teas — because a certain mysterious entity came out through her fingers as she kneaded the dough. I am not talking about the laying on of hands in some kind of spiritual way, but Norm's big mitts, you'd call them, which completely enveloped mine, felt so reassuring, so warming, and they told me that I was not to worry on his behalf, that he had had a contented life from the moment he began wielding an axe and that he was not afraid at all of what lay ahead. Without saying a word, he managed to convey this message, I like to think, through the goodness of his soul as it was manifest in his touch and what his old callused fingers and thumbs and palms had achieved in a lifetime of hard work. He looked at my crooked fingers and knobbly knuckles and shook his head in sympathy. I am sure that he was saying that if he could fix my hands by folding them in his own, he would. But of course he couldn't, and a week later he passed away quite peacefully while I dabbed droplets of perspiration from his brow.

The *Hamilton Spectator* wrote a wonderful obituary. I have the cutting at home. Its heading, in big letters, more or less said that Norm had eased the pain of a lifetime of silence by chopping wood. I can't remember the words exactly, but they had been beautifully put. Then there was his name, also quite big, and under it the single word in bold type, **Woodchopper**, which to me and everyone who had known him, many of whom came from miles around to attend his funeral, carried infinite dignity and said exactly what he had been, Woodchopper. (Flora underlined the word with a forefinger.) We scattered his ashes under his sign, and the new owners of Skye have promised never to take it down.

Flora stopped, sitting in silence, her ice-floe eyes fixed on mine, her bottom lip beginning to quiver. She found a tissue in her handbag and dabbed beneath her eyelids.

I wanted to ask her if she ever felt any danger being near Norm when he was chopping but decided against it. My sister was never worried when I was using the saw that caused her accident, so it's all a matter of moments and circumstances. And fate, and whether it ever signals its intentions, which I doubted but was here to investigate.

I asked Flora if she knew exactly where the theatre used to be, where the stage from which Willy played his last notes in public might have been. She stood, and asked me to follow her as we took a ramp, more steadily this time, towards the Ryrie Street entrance. Once we had reached the building's next level space — a small foyer to our left — she stopped. Beside stairs ascending to what appeared to be glass-encased meeting rooms on a mezzanine high above, a wall of concrete clad with more oblongs of honeyed veneer confronted us. Above double doors of much darker wood, The Playhouse was fixed to the concrete in stern white bas-relief letters. Below it, the words Stalls, Door 1, and Rows A-I directed theatregoers. Flora waved a hand vaguely.

Somewhere in there, she said — indicating an indefinite volume — I sat trembling, listening to Willy. Her eyebrows arched, and I detected a smile in her voice.

I tried the doors, which were locked. I tapped on them, getting no response. I put an ear to them. I stood and stared and held out my hands like a holy man in an effort to try to put myself in a frame of mind that might be most receptive to whatever mystical dregs of past performances, what auras, you might like to call them, echoes, remained from more than sixty years ago. Nothing. There was none. Defined in that narrow sense, my quest, which

I realised again had been idiotic, had failed, but had the failure affected the state of my mind? Had I proved or disproved anything? In that I was near, at last, more or less, the location of a miraculous musical event, my curiosity had been satisfied. But I had partly expected some stones of the old theatre, scraps of the Plaza's foundations to have been conserved, under glass, perhaps, like the medieval crypts of ancient European cathedrals beneath Perspex floors that exhibit dust and old bones, golden chalices and tattered ends of faded ecclesiastical robes. Nothing. The GPAC had failed to recognize, even with a memorial plaque, the Plaza's existence.

I asked Flora if I could drive her somewhere, but she said she wanted to browse in the famous nearby Barwon Booksellers — did I know the shop? — for a nice second-hand copy, as she put it, of Evelyn Waugh's *Helena*, which the writer considered his best work. Did I know it? she asked.

Yes, I said, but I hadn't read it for a long time.

It was about a quest by a Christian mother of a Roman emperor, she said, to find relics of the true cross, the real wood, on which Jesus was crucified. It was a wonderful book, often quite comic, even if its theme was the value of authenticity. If she could come across a nice copy, she said, she wanted to give it to a friend at her church, and we waved goodbye, wishing each other well in our ventures.

A FEAR OF falling short of perfection, I realised — Flora and I had more or less agreed on it — bedevilled the great pianists and was probably at the root of their anxieties. That said, I was keener than ever to explore the abysses above which they walked a wire that was hardly ever taut and could loosen, through their own doing, in an instant. (Nothing unsettles me more than images of wire-walkers, and one immediately came up. It was a clip of Philippe Petit's terrifying journey between the Twin Towers. No film distresses me more than *Man on Wire*, and mustering all my strength, I managed to thrust this particular horror fragment out of frame.)

Two emails of relative importance awaited me at home. A little surprisingly, one was from the mysterious Dr K, whom I had agreed to keep in touch with, to report my progress, so to speak, but he had got in first. Many months had passed since we had been introduced. I was both skeptical and suspicious of him. At our first meeting he seemed unlike other St Sebastian staff, even if he looked as I once did.

Dr M had suggested that we Skype, of course, and as it was late in the afternoon — a weak sun slanting through extruded clouds and ultimately my window — I thought that Dr K might be available. I was a little surprised that I got through to him immediately, one of St Sebastian's walls in institutional cream and a pinboard fluttering with notices and lists behind him, his lab coat as scorching white as ever, his beard as immaculately trimmed. But the picture was blurred, indistinct, as Skype pictures sometimes are because of something in the ether or the digital cloud, which I recently learned is not a cloud at all, or perhaps because of something in the meteorology of the day.

He had emailed me to ask about my progress, he said, what I felt about the state of my mind and whether I was following any plan. I told him that I had come around to thinking, at times, that it was probably ridiculous to hypothesise that the piano could destroy human lives. He smiled and said that that, in itself, amounted to a giant step. *Giant.* I should broaden my research, he suggested, keeping an eye out for pianists who had lived long and happy lives, had performed without fear into old age; there were probably many who had coped very well with a life lived with the stress of trying to perform perfectly.

Long lives perhaps, I said, but surely not angst-free, nominating Horowitz as an example. Don't forget, I said, that he took anti-depressants over decades. He also had had electroconvulsive treatment to attempt to manage his stage fright. More than once he forgot where he was in a piece of music in front of a prestigious audience, and more than once he lost control of his fingers. On stage, on a platform, in front of hypercritical listeners. Yet he was a genius. Was it worth my trying to find *even one* pianist who had been happy? I asked Dr K, with no attempt to be ironic.

He did not reply in words, preferring to respond to my question with utter stillness.

At that instant, a slant of weak sunshine from over my shoulder broke onto the screen and, in the glare, I lost sight of him altogether. By the time a skein of high cloud had obscured the sun and I could see the screen clearly again, my reflection and Dr K's image — still and silent — had become one and the same, and I was shaken in that terrifying silence by the frightening possibility that I had been talking to myself. He so much looked as I had several decades ago, a period during which I was earning good money contributing articles regularly about music and musicians to *Australian Keyboard* and others about joinery to the *Australian Woodworkers' Monthly*. It was also a time when my sister's genius was developing at an extraordinary pace, and her accident, the accident I probably caused, was some way in the future. With whom had I been Skyping? I asked myself, and at that moment the screen went blank.

The second email was from JL, who sometimes thrice weekly messaged me with suggestions he believed would enhance my project, some of them valuable, but many seeming to caress his own ego and demonstrate his considerable knowledge of pianists and pianism. Perhaps he had nothing better to do.

In one email he narrated a follow-up to his story about Miss Fortune. Soon after he had been moved by *The Last Leaf* to the extent that he wanted instantly to become a writer, he had begun to try to put down his own stories. The shortest were three or four sentences, the longest no more than a page, and he had bought a stouter pen than his school one and a box of superior nibs, paying for them out of money from his paper round, to write them. None of the stories was any good, he decided, until he wrote a one-pager that he called *The Duel*, which must have been inspired by tales of the French Revolution and eighteenth-century gallantry that had been rewritten for children. Classic comics, too. He had the idea, wrote JL, that if two duellists fired their pistols at precisely the same moment and with deadly accuracy they would die simultaneously. And that was the story, the arrival by horse-drawn carriages at a forest clearing, the seconds reading the rules, the grim antagonists, back-to-back, deliberately stepping away from each other, steps counted out to ten, the turning, aiming and firing of the pistols, the deaths … and I folded it up carefully and kept it in my wallet for years, JL wrote, not having the courage to show anyone. I even blotted it with ink and rubbed it in places with dripping — young people don't know what dripping is — to give the paper itself an ancient-seemingness, as if it might have been written by one of the duellists' seconds in a cell in the Bastille or some other dungeon.

Then one day Brian McHenry leapt from the school roof onto the hard asphalt three metres below, without hurting himself. Brian was among the more sympathetic of my classmates, and I was so impressed with his bravado that I took *The Duel* out of my wallet and showed it to him. I watched his eyes widen as he read, and when he'd finished, he shook the parchment, by now flimsy, and said that the tale was terrific and that I should submit it to the school magazine. I didn't have the courage to act on his advice, so it has never been published and I have lost it. The folds were frayed from years of taking it out of my wallet and putting it back every so often to read what I had written as an act of reassurance.

JL went on to remind me that if I were writing about pianists, I should not neglect Jascha Spivakovsky, a keyboard exile, so to speak. It was a bottler of a yarn, he wrote, confirming what I had gauged from our meeting: here was a man who loved stories above all else, and with no knowledge of my true quest to understand the fates of pianists, he was simply trying to lead me to good words for my book. He was only trying to help, his messages often repeated. In researching his own book on Kapell, he wrote, he had interviewed a Melbourne music-lover who had found several original acetate discs cut in microgroove from radio broadcasts of Kapell's last concerts, including, of course, the legendary last recital in Geelong. He had mentioned Spivakovsky, and, if his memory served him well, he wrote, the pianist's son was still alive and well and living in the family home in Toorak. He linked me to the email address of the music-lover who had found the acetates. Now there's a story! his note ended.

I was intrigued. If Spivakovsky was an exile, losing his home because he played the piano sublimely, I wanted to know more. I wrote straight away to the music-lover, whose name escapes me but at the time reminded me of a car door slamming, and he replied that night with an email address for Michael Spivakovsky, through which I introduced myself and explained the literary — avoiding the mental — challenges I had set myself. I wanted more details, I wrote, about the famous night after the Geelong concert when Jascha and Willy Kapell allegedly played the piano until dawn. How was Kapell's mood? *Really*? You must have witnessed it. Did he know he was about to die? I asked Michael if he would permit me to record our chat. We scheduled a morning meeting a few days later.

I PARKED the Corolla in a two-hour zone in a leafy, winding, elevated street above the south side of the Yarra River well short of Michael's address, anxious that my time at the kerb might be more restricted if I ventured farther. Fairly narrow, the road was a conduit for the latest of German motoring pride, a stream of Mercedes, Audis and BMWs whooshing by as unceasingly as the river below, blonde women wearing large sunglasses and grim expressions — and sometimes sleek young men — at their wheels. The air smelled of decaying leaves, reminding me of a kind of fresh-tobacco smell that Victoria's moral policemen have eliminated from our lives altogether. (In Victoria, burning leaves is illegal.) Sweeping elegantly to the right, the footpath rose gently, and I wondered who owned the mansions on either side, one after another, each worth many millions of dollars, each behind gardens of European shrubs and trees.

And then I arrived at Michael's wide drive and saw, below and between the eastern side of Edzell House and the boundary fence, the river glinting where sun shone on autumnal ripples, highlighting its usual dull beige.

Modelled on a Scottish fortress, Edzell is one of Melbourne's finest homes, a red-brick Federation-style pile — or Elizabethan revival, if you prefer England to Australia — built in 1892. It has forty-six rooms, extensive half-timber gabling, Marseilles-patterned tiles, terracotta ridging, ornate panelling and architraves, carved enrichments, as the realtors put it, and two asymmetrically placed corner turrets overlooking the river. Originally constructed for James Cooper Stewart, a Melbourne mayor who had arrived from Scotland and wanted to make his mark in the New World, it is renowned for its gorgeous timberwork, expansive rooms, and panelled ceilings. It stands for new-world optimism. The thoughts of Mayor Stewart as he slept his first night in one of Edzell's many bedrooms are beyond our imagining. Or perhaps he just thought he deserved Edzell.

These days it is seven large apartments — Michael and his wife live in one of them — in original condition, as salesman say, millions of dollars probably needing to be spent to fit them out in contemporary styles and to today's plumbing and décor standards. Michael's parents bought Edzell when Jascha moved to Australia in the 1930s — his mother was the only daughter of a wealthy Western Australian gold miner. Michael was downsizing, though, he told me, and by the end of the year he and his wife would move from the house that had been his home since 1940 into something considerably smaller.

He appeared to anticipate my knocking on the heavy timber door of the second portico from the street, and his quick smile illuminated an otherwise dim but large entrance hall, and a corridor behind it. Dressed in a white shirt, sober tie and dark velour jacket, he appeared to be both tall and not so tall, slim, much younger than more than seven decades of a human life usually exhibit, and possessing a charm, courtesy and respect for my interest in discussing his father and Kapell of a magnitude I didn't deserve.

He showed me immediately and with obvious pride to the music room, down the corridor and to the right. An immense

space floored in hardwood, it was exquisitely panelled in a New Zealand timber called rimu, Michael said, which was a native conifer resembling oak. I felt like running my fingertips over the panels, so alive with veins and whorls were the grains. Moreover, they seemed to emit the sweet, beneficent odour of a favourite aunt. Lee's aunt smashing ginger came to mind, and I let the image linger.

Three grand pianos, one on an elevated stage at the rear of the room, hardly made any incursion at all into the space — an audience of perhaps forty or fifty could have been easily accommodated as well. Big windows overlooked the river, the sun entering the room so vehemently that much of the space's detail was obscured for some time, and my eye was led only to the framed black-and-white photographs on top of the biggest piano, a full-sized Steinway concert instrument, its lid strewn with an extravagantly fringed black cloth worked elaborately with what appeared to be scarlet peonies. Resting on it were publicity snaps of Artur Schnabel, Benno Moiseiwitsch and Willy Kapell, among others, studio shots inscribed with thanks to Jascha and his wife Leonore for their hospitality. Overlooking the instrument from a high vantage point on the wall behind was what Michael called a live mask of Beethoven, his eyes closed seemingly in meditation but no doubt to stop the plaster or whatever was used in the initial cast from infiltrating.

Many great musicians had practised and performed here, Michael said. He could come home from school and Claudio Arrau would be playing. Some had given private concerts, Nellie Melba, the esteemed soprano, among them. On his two Australian tours, Willy Kapell often came here, sometimes staying overnight, and I would see him at breakfast but mostly when I got home from school. Dad mentored him, and they often discussed specific pieces of music, how they might be played, what should be in the pianist's mind as he or she played them. I remember overhearing — I was really the only one of three siblings with a strong interest in classical music — their talk about Chopin's *Funeral March* sonata and in particular that magnificent third movement, the funeral march itself. Willy asked Dad about the vantage point from which the pianist should observe the march, how it should affect his playing. Should he be an observer at the church as the funeral cortège leaves, or halfway between the church and the cemetery, or at the cemetery itself? Willy asked. In his view, Dad told Willy, Chopin had positioned himself midway between the church and the grave, and you hear the cortège approach in a sorrowful B-flat minor from far off, very softly. *Da-da-di-da-dee-da-da-da-da-di-da*. A crescendo builds as it draws level with Chopin or the player, as the case may be, and the switch at the fifteenth bar to the brighter relative major key of D-flat, perhaps because of the nearness of the hearse to the observer and the powerful impression it makes, an uncanny shock better conveyed in a brighter major key that makes the heart beat faster — a realisation, perhaps, that death concludes every life, even yours (Michael pointed) — and this brief episode is marked *forte* or loud on the score. The procession passes, arriving at the graveside, fading to *piano*, soft, in the minor key. And the same thing happens, Dad told Willy, said Michael, on the last page of the march when the cortège returns to the church, the hearse empty.

But what about the lyrical middle section? I asked Michael, beginning to hum the tune. What did Jascha tell Willy about that?

It represented the mourners' keening over the grave, said Michael.

It was what Jascha saw, he said, and the piece, its integrity, what it meant, its plangency, and its capacity to draw tears all seemed to add up if you looked at it this way.

Chopin, the reporter at the burial, had written the fourth movement, a torrential *presto* in the minor key in which fingers fly, twelve quavers to the bar cascading as fast as you can play them, your hands acting in unison to conjure wraiths of sound from the piano, spirits that rise and swirl, loudly and softly, for the whole of the ninety seconds that the movement takes to play, lends itself to secret meanings, I thought. What did Jascha think the sonata's last movement amounted to?

It was the wind buffeting the souls of the dead, Michael said. This is what Chopin saw and what Dad told Willy to see. And he did, if you've ever heard the recording of the last concert.

Many times, my father collected Willy from whichever hotel he was staying at in the city and brought him here, where he would often have meals. My mother cooked nice dishes for him, and he was always polite to her. He was a deadly serious musician, and I remember listening to him practise for hours on end on this piano, said Michael, tapping the Steinway. Beyond the music room is a tessellated terrace, he said, pointing, and the other thing Kapell used to do was sit there for hours drawing and painting. The terrace is several metres above the back garden, which slopes down to the river, and at Willy's eye-level was a huge dead tree — Michael could not remember the species — in which kookaburras used to perch on tortuous grey branches and laugh at Willy, who would draw and paint them in watercolours.

I wondered if the birds were laughing at his efforts, I said, quite unintentionally. The words arrived from nowhere, just like the images that haunt me. Did Michael have Kapell paintings? I asked. He shook his head.

He drank a lot of coffee and smoked constantly, and Jascha would say to him, Villy, Villy, you'll get cancer if you keep smoking, you must give up the cigarettes, and Willy would say in his kind of Manhattan drawl, Yeah, yeah, I will sometime. But not today, not today. I said that perhaps his speech made him sound like one of those put-upon, minor-bout boxers in a black-and-white movie from long ago. Michael laughed. Clips of old boxing movies derailed my train of thought, shunting it to the branchline of *Requiem for a Heavyweight*, Rod Serling's masterly script about the primacy of dignity for retired fight-ers. Then came Norman Mailer's description of the flurry of punches that killed Benny Paret and an image of the boxer wedged against a corner post, sinking to the canvas. Emile Griffith's right hand was like a baseball bat demolishing a pumpkin, Mailer wrote, an unforgettable line.

And I can put you in the exact spot, Michael said, where Willy showed me, a teenage boy just home from school, put-ting down his schoolbag, the exact spot by the fireplace where he showed me his hand, the left, I think it was, and pointed to the groove and said it was the life line, and you can't imagine its stopping halfway across the palm of his hand but it did, clear skin taking up where the line faded to flesh. And Willy urged me to look at this peculiar terminated crease in his palm, look at its sudden finish, and said he shouldn't be here, in other words he should be dead, but he declined to put it quite like that. He appeared to be neither serious nor aiming for flip-pancy but somewhere between the two as he made the remark.

It was almost as if he was surprised, somewhat affronted, that he didn't have a long life line.

Piqued by the hand he'd been dealt, I said.

Yes, said Michael. Kapell's remark had dumbfounded him and he didn't know what to say in reply.

Willy's last day in Melbourne, which might have been the day after the Geelong concert, he spent here, in this house, Michael said. Dad collected him from his hotel, and he was supposed to relax with perhaps half-a-dozen guests Jascha and Leonore had invited as a kind of farewell, and he was here when I got back from school. Dad was going to take him back to his hotel then Essendon airport the next day. But Willy stayed all night, and I watched him until I went to bed about eleven o'clock. He was ebullient, and he and Dad strode around this room in great spirits, and Dad would say, What about this? and he'd sit at one of the three pianos — perhaps the Bechstein, which was mainly reserved for practising — and belt out the opening bars of a *Mephisto Waltz*, and Willy would sit at the Steinway and duplicate it, and Willy would say, What about this? and perform *La Campanella*, a ferociously difficult Liszt piece, and Jascha would play along with him at the other piano, and this would go on and on and they'd be jumping from piano to piano, and I saw the music critic of the *Herald*, John Sinclair, out of the corner of my eye, his jaw slack, mouth open in amazement.

Only very occasionally would they need some sheet music. After Dad played a Chopin *Nocturne*, I remember Willy saying, Aah, Jascha, you are a poet. And Dad pulled out the music for Max Reger's *Variations and Fugue on a Theme by Bach* and said, Villy, Villy, what about this? and Dad had been working on it for a performance and Willy flipped through the score and said to Dad, That's impossible. Impossible. It was a very upbeat night. They were smiling and laughing and playing the pianos and generally carrying on and Willy didn't go back to his hotel, and at about six o'clock the next morning they were still playing everything under the sun, Beethoven, Mozart, Chopin, of course, and one would play the solo part of a piano concerto and the other would accompany him with the piano transcription of the orchestral part. And in my mind, said Michael, they would not have done any of that — had this great time, which was lovely to see — if Willy had been depressed.

I had been glancing at Michael's hands, trying to disguise my interest, because I had never seen more perfect almost-rectangular piano hands, the little fingers surprisingly similar in length to their adjacent ring fingers, the palms broad and muscular. But it was not so much their perfect form that had attracted me as their size; they were about a third bigger than average men's hands, I would have guessed, the fingers thick. What powerful devices they were for getting the best out of a keyboard, and I was intrigued to know, of course, if Jascha's had been similar.

Yes, said Michael, referring me to a wonderful photograph on top of the Steinway: Jascha in full flight. His right hand is the image of Michael's, and in the photograph, it is actually above his head, the fingers spread and curved like the talons of a raptor that is about to attack the piano keys beneath as if they were prey. In perhaps his late forties or early fifties — in his prime, anyway — Jascha is intent on the keyboard, looking down, an enormous grin on his face — enormous — his message being that there is no greater joy than playing the piano at a superlative level. He is clearly revelling in the performance, which appears to be taking place, gauging from the background, in a strangely empty restaurant. No one sits at two tables, which are barely visible in the gloom behind. They are spread with cloths on which

there appear to be salt and pepper shakers. Flowers bloom in two big vases, and perhaps Jascha is warming up for an unusual engagement. And the uncanny thing about the power of these enormous hands, I thought, because I had heard recorded morsels of them at work, is the delicacy and speed and softness of the sounds that they were able to produce.

Almost the only recordings of Jascha's playing, despite his touring Europe and North America for fourteen consecutive years after World War II, were made in this room, said Michael, who set up a single microphone and showed me the beige-coloured vinyl case of a small Tandberg reel-to-reel tape recorder on which he, a boy in his teens, had captured his father's performances because someone had to. Many companies asked Jascha to make studio recordings while he was touring, but, when you are playing in different auditoriums and different cities night after night you are never in the one place for the two or three days it takes to put down tracks, said Michael.

The Spivakovskys were born to make music — śpiewak in Polish meaning singer — and Jascha was by 1899, at the age of three, showing prodigious talent by copying on the family piano a busker's tune from the street below. His father, a singer of course, nurtured the boy's gift, and at six he began specialist training in Odessa, almost five hundred kilometres to the south of the small village outside Kiev where he had been born. A year later, he was discovered by Josef Hofmann, who called him a rare, outstanding talent and wanted him to study in Moscow. Because of restrictions on Jews in the Russian capital, said Michael, my grandparents were unable to take up Hofmann's offer and go with him to Moscow, and the boy was too young to live there alone. So he made the best of the local scene and developed a huge reputation in Odessa.

In the 1905 pogrom, the worst of many, a mob of ethnic Russians, Ukrainians and Greeks bent on intimidating Jews, killing them if possible — four hundred were in fact murdered and more than fifteen hundred properties destroyed — targeted the family's apartment block, and Jascha, his parents, and his three sisters climbed onto the roof. Cossack Imperial Guards galloped into the picture, but instead of quelling the rioters they began shooting at the Spivakovskys, who fled down a kind of external fire escape, and at one point, one of Jascha's sisters pushed her nine-year-old brother to hurry him up and he fell forward. A bullet hit the wall behind him just where his head had been. *Exactly where.* In panic, the family took refuge in the building's basement, where the Catholic landlord covered them with straw and told them not to move, and they lived like that for several days, not moving, as still as the dead, breathing through the straw, neither eating nor drinking, until the riots ceased. Jascha played concerts to raise money for his by now bereft family, and in a short while he became a star. With Hofmann's help, the family moved to Berlin, where Jascha entered the Klindworth-Scharwenka Conservatory and, at thirteen, won the academy's first prize and a Blüthner grand piano, which is the one on the platform over there. (Michael pointed.) It was so dear to him and so precious to me, his son, that we play this very special instrument only rarely.

Michael led me to it and opened the lid so that I could read a very big inscription in gold letters: Dem besten aus dem an 20 Juni 1910 abgehaltenen Preisspiel als Sieger herborgegangenen Schüler des Konservatiums 'Klingworth Scharwenka', and in letters twice as large under these, 'Jascha Spiwakowski', under-lined and embraced with *art-moderne* curlicues.

How was my German? Michael asked.

Rudimentary, I said, but I got the gist of the writing.

At thirteen, imagine what the piano and the inscription must have meant to him, how it must have prescribed his destiny, and how obliged he must have felt to fulfil it, I said.

Yes, and he did, said Michael. He astounded the critics, one calling him the new Anton Rubinstein. A teenage sensation, he toured Europe, the *Berliner Lokal-Anzeiger* predicting that he would be called to great things, the *Hamburger Correspondent* saying he was the strongest talent in the past decade, and the *Breslauer Morgen-Zeitung* asking its readers to explain this wonder-genius. He was still only fifteen. He played for the royal families, and even during a blizzard in Odessa: the concert hall was an ice block. After his London debut — at seventeen — a critic dubbed him the king of the keyboard. By his twenties, London newspapers were calling him the pianistic genius of the hour.

He first toured Australia in 1922, during which he met in Adelaide my mother Leonore Krantz, who had come to him for lessons. Concert pianists were the rock stars of those days, and audiences went wild about Jascha, standing on their seats and waving handkerchiefs and scarves and what have you at him, and, at one concert, several people, among them many young women, went up on stage and surrounded the piano while he played a record eleven encores. They wouldn't let him go.

My parents eloped and got married in 1926 over the border in the new state of Czechoslovakia, which Hitler later hyphenated, as you know, the more easily to conquer it. German marriage rules had prevented them from marrying in Berlin. On their honeymoon in the south of France, Dad's agent cabled him to say that Richard Strauss, the greatest living composer, wanted him to play his *Burleske* for piano and orchestra with the Vienna Philharmonic. Strauss himself would be waving the baton, and the piece meant a lot to him because he had composed it when young, and he had had trouble getting pianists to perform it because of its technical challenges. Dad could not refuse, he felt, and, because of it, he and Strauss became very close. Strauss stayed in Germany, as you know, but hated the Nazis, cooperating in some respects with them mainly for reasons of expediency and to try to protect his Jewish daughter-in-law and grandchildren. You might recall that they made him *Reichsmusikkammer* chief without his consent and sacked him two years later after intercepting a letter to his friend Stefan Zweig criticising Nazi attitudes and showing it to Hitler. He tried to perform Mahler and Debussy and Mendelssohn, whom the Nazis banned, and drove to the Theresienstadt concentration camp to try to get his son's mother-in-law and her children released, a ploy that failed.

But most importantly for Jascha, Strauss was a canary in the mine for Jewish artists in Germany, and just before Hitler grabbed power and Jascha had become phenomenally famous but had got up the noses of the new rulers, he received a letter from Strauss. It was a few bars of Rossini's *William Tell* overture scribbled out in Strauss's own hand followed by a big exclamation mark. Michael looked around the room and waved one of his big hands. It was here somewhere, he said. I wish I could find it, but we have packed up everything in preparing to leave all this. I wish I could find it.

Michael's expression *preparing to leave all this* struck me with explosive force, not just because it signified the melancholy that ends each era, but because I realized that the spaces in Edzell House, the timber panelling, the view over the river, the famous all-night recital by two great pianists, the terrace where Kapell painted kookaburras would become for him only memories and images, and even the pianos, removed from their music room, would no longer look as they did now and sound the same when they were elsewhere. Michael would also miss the joinery's sweet caramel odour. I was reminded of Conrad's Stein who was *preparing to leave all this* as he waved his hand sadly at his butterflies.

Which bars of the overture? I asked. Were they the shimmering violins a few minutes into the piece that announce the impending storm, or was it the storm itself, the trombones and bass drum thundering, the strings conjuring *fortissimo* sheets of rain?

He was not absolutely sure, Michael said, but they were from somewhere near the start of the storm, and the exclamation mark was huge. The warning was clear, said Michael, and Jascha quickly organised an Australasian tour of about seventy concerts for his already famous trio — his brother Tossy was the violinist and Edmund Kurtz the cellist — and they boarded a ship only days before the Nazis grabbed power.

No one of my vintage, I said, switching points, could help but remember the *William Tell* overture's rush to the end and the Lone Ranger at full gallop: A fiery horse with the speed of light, a cloud of dust and a hearty, Hi yo, Silver, I recited. Michael smiled, politely, I thought, this time.

Jascha joined the music faculty at the University of Melbourne but for many years did not leave Australia, said Michael. To

deport Jews and other undesirables, Australian border authorities had a dictation test that they could ask foreigners to take
on returning to our shores. An officer would read something
in Gaelic or Maltese or whatever, and if you could not write
down precisely what he said you failed and were refused entry,
or re-entry, as it would have been in my father's case. So Dad's
tenure in Australia was dubious, to say the least. Moreover, in
1938, Goebbels announced that Jascha and several other leading
Jewish musicians had been erased *altogether* from German culture. *Altogether.* They no longer existed in a Germany that would
increase its grasp over Europe not just geographically but over
what people could read and see and hear.

How hard, I said, must it have been for him to feel at home
anywhere? Did he feel an exile everywhere he lived, even in
Australia? Did the notion of home have a meaning for him?

Michael repeated that his father was a big, ebullient Russian,
that that was his character, a very resilient man, and he came to
love Australia and life here. His biggest problem was the travel
needed to sustain his career.

And was he never troubled by piano daemons? I asked, seeking confirmation.

Never, said Michael. He believed that if you worked hard
enough you could overcome — overwhelm — performance
nerves. He never talked about it. After all, he was a professional
pianist. That was his job; making music was his name.

Did you ever play? I asked.

Michael replied with a response he had clearly used many
times: I can play the piano, but I am not a pianist. And, by
accident more or less, he still taught several students, he said,

walking me to the door. His own profession had been architecture, and he had designed and built several hundred of the state's public schools.

In the entrance hall I was overcome by hesitation, preoccupied by the Steinway on which Kapell, Schnabel and other keyboard greats had played so many times. I wanted to hear how it sounded, but I also had the crazy notion that touching the keys would do me good. I would feel what the great pianists had felt. I knew instantly that the idea was ridiculous, the sort of notion that is simultaneously ludicrous, irresistible and inexplicable. Beginning to blush, I asked Michael if I could play something on the Steinway, immediately regretting my request.

Of course, he said, confirming my death sentence. No appeal allowed.

We returned to the music room, and I stammered that I would need music. He pointed to two large glass-fronted cabinets of mahogany joinery with many shelves on which hundreds of scores rested. My hands began to tremble and I tried to calm myself, fearing — even knowing — that I would play badly, that Michael might think I was somehow inauthentic because of it, dumb, and I realised that my confidence would be shredded by this rash and stupid request. The image of my fumbling with music in a packed concert hall vaulted into my thoughts. The spikes that nailed me to the floor followed. The music was upside-down.

Something relatively simple, I said, committing suicide. The slow-movement variations from Beethoven's tenth piano sonata, I suggested.

I did not see him go to the cabinets, my mind by now incapable of forming coherent images, but it seemed that only two or three seconds passed before the music was on the stand in front of me, right way up, and I looked at it, terrified. I stretched my fingers and began to play, and even in the piece's simplest first few bars, which require chords that are easy to grasp and well-separated, I began to hit wrong notes. I was incapable, too, of crisping out the chirpy staccatos that the great Ludwig had dotted above his quavers two centuries before. Mine were flat and dull-sounding.

Standing behind me, Michael began to hum the tune in a kindly sort of way, trying to support the derelict pianist, and he must have noticed the scars on the backs of my hands, too, but was too polite to say anything. I felt as if I should stop, thrust my arms as deep into my pockets as they could go — hide them in shame — and sprint for the door.

He turned the page for me, and I fudged through a few bars of the rest of the movement, including the last and most challenging variation in which the left hand sings a cleverly inverted version of the melody and the right hand accompanies it in semi-quavers. Ironically, amid the blur, the notes on the score had never seemed in such sharp focus. They were either taunting me or pleading with me to play properly. The keys themselves, the ivory veneers and ebony hardwood of the black notes, failed to transmit. Foolishly, I thought they might encourage me. And although I had put this music beneath my fingers many times, though not recently, my hands shook and mistakes were as heavy as the rain in Rossini's overture. Such are performance nerves, lack of practice, lack of professionalism, a reminder, I understood, of the piano's power to terrify those who try to produce artistry from it.

I played the last C-major chord *fortissimo*, as marked, and Michael smiled but said nothing. I was tempted to tell him about my sister's talent but was too embarrassed to take our conversation further. He let me out.

WALKING back to my car, I regained some composure, reflecting on Strauss and Spivakovsky and how confusing and threatening Germany of the 1930s must have been. I was reminded of a doctor friend who had played in a university orchestra made up entirely of medical students. Their conductor was a professor of anatomy, and, at one of the orchestra's concerts quite a while ago, I heard a fine young soprano who had ambitions to be an orthopaedic surgeon sing the last two of Strauss's *Four Last Songs*, which he composed in his eighties, a cycle that ends with the excruciatingly beautiful *Im Abendrot — At Sunset —* and its last line, *Is this perhaps death?* During rehearsals, said my friend, the players had a small competition — the conductor encouraged them — to try to say in a few words what the *Four Last Songs* meant. The winner, a diminutive Jewess who played the viola, lived in Elwood and was training to be a radiologist, my friend told me, called the songs an ultrasound of man's inevitable capitulation to fate.

And if Jascha Spivakovsky had confronted fate without fear, its omnipotence never troubling him, Willy Kapell, in the days after he left for Sydney to catch the flight that killed him, had been far from the upbeat participant in the all-night piano marathon at Edzell House. If he hadn't been depressed when he and Jascha traded Lisztian exhibitions, he was far from happy in the seventy hours or so that followed. JL's book reports that John Sinclair said he left Willy at six in the morning, agreeing to correspond on tragedy in Schubert's songs because, Sinclair said in a radio interview thirty years after the pianist's death, Willy had told him funny things were going on in his head. Three times before he left Melbourne, said the critic, the pianist had held up his hand, pointed out the abrupt end of the life line and said he should not be here.

In Sydney, Willy visited the conductor Joseph Post and was, said Post, in a depressed state. They picked strawberries together in Post's vegetable patch, and Kapell muttered several times that he would never come back to Australia. Reconciling, I realised, Kapell's love of Jascha and other Australian friends with his determination never to return to Australia was an impossible task. I took his last night at the Spivakovskys to be an exception to his usual demeanour, concluding that his enslavement by the piano had destabilised him, fragmenting his character to the point where he no longer cared about putting it back together again. I wish it were otherwise, I said to myself, ripping a parking fine from my windscreen. (I'd been in a loading zone, hadn't noticed the red letters above the green.) A question you might find ridiculous also came to mind: had Kapell somehow caused the plane crash that killed him?

I turned the ignition key, needing a beer and somewhere quiet to think. Across the river was The Googly, a brewpub I knew well in what used to be the working-class, inner-suburb of Richmond but is now a reserve for the gentry and their minute million-dollar labourers' cottages. It made an excellent India pale ale.

RENOVATED ONLY a few years ago, The Googly lays claims to re-creating the authentic atmosphere of the American Deep

South, putting on country, hillbilly and punk nights of live music and trumpeting its shrine to Elvis Presley, which amounts to — as far as I can see — several enormous photographs of the singer performing, Christmas lights flashing in a scintillating series of mute syncopations and gaudy colours around the frame of the biggest. A radiant and naturalistic crucifixion, Jesus dying, his long hair russet — Died for us, says its caption — hangs above the bar, and the floor is timbered in recycled planks of Tasmanian oak. More vertical hardwood supports the bar itself, and the walls are clad in pine strips the colour of ironbark honey. Overhead, a ceiling of tiles made of compressed straw keeps the noise low, and provided no one is performing, The Googly is a good place to think, especially when there are few patrons, which was the case when I arrived and ordered a pint. The lunch crowd had gone.

The pub's smell — of fresh-sawn pine and the floral hoppiness of newly-spilled beer — reminded me of a similar bar called the Lost Coast in a small town in Oregon in the middle of America's north-western forests. (Like the dolphins and bad dreams, these moving pictures emerge unbidden from my unconscious.)

The Oregon bar occupied a three-storey Victorian edifice trimmed in cream that might once have been a draper's shop, its big front windows bordered with elegant moss-green trim. It was clearly once the place to come for bolts of sturdy denims and weekend gabardines. Seeming to be the main street's only lit building at seven o'clock on a mid-week night, it boasted taps that gushed Downtown Brown, Alleycat Amber and 8-ball stout, among many brews. Around the walls, posters, chalkboards and hoardings promoted the bar's beverages: the brown beer's blown-up label, for instance, featured a caricature of a spiv — or bookie perhaps — in bright colours, a tiny black trilby balancing on his thatch, his portrait Picasso-esque, eyes radically askew, disabled, as they are in *Guernica*. A smile beamed from halfway up his right cheek. A Great White Beer was made from malted wheat, a secret blend of regional herbs and ale yeast, among other things, and its label featured a benign-seeming shark holding a surfboard in one fin and a foaming tankard in the other. The whiteness and sharpness of the teeth mesmerised.

Unlike The Googly's afternoon torpor, the Lost Coast had been alive with families, couples and singles the night I visited. It amounted to the town's community living room, I felt, a real public house for local folk who weren't up to cooking or take-out. I loved the clacketty timber floor and the crowd of all ages that ate plateloads of burgers and fries. And the high bar of lacquered and grainy hardwood itself, at which I sat on a stool of glossy red vinyl. I tried to remember the taste of the Lost Coast's ale to compare it with its counterpart in front of me. Both were excellent, I decided, their initial quenchiness — I can think only of the word gulpability — led to the wonderfully bitter and dry, flowery after-taste of hops. They were beers to make a sad man smile. Even someone like me.

At the Lost Coast, a grey-bearded person in perhaps his sixties or even older climbed onto the stool next to mine and introduced himself as Kellogg, and what was I doing in this neck of the woods, anyways, a tourist? I told him that I had been interviewing musicians in San Francisco and thought it would be a pity to miss the coastal redwoods, the world's tallest trees, the *Sequoia sempervirens*, which had, in essence, killed one of the world's greatest pianists. (I'm not sure now if I put it in so many — or so few — words.) He nodded, declining to want to know more about Kapell's story, but wanting to tell me, I had the feeling, one of his own.

The big trees are still there, he said, but not so many.

A gnarled face relieved his beard, and he rested his right hand on the pommel of an enormous hunting knife, which was sheathed in a leather scabbard tooled with whorls. It hung around his waist on a rawhide belt, gunslinger-style. His boots had Cuban heels, and he was frightening in a superficial way — as if he were a fake bad guy got up to play the part for the tourists of Tombstone. He was probably a lamb, I concluded, but a spectral one.

Sipping perhaps our third pints of ale, my elbows planted on the bar for stability's sake, Kellogg drew my attention to the photograph facing us, a huge black-and-white enlargement from the late 1800s perhaps, the figures in it life-sized. None of the Lost Coast's bargirls was ever able to tell him a single thing about it, he said. Dim and faded, it depicted a group of loggers who appeared to be dressed in their Sunday best. Their axes and saws leant against what looked like a quartermaster's store of rough timber slabs, and they numbered fifteen and posed sourly in two ranks in front of the building. They had anticipated the shutter, several expressing scepticism, some suspicion, some both. Some of the lumberjacks are clearly exhausted, I thought, and others are blank, robotic, just choppers and sawyers who had been ground to a dull edge by constant hard labour. Their boots are dusty, bare dirt beneath their feet, and only one of them is without a hat. The others wear modest headgear, including invariably shabby flat caps. I counted a dozen loggers with moustaches, some of them unkempt and most of walrus-style. Eleven show their braces, mostly striped, and two piebald dogs are in the photograph, ropes around their necks. A boy of five or six wearing a battered homburg and sucked-in lips holds one rope, and it occurred to me that the animal is the only living thing in the image that appears to enjoy having itself archived forever. And despite the photograph's detail, I failed to find its centre. It hid what it meant. Almost all the men hold small glasses of a black drink, and one of them has a big white enamel pitcher. Three extend their beakers towards the camera.

Perhaps five minutes passed during which Kellogg, who wore jeans and a tartan shirt, his gaze fixed on the photograph, seemed to become both more vivid yet somewhat translucent, the reds of his shirt brightening intermittently like a lighthouse's slow flash. The size of his hunting knife and its tooled sheath distracted me. Was it merely for show? And I wondered if I should bid him good night and head back to my motel before anything peculiar happened.

Whether I wanted to hear it or not, though, he began a monologue, declaiming as if he owned the story, as if it were forest lore and only he was licensed to recite it. As if he were a shaman of the glades. The photograph behind the bar, he said, captures a celebration, perhaps the final and total depletion of a logging coupe, perhaps the opening of a new one. It was impossible to say why that particular instant, he said, deserved history, and it was a question he had failed to ask the men. Because he himself, he said — when curiosity had got the better of him one night — he himself had walked right inside it to interrogate the loggers.

He did it not because the image was huge and stood over anyone drinking at the Lost Coast's bar — not at all — but because it was the look on the men's faces. He was sure, he said, that they were hiding something.

I sensed a specific kind of tension among them, he said. They were on the point of confessing to something, I was convinced. There was a rawness to their expressions — a bluntness, perhaps out of primitive natures. Shadows behind them exacerbated the intrigue, shadows that stalked them, but cast by what or whom? You see, Kellogg continued, you can look at that photograph and you cannot tell where the light is coming from, how the shadows are made. They were shadowy men bathed in impenetrable shadows, darkness everywhere, so I walked right inside the photograph to find out what was occupying their minds, what was up.

And my first question to the nearest logger was what he was drinking. Bolter, sir, he said. Was it the drink in the pitcher? Yes, sir. Were they all drinking it? Yes. 'Ceptin Pierson, said the lumberjack, smirking. He's drinking lemonade, sir, Pierson. I knew that name, a great name in the north-west, and I looked along the row of faces, up close at the faces, at the dogs on ropes and the boy, passing in front of them, reviewing them as if they were ranks, which was quite an arrogant thing to do, but I wanted answers to the mysteries the photograph was hiding. I stopped in front of a logger. Pierson? It *was* Pierson, *was* him! My heart missed a beat. I wanted to speak to him, warn him, but I was mute, failing entirely to articulate words.

Dwight Pierson needed to be warned. He grew up in the discomfiting South after the Civil War, a farmhand of variable address and income who had also adapted the black music he heard every day of his life to a kind of early species of rag-time piano. He himself composed many tunes long before Scott Joplin, and he played them in a lively manner in honky-tonks in Alabama to make a few dollars more.

(I was tempted to interrupt Kellogg to argue that Beethoven invented honky-tonk in the exquisite *Arietta* of his last piano sonata, but I let the man's soothing oratory flow on, a recitation that echoed sonorously inside my skull as if he himself were trapped there, speaking from the small stage of an empty theatre. His vocal resonances would easily have suited a talking book of a Louis L'Amour wild-west tale, or even the cadences of those uniquely American radio broadcasters who tell wonderful tales of prairies and peaks, farmyards and barns. Real stories, with beginnings, middles and ends. E. B. White's bucolic *New Yorker* columns and Garrison Keillor's yarns came to mind.)

Having lost his parents and their smallholding because of the war, partly because their sympathies were more northern, and lay with the slaves, Kellogg continued, Pierson struggled con-stantly to survive, but like many similar men of good nature, he reckoned such an existence was better with the support of a good woman, and he married Ruth and they had four children in not many more years. Just to keep the mouths fed was a daily chal-lenge. At some moment, possibly as he was counting the pennies in his pocket to see if he and Ruth could afford a loaf of bread, he heard of the regular incomes strong men made in the forests of the north-west. The work would continue forever, it was said, the forests endless. So he went by himself to Oregon, an exile in a way, a foreigner in a vastly different landscape, mindscape, from the South. There was no question of being able to economise enough to take Ruth and the children with him. He promised, of course, to send her money, and he did.

Powerfully built over a fairly small frame, a big small man, you might say, Pierson was perfect for logging, being good in tight corners with an axe. At first, he socialised easily with the rough-hewn work gangs that felled and removed trees, and the loggers liked him because he would play numbers on the banjo-sounding piano at Our House, one of the most popular bars. The loggers would slap their thighs and stamp their boots into the dusty — where it wasn't beer-splashed — plank floors. Kellogg winked. If you listen, you can hear the piano and the boots, he said. I mean, listen and you hear them. They're not in the photograph, but they're there. Among Pierson's own compositions were the *Alligator Allgemeine, Longhorn Lament*, and *Ruth's Own Lullaby*, which his workmates often requested, shouting it from the bar. A romantic in an industry that was brutal and destructive, he saw only merit in what some have called the art of the plain man.

He wrote to Ruth about the smells of his job, the essential sweet, sappy odour of virgin forest, the whiff of wet grass and fresh resin after rain. He told her of the sweeter and even more powerful perfume when sawdust sprayed as a big fir was cut. He told her about the bitter smell of stale sweat from loggers push-pulling a saw and others wielding axes — his own smell, I suppose. And the slatey perfume of oily steam emanating from the donkey engines that sawed the logs into planks, and the smell of ox dung and wet hide that enveloped a bullock team when the animals dragged the logs. He wrote of the sounds of the trade,

the accelerating *whumph* of a crashing tree that, for Pierson,
was like the triumphant crescendos that ended the anthems he
had heard gospel choirs sing in his youth, the harmonics that
had inspired him to sit at a keyboard, some of its ivory veneers
missing, its soprano notes a quarter-tone out. The sounds of
the steam engines, their hissing, their rhythmic clacking and
wheezing, thrilled him. The profanities of the ox drivers as they
yoked up as many as ten of their bulls and whipped them into
enough fury to drag a log made an epic symphony. The mucosal
snorts of the oxen amounted to percussion. The profound bump-
ing — it shook the ground — of a spruce giant as it was hauled
to the mill along a skidroad of logs half-buried in the mud. It
was the essence of logging, he wrote Ruth, kissing the children.
Somehow or other, he made allowances, at least for a while, for
the dirty and unventilated bunkhouses in which the timbermen
lived, the bad food they ate, the lack of baths, the damp rotting
smell that filled the cabins as their heavy woollen work clothes
dried, and the constant dicing with injury and death. And all for
a single dollar a ten-hour day. Big money then.

A thinking white man who knew the Deep South in those
days was at least prompted to ponder right and wrong. That's
my theory, at any rate, for the reason behind Pierson's con-
version. Before too long, he saw the timber industry in a less
glamorous light. Its worst side was exhibited in the saloons he
was obliged to socialise in if he were to get any relief from the
camps. Among them were legendary hangouts such as Adolf's,
The Goo's and Billy the Hobo's. He was happiest in Our House
because its piano was more playable than those of the other
bars. But he became increasingly uneasy in the company of his

fellow-workers, the timber beasts, as townsfolk called them. Proud of their trade, they declined to wash and dress up to go to town, and, as a consequence of their primitive natures, their saloons and whorehouses were strictly assigned and no one who *wasn't* a beast went anywhere near them. In bigger towns such as Portland, the areas the beasts could visit were officially prescribed. These men were out-and-out pariahs to townsfolk and farmers, seen as strays, and were more or less herded back to their camps — out of sight and out of mind, despite their importance to the local economy — once their last dimes had been spent on ale and women.

Strangely enough, it was this disreputable image of the timber-cutter that also compelled Pierson to try to bring a little respectability to logging. Simultaneously, a few townsfolk and farmers began to question the volume of tree-felling thunder that echoed in the forests. They began to visit the coupes and look as well as see, beginning to love these dark, silent colonnades of nature for what they were — natural and disproportionately beautiful. They began to love them simply for their size and majesty, as we do today, and they began to despair over their destruction. Pierson never revealed to Ruth — or anyone else, for that matter — exactly why or how he threw in his lot with the first, tentative north-west conservationists. But join them he did. And he was especially interested in making the logging industry a word we would use today but wasn't used then — professional. He aligned himself with labour organisations arguing for shorter hours, clean sheets and showers in the bunkhouses.

In the camps, Pierson would put down his axe and discuss with foremen and commandants just how much timber actually needed to be cut. *Precise* numbers of trees. How much *really* do we need? Get out and chalk them, he'd say. He would argue the merits of retaining certain bigger specimens, the biggest, slapping a redwood's powdery chocolate bark and declaring — as he wrote to Ruth — she's a beauty, and she should live to a beautiful old age. In the towns, at The Dalles and Portland and Oregon City, he spoke at public meetings, smelling sweeter than his colleagues. The forest was a wonder of nature, he said, and that was that. Tracts of it should stay that way. Off-limits to loggers. And I'm a logger talking, one of those working stiffs, as you call us. He joined discussions with the owners and managers of timber companies, tried to persuade them that there was more than enough wood for everyone. A man of some mental subtlety, he could see that if logging declined, fewer workers would be needed, skills would improve and wages would rise. He spoke with civic leaders and politicians, he urged the construction of logging railheads and the improvement of the industry's technology — better engines, chemical hardening of saw teeth, more efficient pitches on blades, the improvement in the reliability of belt-drives, winches to drag logs instead of oxen. And at night he returned to the camps and rose as high as he ever would, becoming a bull, a foreman. There were the bulls that hauled the logs and the bulls that bellowed orders at their gangs. Pierson was not a bawler, though, and his men generally liked him. He still went with them to town, to the saloons and possibly even the brothels, and tinkled out his tunes at Our House, staying respectably sober. After five years, he had been home to see Ruth and the children only once.

Kellogg paused, sipped his ale and felt for the pommel of his knife, just to make sure it was there, I thought, before continuing.

Nothing could have prepared Pierson for what transpired one fateful night at Our House, though, he said. The saloon was rocking, and an argument arose from nothing, as they do. Several men objected to Pierson's politics. If fewer trees were felled there would be fewer jobs, they argued. Pierson would be fine, because he knew the managers and the politicians and the conservationists. He was like them. But what about the real timber men, the real loggers who did the work, felled the trees, sawed the trunks? Huh? Pierson defended his position as best he could, but the ale and the fetid air inside Our House and the pools of spilled beer on the floor and the state of inebriation set off jostling and more ardent recriminations. Soon the men were brawling — a common enough occurrence, usually over women. Pierson tried to intervene, but was knocked out.

After an amount of time that he was unable even to guess at, he regained consciousness on the back of a wagon being driven at reckless pace along a forest track he was unfamiliar with. He was hog-tied. Four men sharing the vehicle — he recognised them from Our House — beamed at him with drunken smiles. The driver and another logger sat on a sprung seat forward. After what seemed like an hour, they stopped in the forest. Pierson had only a vague idea of where he might be. The actual geographical position. Amid curses and guffaws, he was dragged from the cart and thrown to the ground. The men clumped off a little ways. Soon a voice shouted from a distance that he had found the right one, a giant that Pierson could fall in love with. Above all others. His kidnappers untied him and dragged him to the butt of a big fir. Threw him face-first against the trunk. His arms were stretched around it and secured. You say a tree can make love just like a human being, Lenny? said a voice. Did you say that? Why sure I did, Billy, and trees *can* make love, that is for certain, said another. You ever had a tree make love to you, Pierson? said the first voice. I mean, you love trees, don't you? All the men guffawed. Wait, said someone. He ain't gonna need no more them pretty hands that jig out them honky toons where he goin'. That right, said someone else. No pianers up there 't all. And the next thing Pierson felt were enormous thuds on his hands as one of the loggers rained blows on each of them, cracking the bones and pulping them up good and proper. Pierson screamed from the pain. Couldn't help but, he later told the sheriff. What they hit him with was metal-hard and cold. Then someone said, They're real *animal* lovers trees! Real energetic! Better than them whores at The Goo's, that's for sure. Cheers and more laughter. Tree love-making is something you're gonna love, Dwighty boy. And this little tree, we reckon, is your perfect wife. 'Ceptin' you ain't gonna do the fuckin'. She is! Loud guffaws followed. *She* gonna do the *love*-making! With her own little woodie! This remark preceded the loudest — hysterical, even — cackling as well as whoops of Yeah! And, Let's see her do it! Pierson heard an axe chopping, then some delicate strokes — like whittling, it seemed to him. His trousers were ripped down around his ankles, longjohns next. And he felt the phallus that they had carved enter him. He screamed, loud and long. He tried not to, but the pain was unbearable, made him lose all courage and dignity — all faith and respect in men, he was to tell the sheriff, in anything and anyone he once might have believed in. Panic overwhelmed him, and in a silent pause he heard the horse's soft whinny, which he remembered because it was such an unexpected counterweight. Someone used perhaps an axe to hammer the wood into him until it could go no farther, he told the sheriff, and the men left, their sniggers diminishing as they trotted off.

Pierson was found three days later only because an unusually large number of buzzards circled above him. Admitted to Portland's biggest hospital, he was given the best of care, but there was really nothing anyone could do except to try to keep him comfortable and give him water. He was bloated, his body roaring with infection, his hands wrapped in bandages as big as footballs. Ruth was telegraphed and spent a lot of the money on a rail ticket west. She arrived eleven hours after he died, which was five months after his thirty-first birthday. The culprits never owned up, of course, and no one turned them in. The sheriff failed to act on the few points of identification Pierson was able to whisper from his pillow.

The man is remembered as a martyr. His sacrifice — as some call it — helped improve conditions for the very forest workers who had murdered him. More selective logging became law. But I carry with me an enormous guilt, sir, said Kellogg. For the rest of my life it's the burden of remorse I have to shoulder, which you might probably guess at. You have no idea of my pain. (I was tempted to tell Kellogg that I did.) I wish I could have warned him while I was inside that photograph, said Kellogg, pointing. Warned him about what was coming to him. I could have saved him, sir, saved his life, but I didn't. He's third from the right.

MY PINT MUG was empty, I noticed, by the time the last frame of Kellogg's story had left the projector gate of my memories. It had reminded me of the strangest plantation in Victoria, a place I have never been able to return to after my visit to the Lost Coast. The Otways — coastal hills blanketed by a primeval temperate rainforest of giant tree ferns as well as *Eucalyptus regnans*, or mountain ash, which is said to be the world's tallest tree, or perhaps second-tallest after the redwood, myrtle beeches, messmates, native orchids, irises and lilies as well as *petaloid monocotyledonous* plants, as one expert puts it — is as far to the south-west of Geelong as Geelong is to the south-west of Melbourne.

Inside this vast protected space, in the middle of the forest, is another forest of Californian redwoods that soar to more than sixty metres. No one seems to know how many were planted in 1938 in what was called a logging experiment, and whoever did it and whatever they had in mind are details that appear to have been lost forever. Bordering the Aire river, a narrow creek that bubbles over round pebbles covered with lichens, tree ferns twice the height of a man on either side, the plantation is perhaps sixty metres wide and a couple of hundred long, the handsome ridged chocolate trunks of American *Sequoias* every few steps, the forest floor of dried brown fronds and needles dropped from high above as springy as a trampoline. While beyond these exotic giants the Australian bush is replete with the raucous complaints of rosellas, the throaty cackling of kookaburras and the twittering of smaller birds such as wrens, among the Otways' American flora there is an eerie and eternal silence, and one hears, as long as one knows the story, only Pierson's screams. I like to think that the plantation is a kind of memorial to him, but I can never return there, the dead forever haunting us, shaping our thoughts and actions.

Californian redwoods might flourish in many of Victoria's public gardens and forests, but I have never investigated their general frequency. That Kellogg's story and the Otways's plantation had come to mind, though, prompted my recalling that perhaps half-a-dozen specimens of the *Sequoia* genus, including the species *giganteum*, the giant redwood, which grows naturally these days in only a few groves on the western slopes of the Sierra Nevada in California, were planted in the late nineteenth century in the eleven hectares of grounds of the Beechworth Lunatic Asylum, four hours' drive north-east of Melbourne. A small town in the high country curated for tourism, Beechworth these days has a fine restaurant, a small brewery its equal in quality, several elegant historic buildings, including a courthouse of national significance faced with honey-coloured chipped stone, a gaol of local granite built to accommodate gold-rush convicts and only recently decommissioned, and, on a hill a kilometre to the east of the main street and several hundred metres above sea level, the asylum, which was first known as Mayday Hills, a name usually qualified these days with the adjective *haunted*. The asylum closed its doors to the mentally fragile only in 1995, and for almost a hundred and thirty years it had been one of Victoria's biggest institutions, its campus strewn with forty buildings, some dating from the 1860s. Surrounding it were a further 106 hectares of farmland, which, in a special relationship with the institution to sustain the inmates and staff, provided pigs, fruit, herbs and vegetables, crops, stables and a barn. These days, the remaining structures mix architectural styles from Victorian to a restrained version of modernism. A few buildings are occupied by organisations, including the local shire of Indigo, and a former cellblock and a nurses' quarters have been converted into a hotel. Most of the biggest buildings are empty, and ghost tours of the precinct are popular.

Planted sporadically — and seemingly haphazardly — on undulating grassy fields among the structures, the asylum's trees are its biggest attraction, a gift from Melbourne's Royal Botanic Gardens dating from the 1860s. A patient called Robert Coates decided where the first trees were to go, and one cannot help but wonder if his mental condition contributed to their whimsical scattering. A lilly-pilly, kurrajong, black alder, Chinese elm and Himalayan maple, for instance, are in one relatively tight cluster, and there are many similar examples of heterogeneity. Improvements said to have been made in 1912, 1930, and the 1980s could not have involved uprooting and replanting mature specimens, and every square centimetre of the *haunted* former Mayday grounds retains a kind of agreeable disorder. One never knows what type of tree one will bump into next, and more than two hundred of them are classified as *significant* on state and regional registers.

I have stayed in the hotel several times, mainly to try to navigate my way among the specimens, to find them, name them and admire their robustness. (I also revel in the brewery.) Indeed, the shire, the hotel and the Beechworth Treescape Group have collaborated to publish a modest pamphlet detailing three walks inside the grounds. Each, they advise, takes about an hour to complete and leads the vigilant hiker on a circuit past forty-eight specimens. Comfortable shoes are recommended because there are stretches of rough grass, says the brochure. And one cannot help thinking, as I thought one day, about what patients made of the trees, how those of disturbed minds reacted to the arboreal majesty all around them, presuming, of course, that they were allowed to stroll the grounds in daylight hours, as I am convinced must have been the case, at least for many of the less dangerous among them. Did the trees' stillness and magnificence and variety and beauty calm them, perhaps even spur them to think clearer and better, help with their symptoms if not their maladies? Were they planted for that single purpose? Were they meant to be a tonic for bruised souls, a raveller of addled dreams? No answers have been archived.

On one particular day, the clouds were uniformly lead-grey, presaging snow and so close I felt I could touch them. I had set out from the hotel on what the brochure calls the Ha-ha Wall Walk, which takes you past a bristle-tipped oak, a blue spruce, two Algerian oaks, four Douglas firs, a dawn redwood, a twisted white pine, tulip tree, copper beech, several Himalayan dogwoods, cedars from the same mountain range and Bhutan and Monterey cypresses, when I got momentarily lost — there is no other word for it — in a small forest of a score or more mature poplars that obscured the institution's buildings. I knew exactly where I was but felt adrift, disoriented, as though I had been caught up in a relentless current that was taking me to an unknown destination, away from where I was to somewhere unfamiliar and a little frightening. (An elevator stopped at level thirty-three and I got out. I knew my room was on thirty-seven, but its button had failed to light up, and I'd decided to take the stairs. Why four flights? Dreams never explain themselves.) I had failed to bring my phone, which has a compass, and the winter grass,

the brochure's *rough* grass, was up to my knees where, among
the poplars, it should not have been so luxurious. Why was it
so thick when leaves must block the sun here for much of the
year? The rough grass had slowed my progress, at any rate,
and I wondered if I should fight it or let it arrest me, hoping
that my anxiety would dissipate if I paused.

It occurred to me that the inmates must have gathered in
this place, in hiding and in full view, so to speak, and that they
might have conspired to escape, plotting in low voices, complain-
ing about their treatment at Mayday Hills, the pulling of teeth as
a punishment, the dreadful day that came along once a month

when the electroconvulsive machine was taken from bed to bed
and you could smell the sweetness of burned temples and hear
the screams, of course, and your turn was next, the leather
restraints and straitjackets, all made locally, the leather tanned
in Beechworth at Australia's biggest tannery, we were told, the
padded cells that weren't padded at all but lined with Baltic pine,

a soft wood though it is, and were so small, so small to bang about in, the coarse sackcloth uniform in striped mould-green and no underpants, that was the worst thing, to live your life without underpants, no underwear, year after year, and no chance, no chance at all, of getting the eight signatures you needed to set yourself free. Perhaps here, in the poplar forest, logic and reason replaced the patients' anxieties for once, I thought.

I knew that perhaps two hundred metres to the north (but where was north when the sun was obscured?) I would find

remnants of one of the original ha-ha walls, which surrounded the patients' courtyards, and beyond it the ring road that would take me back to the hotel. Three metres high and several red bricks thick, ha-ha barriers were designed to appear to patients to be formidable obstacles, discouraging flight. For the free men and women of Beechworth on the other side of them, though, gentle grassy embankments sloping up to nearly the height of the top course of bricks obscured their practical function. Don't they treat the madmen well, high-country graziers and tannery workers must have said, ceding to the illusion. Look, the walls aren't at all foreboding. I could jump over them, I'm sure. Of course, some of the locals would have been worried that they didn't provide a *high enough* barrier.

I spread over the grass an old SOS-blue parka that lives in my backpack, sat down, and listened for the lunatics' voices, hearing only the whisper of a chill wind as it sluiced among the whiteness of the poplar trunks, whistling softly in their horizontal scars.

In my room at the hotel I had found a short pamphlet explaining in five small pages of plain paper the history of Mayday Hills, and I remembered that I had put it in my pocket before setting out. No better place to read it was in the poplar grove, and in a few hundred words I became acquainted with the various ways in which the disturbed could be admitted here, including voluntarily, which reminded me of St Sebastian House. While I suspected that many patients had left narratives of life in the asylum, the stapled summary provided two short versions of what it called *accounts*.

Declan Murphy, for instance, who was fifty-nine when he was brought to Beechworth in 1883, said a policeman had taken him there because he was silly and masturbated. He had the habit of saying his prayers, he said, and one night he had stayed out looking for a quartz reef that would be worth three hundred pounds if it were worth nothing to him and his Nessa, his aisling, when she arrived by and by from Galway. When I was in Dunolly, he said, some larrikins burned my tent and I could not find it, even the ashes of it. I asked five men dressed like navvies if they saw my tent go up in flames and who lit the fire and where it might be now, the remains, the ashes that are left, and they did not answer. I spoke to them a second time, and they said they were ghosts and had no manner of putting words into their own mouths. I found a house to shelter in, but the navvies told me it was haunted, so I stood by the door, not wanting to frighten the ghosts by entering in, so I didn't. Then I saw the devil like a gigantic steam engine, puffing and panting and blowing out flames and smoke and sparks, and when he had passed me by my clothes were covered in ash and smoke. I next saw the Blessed Virgin and shook her hand, and she smiled at my act of kindness. She uprooted a tree pulling it just like that, flat out of the ground, sir, and made slabs from it and made me a house from the slabs and sent Jesus for more wood to build a roof for my house. The Blessed Virgin built my house in a tree for safety's sake and lifted me up into it, into the topmost branches of the tree as easy as I can lift this stylograph off your desk, sir, and I said Hail Mary countless times over and over above the choir and its singing. And Jesus made me a roof, and I watched him saw the timber and plane the planks in a jiffy, sir, a real carpenter, and build the roof, nailing in wooden spikes as big as your arm, sir. I asked the Blessed Virgin for money, but she had a bird in her hand and put it on a perch. One of the men had a purse full of coins but he gave me none. A priest came by and I told him about the generous navvy with the purse and he said to me, Be off with you.

The following morning, I cleared a blanket of snow from my windscreen and drove home.

OF THE THREE pianists whose lives had ended violently at thirty-one, the Australian Noel Mewton-Wood, who was born in

Melbourne and grew up in an affluent suburb, the son of what the *Australian Dictionary of Biography* calls an English secretary but who was, in fact, an embezzler, seemed the most opaque and mercurial. Of one thing is certain; his Australian mother Dulcie catalysed his success.

When I investigated, few clouds in the ether detailed his life; they revealed only that from a very young age he had been enormously talented, a formidable pianist. The person who had almost certainly accumulated most facts about him was Sonia Orchard, a Melbourne writer, and it was to her book *The Virtuoso* that I turned.

Dr Orchard admits from the start that her work is a hybrid — fiction in which she has tried to record faithfully the significant events in the pianist's life, as she puts it. When, late in the text, we learn of the demise following an appendectomy of Bill Federick or Frederick or Fedrick — sources vary — Mewton-Wood's partner and factotum, and only a dozen pages later of the pianist's death at his own hands, one of which held a glass tumbler containing a cocktail of gin and prussic acid before he threw it against the wall of his living room and it shattered and he crumpled, the reader is, to use that unparalleled French word, *bouleversé*. The surprise devastates, arising from nowhere, it seems, having no discernible origin, like a nightmare or a perfect storm. (Or the images that leap unbidden into my mind.)

For more than two hundred pages she describes a man seemingly blessed by endless good fortune, which began when Dulcie recognised early his talent and nurtured it by getting him trained from the age of nine at the University of Melbourne's conservatorium, promoting his first public performance with the Victorian Symphony Orchestra under the baton of Bernard

Heinze only three years later, and, with public financial support, enrolling him at the Royal Academy of Music in London, which was a kind of finishing school for the most talented British musicians and those of its empire. Dr Orchard's narrator tells the story of a young man who, settled and already famous in Britain, bred geese and Alsatian dogs, could expound at length and with accuracy about literature, art, antiques, tennis and marionette theatre — apparently he made his own puppets — a musician who prepared meticulously and performed perfectly and seemingly without effort, a trait I questioned immediately, who could explain in easily understood terms atomic physics, how a virus replicates and why the ancient Egyptians lost their empire, subscribed to the academic science journal *Nature*, wrote musical compositions from the age of five — Dr Orchard describes his first piece as a rollicking number about going to a corner shop to buy cheese sticks — was seductive in looks, dark, thick tousled hair no doubt helping, would tell those who asked that he would prefer death to an inability to play the piano, signed his name with an umlaut, Noël, even if diareses might have been misconstrued among the Australians of his generation as perhaps the name of a new species of prehistoric fish or a type of hooligan that posed an even greater challenge than normal to the Victoria Police's flying squads, which used lead-filled rubber hoses on delinquent teenagers in those days, a pianist who wore sweet and dewy cologne, as the narrator puts it, and who was close friends with Britain's greatest musicians, including the composer Benjamin Britten and his partner, the tenor Peter Pears, as well as the composer Michael Tippett. Mewton-Wood, who believed that his fellow Australians were unsophisticated, was a promiscuous homosexual, a keen drinker of gin, and a smoker. But when I discovered that forty-three pages of suicide notes had been left scattered around his house and that, in essence, their message was that he had decided that he could no longer play the piano, that music *was* his life, and that there was no point pressing on without it, my interest in the state of his mind intensified, the possibility of the piano's role in his demise obvious. I was heartened that Dr Orchard's narrator felt similarly, noting his opinion that a type of love that had provided a refuge from the world — which of Mewton-Wood's many worlds? one might ask — could hardly be described as love at all. I found it a telling phrase.

FORTUNE SMILED on my investigations when Dr Orchard sent me the email address of one of Mewton-Wood's last remaining relatives. I launched a message into the ether, and a woman that I shall refer to as SH said that she would be delighted to chat, but she lived in Sydney. She had material — a trove of letters, photographs, miscellaneous documents, a piano stool, briefcase and gloves — that, in its entirety, amounted to the pianist's most significant archive, she added. Her mother was the pianist's first cousin, and she could tell me a lot about him.

The next day, JL began an email with, I suppose you know that the Sydney International Piano Competition is on, an event like the Olympics that comes around only every four years. I had not known, and his email continued that he had once written about it, and if *I* wanted to write about pianists and their hands, I could do worse than watch the freshest batch of up-and-comers perform in the pressure-cooker of a prestigious tournament, the words he used. It had become one of the majors, he wrote, alongside the Queen Elisabeth in Brussels, and the Chopin, Busoni, and Tchaikovsky competitions.

It appeared to me as though he were writing about sport, the Australian tennis Open or the American Masters golf, say, which in a way he was. His email went on to say — with typical JL bombast — that he had been among the first Australians to give the Sydney competition any public prominence, penning an article about it for a widely circulated American music journal that he declined to name.

He said he had been flown to Sydney in the 1980s at the competition's expense and had been invited to stay with Claire Dan, the former Hungarian cabaret dancer and singer who had founded SIPC, as it is known. Ms Dan had married her compatriot Peter Abeles, a nightclub entrepreneur, when they were on tour in Romania just after the war. They lived in London, Paris and Rome before emigrating to Australia in 1949 and adopting two daughters, with whom, JL wrote, he had spent a delightful evening. For no reason that he could determine, the night he had spent playing card games, mainly poker, which he knew little about until the sisters, or step-sisters, taught him, women who must have been in their late teens or early twenties, had always reminded him, he had no idea why, of the Yarra River's flooding when he was a child and the hundreds, perhaps thousands, of carp that were stranded on the flats when the water receded. He and a friend had ridden their bicycles through mud and slush and long grass as tangled as wet hair to inspect the fish, some of them the size of toddlers and in their death throes, still gasping, in puddles no more than two or three centimetres deep. The fish were no good for anything, we had been told, wrote JL, and certainly not edible. Many were beginning to rot, and the smell was repulsive.

By the 1970s, Abeles was a wealthy trucking magnate, a knight of the Queen's realm, and was divorced from Claire, who was obsessed with the arts and establishing SIPC, and disliked being known as Lady Abeles. She charmed me, JL continued, giving me a large bedroom on the top floor of her Bellevue Hill mansion, which had a view of the harbour and was sold only recently for $15.5 million to a nearby private school. Had I read about it? The room overlooked the swimming pool, and every morning he watched Claire swim lap after lap of backstroke, free of a bathing suit.

By now, I was beginning to take JL's missives with not just a grain but several bagfuls of salt, extracting from them only the biggest crystals of greatest clarity. But it disappointed me that he had had to mention a naked swimmer when young pianists' careers — and therefore their lives — were on the line.

I looked online and discovered that on the eve of my meeting with Mewton-Wood's relative, the first of four finals was to be held. The half-dozen finalists — born between 24 July 1983 and 6 July 1998, that is, less than thirty-three years of age — would by then be decided from thirty-two who had commenced the journey almost a fortnight earlier. They would have played solo recitals of twenty and thirty minutes, semi-finals of chamber music with a violinist and a string quartet, a further recital of sixty-five minutes, and would need to endure the final rounds by performing two concertos with the Sydney Symphony Orchestra, choosing one from a list of 18th-century works and

the second from a counterpart of 19th- and 20th-century pieces. I
began to feel light-headed just reading the extensive rules, and
I was shocked to recall that Anna had been working up a repertoire for the first SIPC, or sip-see, as she called it, not long before
my saw took off her fingers. I began to perspire, and it was with
difficulty that, on the verge of toppling, I stayed upright on my
chair long enough to close my laptop and lie on the floor until
I recovered my composure. It was only the following day that I
felt well enough to buy a ticket.

Three weeks later, I flew to Sydney and went first to the
Opera House to pick up my ticket and a program, a glossy and
expensive publication that I took back to the hotel to read. The
finalists were Kenneth Broberg from the United States, Moye
Chen and Jianing Kong from China, Andrey Gugnin and Arseny
Tarasevich-Nikolaev from Russia, and Oxana Shevchenko, the
only woman, from Kazakhstan. They had all won first, second
and third prizes — gold medals even — at other recent events,
and the youngest was Broberg, who a week or so after the competition had run its course would turn twenty-three. Oxana,
who in the program had long red hair and big blue eyes, had
won a Liszt competition in Italy the year before; her hands did
not appear to be especially large, compelling me to wonder how
she managed the composer's daunting leaps, arpeggios, scales
and octave runs that must often be executed *fortissimo*.

Tonight I was to hear Broberg and the two Russians play
Mozart concertos, and I spent the rest of the afternoon wondering what went through the competitors' minds in the hours
before the shuffle to the scaffold, bowels rumbling, anal-sphinc-
ter taut, feet dragging, a burly guard under each armpit, across

the execution clearing to the post, to be tied to it, wrists bound behind your back, a *hi-vis* bull's-eye in a hideous and inartistic luminous orange pinned to your chest. Jesus came to mind. What was it he said? Into your hands I commend my spirit? Or was it their hands? Or the concertgoers'? Or the piano's? Or the judges'? I wondered, too, if Schnabel's remark that Beethoven's greatest works were greater than they could be performed sprang into their young minds, threatening. Because if it was a truism for Beethoven, it also had to be true for the works of Mozart and Bach and Haydn and a few others. I expected that the finalists spent the depths of the afternoon exploring the deepest crevices of their psyches, loci where doubts lurked, dark places where the black monk would visit uninvited to advise, as he did Chekhov's poor Andrei Kovrin, that their dazzling playing had come about only after an enormous sacrifice that they had worn themselves out making. That their health would go first, and it wouldn't be too long, the monk warned Kovrin, before you sacrifice your very life to your scholarship and artistry. But what could be better? the monk rhetorically posited. All noble spirits blessed with gifts from on high have this as their aim, he says. And I thought of Kapell and Farrell and Mewton-Wood and Lipatti and all of the others — of my sister, too, of course — who had given their lives early to the keyboard.

A SLEEK CLOAK as black as wet tarmac had fallen over the city by the time I walked down the Macquarie Street hill to the Opera House, and I imagined again that somewhere near here Richard Farrell might have told his friend Trent that he would die young. Then, soon, I was confronted by a view that, every time I see it, entrances me to the point that I feel myself rising above the pavement in a burst of ecstasy. The night was still, the mid-winter temperature an unusual and balmy nineteen degrees. The illuminated sails of the Opera House glowed their delicious ice-blue-white, as if this gigantic structure were a kind of celebratory cake, and below them ripples on the great expanse of the harbour caught flashes of illumination reflected from the tall buildings behind Circular Quay. Brightly lit ferries slid in and out of their berths on the quay, the turquoise of the harbour churning to smoke-green behind them. In the middle distance and to the left, scintillating points of light outlined the Harbour Bridge, sketching an architectural colossus that stands for Australia but is not even remotely like it. On the northern shoreline, waterside apartments were illuminated trellises, and a thousand metres away across the water, as clear as if it were only a handspan from my eyes, the giant mouth of Luna Park smiled and the park's Ferris wheel turned as slowly as life.

As if to rebuff this sensational landscape, a truly unexpected and shocking sight confronted me. On the Opera House's paved and pebbled forecourt, perhaps a couple of hundred people of similar ages to the pianists who would be playing tonight took part in a kind of frenetic Brownian motion, staring zombie-like into electronic devices, most of them mobile telephones. Light from the screens revealed their wide-eyed concentration, the grimness with which they focused on whatever it was on the machines to which they were devoted. Instead of being micro-scopic particles being pushed around by molecules, as happens in Brownian motion, these were real people being shoved erratically by a digital application, a game, if you prefer, called Pokémon Go, I learned. They might have noticed, at some point, the view of the Opera House and the harbour and the bridge, its stunning magnificence, drawn their collective breath, so to speak, and revelled in it. But not a single pair of eyes was looking at it now. So strange was the scene, so weird the fixation on screens, so random the trajectories, collisions so frequent, entrapment so total, appearance as automatons so real, that I took refuge by the railing to gather my breath.

A man in his twenties, his skin scrubbed, his short hair and beard ginger and spiky, his round face beaming, joined me at the rail. He, too, was holding a device, and I waved a hand at the crowd and asked what it was all about. He said he was Sven, smiled a smile that divided his face into quarter and three-quarter moons, and showed me his phone. The crowd was catching Pokémon monsters, he said, like the one here, an awful-looking cartoon marsupial called Kangaskhan. There were many others bearing names such as Zubat, Metapod, Kakuna and Rattata, he said, flicking them onto his screen to show me. Satellites direct you to hot spots where they may be trapped, he explained, and you can throw Poké balls at them to capture them. Then you may train them to fight, said Sven, beaming.

Dredging my experience of the world, I failed to come up with a single context in which to fit any of this new knowledge, and I was tempted to say something as banal as, I don't understand. What are you telling me? Another question came to mind. What about the view? But I realised that it would have had not the slightest relevance to the Pokémon Go players. What did interest me, though, was the gulf between what the people on the forecourt were doing and what the SIPC finalists — humans, not directed hubots — would be achieving within the next couple of hours, feats that can be performed by perhaps only hundreds of people, at most a few thousand, worldwide. I felt like telling Sven about that, about the concert, about the skills of the pianists, what the hands of pianists can do, but I found no words by which to do it, and he left me at the railing to go off and hunt monsters. I suspected that no black monks would ever visit him and the other Pokémon Go players, and that they were sure to lead long and happy lives.

KENNETH BROBERG, pale, thin, dark-haired, and of medium height, willed himself onto the platform in white tie and formal attire. He floated a little in his tailcoat, which appeared to be too big for him, and I got the strange impression that he was chewing gum. His smile was gentle and he sat at the piano as cautiously as a condemned man being coaxed onto an execution gurney. I tried to imagine what was going through his head. Did he wish that an incalculable number of clocks would somehow invade the Opera House and manage to stop time dead in its tracks, so that he would not have to play? Or did he wish for the opposite, that the clocks would somehow swallow up the next twenty-odd minutes and he would arrive instantly at the moment when he struck the piece's last chord, quelling his anxiety and getting over and done with what he had to do?

Mozart's twenty-fifth piano concerto has a long orchestral introduction in which the first movement's major themes are announced and the pianist must sit there, cooling his heels, as the saying goes, camouflaging his intense anxiety. Kenneth,

who in the past two years had won and placed in five competitions, now stroked the keys several times, as if to remove dust
from them, and at one stage his hands dropped to the lever that
adjusts the stool's height, and I noticed that the right one trem-
bled. I had interpreted his dust-removal poorly; as the orchestra
progressed towards the piano's entry, I perceived that he was
vulnerable, that what he was doing to the keys was reassuring
them, hoping to caress the black and white devils in front of him
into cooperating. He was not about to hurt them, he was saying.
They were friends, and he and they would have to work together
for both the foreseeable and unforeseeable futures.

From that flash of recognition, I prepared myself to love the
boy and his playing. And so it was. Despite an unsteady entry,
a few missed notes in the relatively easy opening bars, Kenneth
played from the heart, poetry and passion radiating in a glorious
continuum from the Fazioli's red-spruce soundboard, the soundboard's being a piano's beating heart, the essential organ without
which keyboard music has no life. Executed by hands that were
neither big nor small, his scales and runs were, in particular, beautifully executed, just lovely phrases, swelling and dying, as we
must presume Mozart would have liked them to sound, and his
head and other body movements in time with the pulse of the
music were minimal. (I was reminded of Géza Anda, the great
Hungarian Mozart player, who moved scarcely at all on the stool.)

Kenneth had gone to the trouble — his co-finalists didn't —
of writing his own cadenza for the first movement, and when
the orchestra stopped for a minute or two and he played alone,
he demonstrated not only intimacy with the way Mozart penned
piano music but an especially touching flourish. Included in the

last few seconds of his solo were the first three bars, or perhaps five, of *La Marseillaise* — converting them to a Mozartian call to arms. Only five days earlier, I recalled, a madman had driven a truck along the Promenade des Anglais in Nice, killing eighty-four and injuring hundreds.

No such sympathy was shown by the Russians. Graduates of the Tchaikovsky Moscow State Conservatoire, their playing was perfect, technically unblemished and emotionally a little too forced, too well-shaped and immaculately projected to appear the product of organisms in which blood ran. At their ages, they already dominated grand pianos, letting them know from first note to last just who was boss. I suspect that Russian conservatories train pianists to stand over pianos, bully them, be unafraid of them, *à la* Jascha Spivakovsky. It is perhaps a valid strategy, I thought, if the anxiety of performing can be suppressed by a technical ability so comprehensive that terror itself is conquered, that you are confident that you can escape from any potentially fatal situation halfway through a piece.

Arseny Tarasevich-Nikolaev, in a dark business suit, a satin bow tie the darkest possible shade of navy blue, and black patent-leather shoes, had a striking resemblance to Kenneth. Andrey Gugnin, who was equally thin and pale but taller than the other two, his hair a lighter shade, his gleaming bow tie off-white, and his hands enormous, the little fingers especially long, broadcast an unambiguous message to the audience as soon as he sat down: he would win SIPC, his body said. Both the Russians marketed their playing more than Kenneth, rocking on the stool and bobbing their heads in time with the music much more than had the American. Their playing was also more insistently perfect, as precise in its execution as the Russian microsurgery on corneas, say, for which their compatriot, the ophthalmologist Svyatoslav Nikolayevich Fyodorov, for instance, became famous around the world. But I would have liked to have heard louder heartbeats when they played, and Andrey had a habit of raising his left hand almost to obscure his face, palm facing the audience, when the right hand was playing unaccompanied solo passages. I found it distracting, but the jurors clearly thought that it was no obstacle to his winning, which he did, pocketing $50,000 and a host of engagements worldwide, including a concert with the London Philharmonic, another at the Mariinsky International Piano Festival in St Petersburg and a tour of Australia. Arseny came second, and Kenneth fourth, deprived of a podium finish, as the sportswriters say, by Moye Chen. But if you ask me whose concerts I would prefer to attend in the next few years, Kenneth Broberg's would lead the list. He looked just a little vulnerable, which is, I suggest, the default attitude no great pianist should — or can — avoid. Will I or won't I succeed tonight? And what miracles will I need to create on the way to evading fatal mistakes? How can I demonstrate that the black monk is right without killing myself?

OVERNIGHT, a low-pressure system had rolled in from the sea and Sydney's weather had got diametrically different. When I left the hotel mid-morning fine rain was drowning the city, the droplets so tiny and densely delivered that it appeared as if a giant device obscured by the clouds was spraying the city and all its inhabitants, parks and gardens, birds and animals, in drenching mist. I walked uphill from Edgecliff station, taking steep footpaths along winding narrow roads on each side of which apartment towers jostled for better views of the harbour.

By the time I had reached the one in which SH and her husband T lived at an indeterminate height above the road, I was saturated and they were sympathetic. A small but light-filled home, as real-estate agents like to say, it had a spectacular view on a clear day to the north and east, said T, waving a hand. You could see as far as North Head, even Manly, perhaps half-a-dozen kilometres distant across the harbour. I saw moored yachts in a bay three or four hundred metres below, but beyond them was a grey veil that thickened the farther your vision tried to penetrate it; attempting to see anything beyond the boats was as rewarding as peering into the future, I thought.

T left SH and me to talk about Mewton-Wood, and she produced a big cardboard box and placed it on a chair alongside me. Her mother, SH repeated, was Mewton-Wood's first cousin, and that was how she came to own these archives, she said, tapping the lid of the box. A pretty woman, her short grey-blond hair cut in a bob, her lips glossed in medium schev red, a wrist and a finger hosting stout modern silver pieces designed by Georg Jensen, she told me later, she said that Noel deserved an archive-keeper who had an appreciation of style and good design. I estimated she might have been anywhere between her early fifties and early seventies. At one point, she did in fact mention how old she was, but its irrelevance led to my instantly forgetting the number.

I wondered if she knew, I began, pulling out the SIPC program, that the competition's sixth prize of $7,500 was named after Noel, or Noël, if you like. She hadn't known, she said. His was the last of seven placings' prizes, preceding a host of others for performances such as best overall concerto, best semi-final recital and best piano quintet, for instance, and following the Ernest Hutcheson first prize, Percy Grainger second, George Frederick Boyle third, William Murdoch fourth, and so on.

We read the program's brief biography on Noel, discovering that Benjamin Britten had composed his third Canticle for a memorial concert honouring the Australian. She opened the box and began drawing out folders, a pink one and a cardboard one, loose photographs, one in a frame, its glass cracked, bundled letters, sheet music, a pair of leather gloves in which my hands would have floated, a leather satchel and a red and white pure-wool scarf woven in a houndstooth pattern and bearing

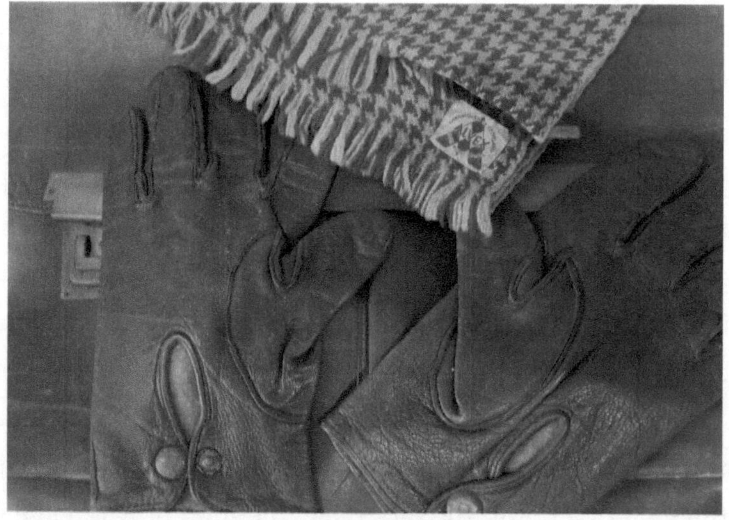

the label, Alvex, handmade in Scotland. They were all Noel's, she said, and she was as curious as I was about his demise, she added. That was his piano stool, she pointed, indicating a mahogany piece with two drawers beneath a seat upholstered in a striped, glaringly multi-coloured fabric.

She had discovered that there were twenty to thirty farewell notes, as she called them, scattered around the room in which Noel had killed himself, and she understood that they had been archived in Britain with the coroner's report. The only way an interested person could get access to them, she said, was by obtaining permission from a family relative. I asked if she would write me such a licence, and she said that she would have to think about it, which must have appeared to be, from her side, an obvious and careful response. From mine, it was, as you might imagine, frustrating.

Noel's mother Dulcie had put a commemorative note on the anniversary of her son's death each year in *The Times* until she left to return to Australia, said SH. Her grief was utterly overwhelming, and she herself, SH, was able to measure its magnitude only because she and a cousin took piano lessons with Aunt Dulcie. My mother, said SH, was highly dominating and religious, so Aunt Dulcie was more reserved in what she said to me. But my cousin had an endlessly sick and passive mother, and Aunt Dulcie probably felt she could unburden herself to her more easily, and she did, my cousin experiencing her sadness to a considerable degree. My own mother might have been a wonderful support for Aunt Dulcie's despair, except that Dulcie did not believe in death and any attempts to seek comfort from her would have hit a brick wall.

Parenting is designed for guilt, said SH, and as a theorist on family systems, as she put it, I have worked with mothers and fathers who have lost children to suicide. Their guilt is endless, and as those words left SH's mouth I could not help thinking about Anna and my own guilt, of course. The frightening image of her fingers twitching on the pavers came up. The one that curls into a hook had never been so graphic, and vertigo invaded. I was glad to be sitting down.

SH asked me if I was all right, and when I steadied myself, nodded, and said that I suffered turns like this without explaining why, she waited half a minute or so before asking if she should continue. I nodded and said I was fine.

Suicide produces a type of grief that can last in varying degrees of intensity throughout a life, she said, and children without siblings have little room beyond the projections of their parents, the witting and unwitting attitudes and gestures they make that they think are best for them. Noel would have been Aunt Dulcie's total focus. Moreover, she said, Aunt Dulcie had been a widow since 1941, and her husband, Noel's father, was scarcely memorable, having been a thief, you know, a petty white-collar criminal who did time in Long Bay. My grandfather had a service station in Double Bay, and Uncle Son took even *his* money, a relative's money.

Aunt Dulcie retained her dignity and had something of a life when she returned to Sydney, running deportment classes and modelling, once for a cover of a Player's cigarette packet that depicted Whistler's mother. She used to claim that she had been chosen for the advertisement because of her classical features, but the mother in the painting looks glum, elderly and ugly, don't you think? She surrounded herself in her tiny apartment on New Beach Road with homosexual men whom she would entertain. She called silhouettes sillo-ways, which shows you how much she knew about the French language, and profiles pro-feels. SH stopped and smiled.

I suggested without much conviction that Dulcie Mewton-Wood might have taken Noel to London partly to escape from the shadow of her husband's criminality and to further her social ascent, but SH said it was only to develop Noel's talent. Australians with artistic flair all went to London in those days and even earlier and later. Think of Barry Humphries and Clive James and Germaine Greer.

She went to the kitchen to make us coffee and left me with the contents of the box.

Most of the documents and letters I skimmed were insignificant, giving up no clues as to why a hugely talented and famous pianist had taken his own life. I read a cutting from *The Times of Ceylon* dated the 22nd of June 1937, for instance, saying that the thirteen-year-old Australian prodigy Noel Mewton-Wood was going to provide first-class entertainment tomorrow night at the Royal College Hall. And the photograph under cracked glass showed a not-much-older Noel in the garden of Artur Schnabel's home in Switzerland, where he had stayed and studied with the great Beethoven master. There were photographs of Noel patting both a goose and a dog and sitting at a keyboard when very young. Among the documents were Noel's will and a rollicking piano piece in four-four time called *Kraft Relish*. Above the first bar, the player is directed to play as if he or she were going to the grocer to buy the relish. In the sixth bar he or she must ask for the relish, and the eighth bar, to be played *presto*, or as fast as you can play it, is marked joy at getting relish. Above the last three bars, which are cascades of scales, is scribbled relish slipping down throat.

The will was a less cheerful affair. Dated the 20th of November 1953, exactly thirty-one years after Mewton-Wood's birth, a fortnight before his death and three weeks after the death of William Kapell, it bequeathed to John Amis his radio-gramophone, records and two pianos, one his practice grand. To his mother he left all his effects and his double-storey townhouse at No. X Hillgate Place, which was mortgaged, and, as Mewton-Wood notes, it might not be mine to give. He hopes that his mother will be able to keep up the payments because it is the first house he had ever owned, he writes, and in it his friend and he had been wonderfully happy, the expression he uses, and that he had hoped for much longer but it wasn't to be the case. He nominates two more friends, Raymond Russell and Patrick Trevor-Roper, to have some of his possessions, but he cannot think what they would like. They should take from my mother whatever they want. I am sure she will have no objection, he writes.

Of all the documents I read, only one was outstandingly helpful. Of about half-foolscap size in landscape format, the *pro forma*

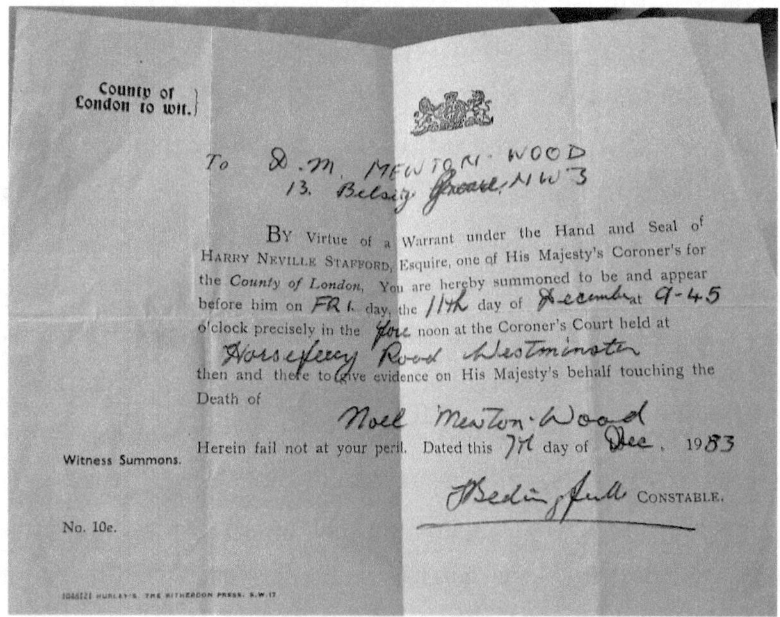

was headed by a lion-and-unicorn crest and in Old English script, set left, *County of London to wit. By the hand and seal of Harry Neville Stafford*, it said, *one of His Majesty's Coroner's*, as it was written, the second apostrophe strangely erring in the grammatical 1950s, *for the County of London, D. M. Mewton-Wood of 13 Belsize Grove, NW3*, the name and address written in ballpoint pen to fill in gaps, Dulcie, in other words, was summoned to appear before him on Friday the eleventh day of December at 9.45 o'clock precisely in the forenoon at Horseferry Road, Westminster, to give evidence on His Majesty's behalf touching the death of Noel Mewton-Wood. The summons ended ominously: *Herein fail not at your peril*. Not only was I convinced that Dulcie would have failed not, but I had a good lead, at last, on where the coroner's report might eventually have been archived.

SH returned with very strong coffee. It was the way she made it, she said, offering to water it down. Might she have detected my febrile nature? I thought. Without my prompting, she said that part of the mystery about Noel's death that needed to be clarified was a rumour that he had been the subject of sinister visits in the weeks, and possibly months, before his suicide. The pianist had cruised, to use the demotic term, for promiscuous homosexuals in certain parts of London that were well-known to police, and homosexuality between consenting men more than twenty-one years of age became legal only fourteen years after his death. Might police have threatened him? Might someone who knew his habits have been blackmailing him? Could his illegal behaviour have been all too much? Got to him? Got *at* him? SH and I were without answers, but I promised to try hard to find them, leaving her soon afterwards for the short walk, this time downhill in the rain, which had lessened, to the station.

JOHN AMIS, who acquired Mewton-Wood's radio-gramophone, records and pianos, was among the pianist's most ardent heterosexual friends. Amis managed symphony orchestras, organised music festivals, and was a well-known critic and man about musical London in the mid-twentieth-century. He became best-known for his membership of the panel that, with quick wit, grace, immaculate articulation and vast musical knowledge, presented the weekly *My Music* game show on radio and television. He was a friend of many of Britain's musical greats, including Britten, Tippett, William Walton, and Sir Thomas Beecham, who, perhaps because he was a little older than the others, was always known as Sir Thomas, even if most of Amis's other musical friends were also eventually knighted. (In the last year of his life, Britten accepted a life peerage, becoming Baron Britten of Aldeburgh, an even higher accolade.) But I was interested to read *Amiscellany*, Amis's cleverly titled autobiography for what it might say about Mewton-Wood, and I discovered that a copy was retained in the State Library of Victoria. I found my library card and arranged to read it.

Its foundation stone laid in 1854, the library is a vast, grey edifice occupying half a city block and is said to be one of the biggest publicly accessible collections of books, periodicals, newspapers and sundry knowledge anywhere. Home for more than two million volumes, the diaries of city founders and folios concerning Captain Cook, it also displays Ned Kelly's armour. You enter through an octastyle portico of Corinthian columns that were erected in 1870, and beyond them are enormous high-ceilinged Victorian spaces, usually alive with either young students or old researchers. Canvases of colonial Melbourne hang. It is a noisier library than most, hundreds of students, most of them from South-East Asian nations, pooling their knowledge and ideas in small groups and riveted to the scores of screens sprouting above neat ranks of desks. Beyond all this, though, is the much-vaunted octagonal reading room, one of Australia's most beautiful covered spaces, as the art historian Kenneth Clark might have called it.

Opened in 1913, it is a cathedral of the intellect, its dome almost thirty-five metres high and its floor the same number of metres in diameter. The ether says it is able to hold more than a million books and six hundred readers. Renovated only recently, it is lit naturally from above by sixteen panels, each of two lights, that form a gigantic disc, its central oculus almost five metres wide. Twenty-six readers may sit on U-backed timber swivel chairs at each of eight hardwood desks radiating from the centre of the room and illuminated by small Tiffany-style lamps with luminous shades in a colour I like to call sub-editor's green. No digital screens are allowed to blight the space. On every side of the octagon, arched galleries and tiers of books on three levels rise to the dome. The reading room says many things, I believe. It can remind us of the leisured serious-ness of the past, or of the importance of the intellect. Repainted in a matt-finish antique white, it is a brilliant space, its bright-ness soft, its illumination outstanding. Perhaps because of the altitudinous dome, the air seems mountainous, fresh, ideal for thinking in.

Yet I am ambivalent about this exceptional intellectual locus because of its books. They mass in their shelves, becoming aggressive intellectual foot soldiers that crowd in upon you, intimidate you with their erudition, suggest that a disorderly mind such as mine has no right to be here, and that the longer you spend in this room the more its walls might press in upon you, demanding your authenticity, checking to see how much you really know, discovering that you are an imposter.

The books ridicule even the most recondite quests for meaning, let alone one so feeble as mine, insisting on answers to questions such as, Do you really know what you're doing here? Have you read us? Have you read *Ulysses* or Proust, really read them, read all the studies about them, and Socrates and the Theban plays? *Nostromo*? Do you understand general relativity? Could you take a pipe with Einstein? You dare to enter here, you, someone who is so ignorant, so naïve? So I opened *Amiscellany* and put my head down, trying to look studious, as people in libraries tend to do, trying to get the job done and leave, trying to prevent the books from rising up against me.

Amis devoted several pages to Mewton-Wood. Indeed, he calls him a *great* friend, admiring most of all his polymathematical abilities. He could mend a radio, repair a car or a piano, breed Alsatian dogs and compose a string trio, as Amis puts it. He knew the lives and works of painters, poets, writers and all of the music from Bach onwards. He was a brilliant sight-reader and had most of the piano music of Mozart, Chopin and Beethoven, among others, in his head. He had also made a thorough study of medicine and was a person who gobbled up life, in Amis's words. He and Mewton-Wood were playing duos on two pianos one day when Mewton-Wood broke a string. He yanked it out straight away and replaced it, and Amis knew, at the time, he writes, of no other pianist who could have done that. Pianists in general, he remarks, fail to know how to repair their instruments. In Mewton-Wood's case, how to fix a piano was probably crucial, because when he played Hindemith's *Ludus Tonalis* on the little brown Steinway in the Holst Room at Morley College, those who were listening feared for the piano's safety. Now and then the physicality of this young god-like creature, writes Amis, would run away with him and he would bang the keys — go through his tone, as professionals say. God-like, he might have appeared, but Amis says that he was also a little too coarse-featured to be truly handsome, and his exuberance disguised shyness.

Amis also knew Dulcie, whom he describes as great fun, a craggy witch like a thinner and older Dame Edna Everage, a woman who was crafty and bossy and had a dangerous habit, he says, of giving you a friendly tap on the balls if she liked you. Her son never quite made the big time as Clifford Curzon, Solomon and Dame Myra Hess had done because he lacked enough popular appeal and played too much out-of-the-way and modern music. He never got around to asking Noel if he was queer, and his friendship was tainted when Noel and Bill Federick told a joke that ridiculed heterosexuality. Amis had just married Olive. Amis once told Noel that he appeared to mince as he walked on stage. The pianist was so horrified that he never walked that way again, although he did take to wearing medallions on chains. He says that Noel never forgave himself for ignoring Bill's last bout of abdominal pains, which preceded his death. Almost immediately, the pianist tried to kill himself with umpteen aspirins, writes Amis, surviving only because medical friends washed him out. A week or so later, Noel telephoned him, and they chatted for more than an hour. Noel said he thought he was getting over Bill's death, and they discussed his plans for the future. Amis thinks the telephone call was an attempt to say goodbye, because the next day, the 5th of December, 1953, Noel drained his fatal draught of prussic acid — liquid cyanide.

Two or three days later, Dulcie asked Amis to come with her to Noel's little house in Notting Hill Gate to do some sorting-out. He saw Noel's notes, as he calls them, but fails to say what kind of paper they were written on and the tone of the writing, let alone the burden of their message. More remarkable was a stain on the wall, as he puts it, the remains of acid that Noel had thrown away — surplus to needs, he surmises.

Dulcie told Amis that she needed to go to a bank and asked him if he would mind being alone in his friend's room. Amis began sorting through sheet music on one of the pianos. On the top of a pile he finds his own copy of the Busoni piano concerto, he writes. He goes to the upright of the two pianos he had inherited and begins to play the keyboard transcription of its long orchestral introduction, three or four minutes of calm before the solo piano crashes in, as he puts it. He plays on, right up to the pianist's entry, and the instant the soloist is supposed to articulate very loudly — *fortissimo* — C-major chords from the bottom of the keyboard to the top — crashing in — Amis hears a hell of a twang from the concert grand, right on the beat, on the first of the chords. He leaps up, terrified, and opens the piano's lid to discover that a C-string had snapped. He says that his horror soon turned to joy, so much so that when Dulcie got back from the bank he was in fits of uncontrollable laughter.

The shock of Amis's story twanged me, and when I looked up I discovered that the walls of the octagon and their shelves of books were much closer than they had been when I had begun reading, their antique whiteness and the books' old-leather bindings — I could smell the cured pelts — intimidating me, their capacity to threaten suddenly more frightening than ever. They loomed, and, feeling ill at ease and hoping I could get to the exit without tripping or fainting, I closed *Amiscellany* and left.

AT HOME, I began to acquire a new skill that surprised me. By sending signals, mere clicks of a mouse, via the ether — I strive to imagine what they must be like, these miraculous pulses, their invisibility, their particularity, their soundlessness, even their lack of aroma — I mined the archives of the newspapers of the 1950s, importing to my screen whole pages of *The Times* of London, in particular, discovering first of all that Dulcie had failed not to tempt peril, not only attending her son's coronial inquest but giving evidence at it, an investigation that took place, you will have noticed, less than a week after his death. No doubt in a state of intense grief, she was nonetheless able to tell the West London Coroner, Mr. H. NEVILLE STAFFORD, as *The Times* put it, that Mr. Fedrick, who had lived with her son, was Noel's *very dear friend*, and that her son had been terribly distressed when Mr. Fedrick died in hospital. Mr. P. D. Trevor-Roper, of Harley Street, a distinguished eye surgeon and brother of the historian, said that three weeks ago Mr. Fedrick had become ill with acute appendicitis and two or three days had elapsed before a doctor was called. Mr. Fedrick was eventually admitted to Westminster Hospital, underwent a *major* operation, but died nine days later. Mr. Stafford asked Mr. Trevor-Roper how Mr. Mewton-Wood took the loss. He was extremely distressed, said Mr. Trevor-Roper, not only because he had lost a *close friend* but because he felt that he had overlooked Mr. Fedrick's early symptoms. He said that it was his impression that Mr. Mewton-Wood felt he was in some measure to blame for his friend's death. His grief was so great that he had taken an overdose of aspirin. Unusually, *The Times* report becomes ambiguous at this point, and it is unclear if Mr. Mewton-Wood or Mr. Trevor-Roper himself, in the witness box, had a discussion with a psychiatrist, after which Mr. Mewton-Wood was advised to be removed to the Atkinson Morley Hospital, which specialised in treating neurological disorders. He stayed there five days. On his discharge, he was *very* cheerful, although pre-occupied, and he had recovered from the aspirin poisoning; it was presumed that he would make no further attempts on his life.

On the 5th of December, Mr. Mewton-Wood left Mr. Trevor-Roper's house, saying that he would be back for tea, as was his custom, but when he did not return in the evening, *The Times* goes on, reporting the inquest but not naming the witness, police forced an entry into Hillgate Place, where they found Mr. Mewton-Wood lying dead across the sofa of the music room (which in houses without a grand piano would have been called a parlour). Dr R. D. Teare stated that the cause of Mr. Mewton-Wood's death was prussic-acid poisoning and that the poison had been ingested, not merely inhaled. Attempts to trace its source had been unsuccessful. Mr. H. NEVILLE STAFFORD recorded a verdict that Mr. MEWTON-WOOD had died from prussic-acid poisoning, self-administered, while the balance of his mind was disturbed. On the same page, *The Times* noted that there had been a record attendance at the Smithfield Show, that masked men had attacked council clerks and stolen £870 in wages, that eighty employees at a Grimsby fish factory had been dismissed, and that five thousand people had signed a petition against plans for a riverside garden in Windsor.

I also found a story in *The Evening News*, which reported the inquest in more detail, describing Trevor-Roper, who was among Britain's first activists for homosexual rights, as Mewton-Wood's doctor, and that when the pianist had not returned for dinner, not tea, as *The Times* had described it, he and a Mr. Russell had gone around to Hillgate Place, where police forced an entrance and found Mewton-Wood dead. Police-Sergt John Prynn said the pianist was crouching on the floor, his head resting on his right arm. He was dressed in khaki shorts, a red plaid open-necked shirt, and white plimsolls, the sergeant reported, probably adding, Your Worship. Trevor-Roper, whom *The Evening News* erroneously called Dr. Trevor Roper, told the court that he saw a broken tumbler, which looked as if it had been thrown against the wall, probably as Mewton-Wood collapsed, and on the wall there was a stain and some crystals where the glass had shattered. *The Evening News* also clarified Mewton-Wood's admission to the Atkinson Morley Hospital; Dr. Roper had advised it for the pianist's wellbeing. Released, he was in good enough health for the doctor to form the opinion, said the report, that Mewton-Wood would make no further attempt on his life. Indeed, he came to stay with Dr. Roper, returning to his own rooms each day only to practise the piano.

IN THE following days I exchanged emails with the coroner's office, which I discovered was still at Horseferry Road, Westminster, in what appeared to be, judging from photos in the ether, a nondescript two-storeyed, red-brick building on a street corner. The images suggested that nothing might have changed in the six decades since Mr H. Neville Stafford decided that Mewton-Wood's mind had been disturbed at the moment he drained his liquid cyanide. I had high hopes, at any rate, that the records pertaining to the verdict, the words even, faithful dictation of the witnesses' testimony, had been safely archived if not in Horseferry Road then somewhere else and that I could read them.

After ambiguous reactions to my request for access to the Mewton-Wood file, I finally received an emphatic email from one Clairette Bingley, a clerk to Her Majesty's coroner, who told me that records were kept for only twenty years, only a small sample, as she put it, held for historical reference. Details of Mr Stafford's finding on the death of Noel Mewton-Wood would no longer exist. It was the way things *were* in British coronial record-keeping, and she could do nothing about it. Too many people die, she added.

And it crossed my mind that if records fail to be kept, the past is anyone's to invent, and if the *real* remnants of events long ago — those that were made contemporaneously — fail to be archived, then the construction of any *reliable* version of what happens anywhere at any time is impossible. If only we let it, the past has the capacity to guide the present, say many clever people, but whose past is it and what credence may we place on its remnants? The *true* past, it seems, is as difficult to retrieve as Helena's true cross. It remains a mystery.

MANY UNRESOLVED questions remained, and it pleased me that I was contemplating them and not my obsession with Anna's death. My detective work was bearing fruit, my hand on the dead-man's handle secure. The silly thought crossed my mind that I might be — *might be* — fixing myself. I dared not use the word *cured*. But I would need to persist to be safe, and a trip to London was the logical next step. I would pillage the British Library, archives in Sussex about Farrell's car accident, talk to contacts whom Dr Orchard had very kindly provided. For several years, too, I had been corresponding with a piano maker in the Czech Republic whose partner was the daughter of the great Russian pianist Vladimir Sofronitsky. Did Steinways/Bechsteins/Bösendorfers ever terrify him? I should ask. Over the next few days I took enormous pleasure — I couldn't believe I was actually enjoying myself — in drafting an itinerary and buying cheap air tickets, which drifted about in cyberspace like sirens.

FOR TWO REASONS, the small town of Saint-Maximin-La-Sainte-Baume drew me to it *en route* to London. In a valley of Provence, undulating vineyards all around, it is famed for its basilica, which was constructed between 1295 and 1532 and is said to be the most important Gothic edifice in south-eastern France. An immense grey block without spires, its outside walls ulcerated, it soars above the plain and may be seen from kilometres around. Its modesty belies its cultural value, and in

the gloom of the crypt you may witness its principal treasure, a reliquary said to contain the remains of Mary Magdalene.

But I was more interested in the basilica's organ, an instrument of 2960 pipes and four manuals, which was built in 1773 by the Dominican friar Jean-Esprit Isnard. One of the last great baroque organs, its eighteen ranks and columns of pipes are contained within an exquisite two-tiered case of carved and polished fruitwood urns and garlands. Visiting on a Sunday, I not only heard the instrument during a mass but at the weekly noon recital during which a visiting organist, a woman from Kazakhstan called Darina Marat, who was studying in St Petersburg, played Bach's BWV 552, commonly known as the *'St Anne' Prelude and Fugue* and among the most exquisite quarter-hours of sound the world and its people will ever hear. Would it not be marvellous if it became the legacy of humans, echoing eternally, a gift to the universe, after we are gone? Which will occur soon. Shoot it out to all those beings in far distant galaxies and wait several million years to hear what they make of Bach's genius. If only …

When everyone had left, I stayed to achieve the second of my aims. While the organ's casement, a few of the basilica's chapels and its immense pulpit are known for the intricacy of their carving, the ninety-four darkly glowing choir-stalls in their entirety amount to a masterpiece of sculpting. For me, they are a site of pilgrimage. I know of no better example of complex and refined chiselling on a grand scale. And while great art is required only to live, great craft must be perfect, I remember hearing someone say, an idea that I agree with. The choir-stalls are perfect.

I took a loupe from my pocket to verify the adage. Executed late in the seventeenth century by Friar Vincent Funel and his team of carvers, they show in oval medallions surrounded by garlands of peonies and topped by streamers, all whittled from darkly tanned walnut, various Dominican martyrs and miracles.

So smooth and sinuous appear the streamers that they might be silk, so real the figures that they might be alive. Represented are the saints Pierre of Verona, Ambroise of Sienna, Agnès of Montepulciano, Jean of Cologne and Rose of Lima, among others, as well as arguably the most important Dominican, Thomas Aquinas. Identical in size, the medallions have a long axis that is about the height of a small child, and within each several personages make up *tableaux vivants*.

The Blessed Ambroise, for instance, is shown teaching — perhaps pilgrims or prisoners or the sick — doing what he is said to have done best, anyway, and he leans forward from a kind of throne, his right arm outstretched, his left preventing his robe from falling open. Four of the six men in front of him pay rapt attention, one open-mouthed and gesturing as if he has suddenly become privy to a miracle. Ambroise is pausing, his mouth closed, and what appears to be a dove is about to perch in a cowl of many folds at the nape of his neck. His voluminous habit has perhaps six major gathers between shoulder and a small elevated platform on which the throne rests, his toes protruding. I trained my magnifier on them, looking for a slip of the chisel that needed camouflaging by removing wood, thereby creating something unnatural in the fabric's fall. There was none. The work was indeed perfect. And then I thought about the dove; its presence seemed odd. Moreover, its wings were half-retracted, as if in a dive, and it appeared as if it was about to attack the saint. Perhaps it obscured a knot in the wood, say, but on close examination this seemed not to be the case. The dove and its dive, nonetheless, seemed strangely out of place, and I was disconcerted enough to be visited by my hotel nightmare. This time, I had alighted at the right floor — its number said so — but it contained only building materials, mainly shiny metallic wall-frames for new rooms. A circular saw idled amid bags of plaster and I shuddered.

If I had found something eerie in Saint Ambroise's panel, nothing was amiss in the next to the right, which features Saint Pius V, who is on his knees, praying to Mary, who nurses Jesus. In the background, a figure, perhaps a warrior, holds a three-barred cross similar to the heraldic cross of Lorraine. Pius's prayers, we should remember, the ones depicted in the medallion, resulted in a victory over Turkish forces. As perfect were the medallions devoted to the Blessed Jean de Verceil and St Catherine of Siena. Running my loupe over them, I wondered in a start whether one of the basilica's clerics might drift into the choir behind me and notice this strange man examining the *boiseries*, as they're called, and interrupt my investigation. Nothing. Neither priests nor imperfections shortened my observations, and the faultless brilliance of the carving reminded me that humans constantly create perfection. I myself once copied a Bente Strand cabinet in Tasmanian blackwood and Huon pine from one of her books, and apart from a gap of perhaps half a millimetre or even less between one of the pins and one of the tails of a dovetail joint at the back of a drawer, a fault that few would notice even if they saw it but I knew was there, the piece was unblemished.

Moreover, I have never heard anyone say that a note should be added or subtracted, a pause lengthened or shortened in any of Bach's hundreds of works. He revised them until they were flawless, musicologists say. And one could say much the same thing about the works of Beethoven and Mozart and Haydn. I am also convinced that literary scholars could emphatically declare that many of Shakespeare's plays and the poems of Keats and

Eliot, just to name two, are without fault. Not a word could be added or subtracted that would make them in any way better. (I thought, too, of Hope's wonderful poem about the death of a bird.) To cite a more demotic demonstration of perfection, a score of ten for an intricate dive from a ten-metre platform is not all that unusual, JL once reminded me in an exchange of emails about the anxiety the pursuit of perfection must cause elite pianists. Competent chefs (he went on in his usual florid style) could create perfect sauces every time they placed a pot on their *pianos*, that wonderful description they use for their stove-tops. It's not difficult, he insisted. Among other juices, he had many times consumed perfect *beurre blanc* confections, he said, the balance of the four basic flavours — salt, sour, sweet and bitter — impeccable, the integration of Muscadet white wine, fish *fumet*, shallots and butter, which must melt but never to the point that it separates, perfection itself.

On contemplating the prevalence of faultlessness, I became even more pre-occupied with the angst of elite pianists who strive for it. They know that, for them, it is much more difficult, if not impossible, to achieve. Another dimension governs what they do: time is their enemy, and, being people of high intelligence, they are fully aware that they must perform something that is a terri-fying challenge in its own right but whose difficulty is doubled by the imposition of the four-four, three-four, six-eight markings and composers' metronome *diktats*, which say at what speed the music should be played. These directions glare at them from the top of each piece. They don't have the luxury of revising words and music; they must push on over the bumps and slips, the lapses of concentration and inadequacies of muscles and mind, the music insisting on continuity. No corrections are allowed as they go along. How they must envy other creators — writers and painters and composers — who are afforded the privilege of editing, of laying on another corrective brush-dab, a word crossed out and replaced, a note erased, a pause lengthened.

In most things humans do, escape chutes for the weak and fraudulent are clearly marked. Elite musicians have none. And as I pocketed my loupe and left the basilica, I was reminded of Flora's remark about the flying Wallendas — her contention that elite pianists confront a death threat, walk a slack wire many metres above the ground, every time they sit down to play. I had to believe it.

THAT NIGHT, I stayed a few kilometres out of Saint-Maximin-la-Sainte-Baume in a *chambre d'hôte* on the summit of a hill opposite the tiny hamlet of Le Revest-Agate. From a kilometre away it imposed itself on the horizon, a block of several storeys painted in the deep Naples yellow — brighter than ochre — that so suits the Provençal landscape and, in spring and summer, complements the lush cinnabar greens of the vine leaves and in autumn their barok and cadmium reds.

On closer inspection, the surface of the building, however, had lost much of its integrity, its bagged walls revealing patches in many shapes and sizes where render had fallen away to reveal bare crumbling bricks. Greeting me at the front door, Madame Chantal Pic said a mountain of work was needed to return the place to its former glory, especially outside. She had been concentrating on renovating the bedrooms; when they were finished, she would move on to the exterior. The building was once a hotel of considerable esteem, hosting up to seventy-four guests a night, she said, dignitaries such as President Jules Grévy, famous politicians and their mistresses, mayors of Marseille, the writer Marcel Pagnol, and the painter Paul Cézanne, who had once come to lunch and was so captivated by a view framed by shutters from one of the top-floor rooms — she had never found out which among several possible candidates — that he had wanted to take it for a week to paint the vine-covered hills and valleys in the foreground and the Gros Bessillon and Vieux-Rougiers, faint violet and breast-shaped, on the horizon. He had eaten *andouillette* — the famous lower-bowel sausage — with

mustard at lunch, but had failed to return to paint, said Madame Pic, a plumpish woman dressed in a flower-printed housecoat, her short straw-blonde hair barely infringing precisely drawn chocolate-brown eyebrows.

At first, she and her husband had contracted a kind of mania about the hotel, which was built in the 1850s. It was their *da-da*. They had bought it and its chattels rundown and had the lovely idea of resurrecting it in some manner, blowing off its dust, giving it back a life, a task that was proving impossible, she said. It would be years yet before a project that they had begun together a decade ago would be completed. Much of the building was already apartments when they purchased the property, which explained the half-dozen vehicles in the gravelled car park. The tenants would be left alone. Two years into our challenge, Madame Pic said, a brunette came by and my husband followed her out the door, leaving me with three teenage sons to bring up. The boys have gone now, and I live with only my two girls, a poodle called Lou, short for Louise, and Sophie, a bolognese I have no contraction for. They are playing in the garden somewhere.

Madame Pic took me inside, telling me that she made her own *confiture* and I would taste apricot and blackberry in the morning with fresh croissants and *pains au chocolat*. A spiral staircase in a large and well-lit stairwell immediately ascended to the top floor, its hardwood banister an open coil that climbed almost vertically to the heavens. I marvelled at it. Trapezoidal, the staircase's treads were of pale maroon tiles bordered by oak. Stopping off floor by floor, Madame Pic showed me five renovated bedrooms, rarities in France because of their immensity, their brightness, their exquisite views, their taste — she alone had collected the artefacts, the models, the ancient photographs and certificates, the small raffia dolls and so on, all of them — that gave each room its character and charm. So unusual were the renovations that whole families could have been accommodated in the showers of two or three of the bathrooms, all of which were *en suite* with the bedrooms. Everything was new, she said — new, at any rate, over the past few years. I could have any room I liked; I was the only guest tonight. I chose one floored with bare pine planks and the most modest décor. Small straw dolls of a girl wearing a large floppy sunhat holding a shopping basket and a fisherman holding a net stood on an ancient chest of drawers in oak, its modern knobs of white ceramic. A curious model yacht made of bark and paper stood on a high pedestal beside the dolls. On a fold-up walnut coaching table, a tiny mariner wearing a Greek captain's hat and smoking a pipe had been placed beside an old black-and-white photograph in a wide timber frame of what appeared to be identical twin urchins from perhaps the 1910s. The scheming eyes and pout of one of them conveyed what most might call a natural naughtiness but what I took to be malevolence. Her sister looked a little angel. Madame Pic said that she had done all she could to make the rooms contemporary and attractive and that the plumbing was modern — I would not have to wrestle with the taps to get the water temperature right or wonder why the lavatory failed to flush as one must in many other provincial French *chambres*.

She was a collector, by the way, and she would show me downstairs her dozens of ancient pewter coffee pots and painted ceramic hens. She had the world's first pressure-cooker in her kitchen, and it stood on the hob of an Alpine Larians fuel stove, if the name meant anything to me, in the heaviest of black iron. She paused and waved at a little doll in a sailor's suit. All her collectibles and her quest to create charming spaces in which people could restore themselves for two or three days gave her enormous pleasure. For several seconds she paused. Perhaps the charm of her bedrooms and the thrill she had had from decorating them somehow compensated for what she called the crypt, the existence of the hotel's skeleton, its relics, as she called them, which were buried downstairs and wouldn't go away, reminding her of the future and its single message — decay, not that she put it exactly like that. They scared her in a way she couldn't quite understand. She couldn't bear the thought of sorting through them, cleaning them up, disposing of them, and they remained there, the relics, beneath our feet at this very moment, she said, gathering dust, lurking, intimidating, existing in a kind of limbo, taunting her renovations. In a way, she said, they reminded her that all the beauty she was creating up here, she gestured, would, in turn, become dust. We descended the spiral staircase.

At the farthest end of her large renovated kitchen and its magnificent brass-knobbed Alpine Larians stove — as black

as coal, its muscles about to burst, a quaint and stocky ancient pressure-cooker resting on it — a plethora of ceramic chickens lacquered in bright colours and pewter coffee pots stood on high shelves. Madame Pic opened the door beneath them onto a darkened staircase of rough timber treads that descended abruptly to … Who knew where? She beckoned me to follow as she reached for a switch. The staircase was relatively short and dropped beneath the level of the kitchen perhaps only a couple of metres, finishing at another plain door. She opened it and turned on lights, revealing a cellar extending an indeterminate distance into the gloom, even, it seemed, beyond the already large footprint of the hotel. It was as if Madame Pic's *chambre* was the poppet head of a mine shaft and the cellar was a first level of endless galleries.

Old bones, as she called them, were everywhere, a skeleton shattered. Piles of white dinner plates bearing the florid gold inscription HB—the hotel was called the Bellevue, she explained — rose to the low ceiling, as did mattresses, piles of them, the topmost wedged in under exposed beams. Balloon-backed dining chairs, most without their upholstery, the backs hollow, many broken, numbered perhaps in the thirties or forties, and tables of several types and sizes, some of them of obvious antiquarian value, were stacked one on top of the other. Cardboard boxes, their seams cracking, and rough timber crates held decrepit shoes — for no reason I could think of — cooks' trousers, aprons, and cutlery by the kilogram engraved with the hotel's initials. Bedside tables and their lamps were scattered at crazy angles, and everywhere cartons of light bulbs and lavatory paper overflowed, pillows made clouds, and I noticed mountains of neatly folded sheets, jugs and urns, commercial toasters, pots and pans, meat slicers, bread baskets, chefs' knives, glasses, including champagne flutes and burgundy balloons, green-stemmed, fine-lipped Alsatian glasses even, and salt and pepper salvers. Brass taps were strewn in rough timber shelves, and lengths of plumbing that finished in U-bends and elbows lay in the dust. Among the artefacts right-side-up were three grand pianos, one a Bechstein model M with the serial number — I wiped away the dust — 147331, which meant, I later discovered, that it had been made between 1890 and 1895. The air smelled damp but was dry and fungal and had the dank, nutty aroma of a decaying mushroom. Thick dust blanketed everything to such an extent that I feared that, had I sneezed, the whole depressing landscape might have been obscured. The silence was as thick. Overhead, the low ceiling was vaulted; rough red-brick arches were interrupted every half-metre or so by oak beams. Many of the bricks had come loose and fallen, the gaps like missing teeth, the fallen bricks in the dust on a floor of indeterminate composition. Madame Pic waved her hand at the hotel's bones, as she repeatedly called them, and said in a quiet and exhausted voice, *Je n'en peux plus, monsieur, je n'en peux plus* … I can't go on, I can't go on.

She led me through the detritus — wading through bones, as it were — to another door and a steeply descending staircase to a deeper cellar, dark vaults almost three metres high and two or three wide heading into the distance on the cardinal points of the compass. Each was feebly lit by dull yellow bulbs in translucent plastic cowls attached to a beam. Shelves constructed from timber and crumbling bricks lined walls of big glazed tiles in what appeared, in the gloom, to be a beige colour, and I noticed, daubed on the shelves as if with a thick paint brush, the rubrics, BOURGOGNE, ALSACE, MEDOC, ENTRE-DEUX-MERS, MOULIN-A-VENT, ETRANGERS, among others. Only three of

the hundreds of shelves held bottles. Beneath this cellar was another, said Madame Pic, who shook her head. Every time she came down here she felt faint, overwhelmed, and the thought of paying someone to take it all away, of tidying up to a certain degree or of memorialising the former glory of the hotel in some way, perhaps a kind of *cabinet de curiosités* upstairs, brought her almost to the point of collapse. Several times she repeated, *Je n'en peux plus*. At that moment, I, too, felt faint and leant on ALSACE to steady myself, not the most stable of regions, I realised later. I must have appeared unwell, because Madame Pic glanced at me sympathetically and said that to linger here terrified her, and I gestured towards the stairs, relieved.

And it crossed my mind that the crypt of Madame Pic's *chambre d'hôte* was nonetheless a last resort, somewhere — perhaps among many throughout the world — where the last men and women would gather after climatic annihilation, say. Or almost annihilation, because the remnants of humanity would have at their disposal in the basements of the former Hôtel Bellevue everything they needed, even mattresses and clean sheets, and they could exist on what uncontaminated food and water they could bring with them, camping by candlelight presumably, until the wax ran out and they too perished, their bones — human bones — settling into the dust with the hotel's cast-offs.

AND SO TO London. I had rented an apartment at Kew Bridge about fifteen kilometres south-west of the capital mostly to avoid driving a hired car through dense inner-city traffic to the West Sussex Record Office in Chichester. But I also wanted to visit — an easy walk away — The Musical Museum, which calls itself one of the world's largest collections of self-playing instruments.

At the intersection of the South Circular Road and the A315, I strolled west in air only a few degrees above zero along a wide footpath of concrete pavers on the southern side of Kew Bridge Road, which runs east-west on the northern side of the Thames. In an ice-blue sky, a few wispy cirrus clouds seemed

to float halfway between Earth and Moon. Impossible to miss on the other side of the road, beyond the constant traffic, was the Italianate tower of the London Museum of Water & Steam, a spire of dull grey-brown brickwork and the area's only significant landmark. It soars sixty-one metres, in fact, a confident edifice completed in 1867, a year of undue optimism in which ships first navigated the Suez Canal, African-Americans were granted the vote in the District of Columbia, the Dominion of Canada was created, diplomatic and political compromises resolved several hostilities among nations, and Alfred Nobel patented dynamite. I suspected that it must have reassured the people of Kew Bridge and adjacent Brentford that the system of pipes the tower's four sides enclosed would provide them, at last, with a reliably potable source of water at a constant pressure. With its elegant arches and corbelled narrow balconies a third of the way and five-sixths of the way up, it must have trumpeted a rosy future for those who would live on into the fast-approaching twentieth century. Could anything follow the miracle of steam-power? they must have asked themselves, probably answering no.

The spire's open octagonal crown is its greatest conceit. Sixty metres above ground level, it appears to be an observation post from which water authorities might have been able to see the sluggish Thames far below and congratulate themselves for their engineering mastery over it. They must have barely believed that they could sequester the river, purify it and distribute life to the people from the unprepossessing pumping station, which has only fairly recently become the museum. The watchtower also appeared to me to be strangely

Islamic in character, a minaret from which a kind of muezzin representing the precious nature of water itself, could call upon worshippers of Brentford and Kew Bridge to thank the Allah of all things for the gift that the tower provided. It was, at any rate, the strangest of constructions in that it insisted on camouflaging its age and function, as if its designers and engineers — and even the water authorities of the 1860s — had taken into account its inevitable redundancy.

A few minutes later I passed O'Riordan's Tavern (at an hour too early for a pint) and took the Thames Path on a diagonal down to the eastern end of Watermans Park and the balustraded walkway of timber plinths above the muddy banks of

the river itself. Stuck in the slime, sometimes at crazy angles, was a variety of decaying houseboats, most of them fifteen to twenty metres long and broad-beamed. Indeed, one appeared to have been a tug boat in an earlier life, and another boasted that it had served in both world wars. And the farther up-river I walked, the more decrepit became the boats, until, eventually, at a footbridge near the western tip of the Brentford Ait, a narrow island several hundred metres long, its muddy banks completely obscured by clouds of white gulls, I was shocked to discover a vessel's skeleton, its curved ribs just showing above the slime. It was as if I'd discovered a corpse, and I reached for the freezing steel banister to steady myself.

With names such as VIECO 223, ROTTERDAM, LYSLAND, and FRESHWATER, the hulks appeared to be not just falling apart as I watched, rusting away, decaying and disintegrating, but gently subsiding into the mould-green ooze at the edge of the Thames to join dozens of discarded car tyres, broken bicycles, coils of old rope by the kilometre, rusted garden furniture, dislocated plumbing, besmirched soft toys, including a fearful teddy knee-deep in mud, its arms up, appealing for help, broken windows, plastic of all sorts and colours, gas bottles, rotting and begrimed timber of all shapes and sizes and what appeared to be enormous pieces of broken concrete breakwater. In the middle of the river, narrow here, three white swans and two with tawny dapples, paddled away from the wrecks as if in disgust. No one came or went along the narrow gangplanks connecting the boats to the boardwalk. Indeed, the whole area appeared deserted until a young man so enveloped against the cold that barely a square centimetre of his skin was exposed, threw a Frisbee to his black-and-white border collie.

Despite their decrepitude, the powerful decay that they projected, the houseboats gave every indication of recent habitation. An empty wine glass stood on a table made from a converted cable spool. Fold-up aluminium chairs, lifebuoys, a canoe, tarpaulins of sky-blue plastic, pots and pans, bicycles, thirsty potted plants, a ladder and fruit boxes of timber palings rested on one deck, and chopped firewood had been stacked on the roof of another vessel's wheelhouse. In the unbroken window of one of the smaller ships, a large printed notice urged readers to stop the eviction of the Brentford houseboat community by signing a petition. A new marina would close off the park to the public, said the notice, damaging the environment and endangering the nesting sites of heron, kingfisher and other avian species.

The digital ether later provided me with the most recent news: Hounslow Council would replace the hulks with docks for twenty-six vessels at a cost of many millions of pounds. The new facility would smarten up the bank, it alleged, and stop sewage from being discharged into the river. Watermans Park itself would be renovated and feature a new café, play equipment and a performance space. I wondered if the park would soon be plastered with advertisements for a festival of English folksong or a rock band with an outlandish name. Rotting Hulks?

Arriving in the eastern sky and passing overhead every minute, it seemed, passenger aircraft descended, wheels down, heading for Heathrow, and as I left the park, confused, not knowing which side to take or even whether in this instance sides needed to be taken, two white geese honked loudly as they flapped in ascent not more than a couple of metres above my cap.

ON THE OTHER side of the High Street, opposite the eastern end of the park, The Musical Museum is a stern contemporary blockhouse painted in tones of grey and blue-grey, three narrow decorative pillars in salmon, carmine and mauve appearing to have been glued onto the longest side. High up on the wall facing the street, it announces its name in bold black capitals and a modern typeface, THE MUSICAL MUSEUM. Alongside the

name is the museum's logo, seven short lines of dots and dashes resembling the holes in a piano roll.

Inside the museum, I inspected the self-playing instruments for which it is famous. Until recorded sounds superseded them in the 1930s, orchestrions, player-pianos and hurdy-gurdies were the toys of the rich and the boasts of the smartest cafes and bars. They superseded the hands of pianists and organists, which were no longer needed if music could be made without them. Or, to be more precise, one person's playing — that of the musician who cut the rolls — could be made available to everyone. And humanity has trod that path ever since.

Constructed in Leipzig, for instance, arguably the centre of the world in those days for manufacturing musical instruments of all sorts, the Popper Clarabella was operated by a coin in a slot and featured an animated backlit picture, a Watteau-like landscape of cliffs and rocks, trees and pond and river, a decaying marble arch at the top of a waterfall and a windmill in the distance, as well as flashing light bulbs alternating in scarlet and kingfisher-blue. Encased in carved mahogany, it has a couple of dozen visible pipes in what appear to be zinc alloy, several of them topped with highly polished brass bells, a drum to the left, its stick finishing in what appeared to be a black Bakelite knob, some sort of percussive device in a window to the right, and centre-stage, above a box in ornately chased solid silver, or so it appeared, a horizontal cylinder, its gears exposed, a roll of puce-coloured punched paper ready to be fed into it and ultimately the machine's bowels, where mechanical bellows would blow air through the pipes, making each of them sound a different note according to which holes passed over the machine's tracker bar at any given moment.

Farther on, I was reading about two barrel organs in tall mahogany cabinets, Michael Woodward's instrument having two ranks of pipes and a triangle and having delighted the people of Birmingham since 1813, the year it was built, when an elderly woman tapped me on the shoulder to tell me that the museum's mighty Wurlitzer was about to be demonstrated in the auditorium upstairs. Everyone had gone up, she said. Didn't I want to hear it? I looked about, realising that Dorothy, the name to which she was pinned, and I appeared to be the only occupants of the museum's ground floor. We were alone, and having heard Wurlitzers and the sounds they can emit several times, I was more interested in how this exhibition of instruments could exist in a digital age, when dizzying cacophonies made by successions of ones and zeroes constantly surround us.

Her grey hair rolled into a tight bun, her square-framed

spectacles balancing on a small nose above taut thin lips, which infrequently broke into a smile, exposing prominent front teeth, one protruding farther than the other, she failed to answer my question but told me instead that she was one of many volunteer guides who were indispensable to the museum's general running. As she spoke, she wagged a turquoise pipe-cleaner. Three more — in puce and saffron — sprouted from the top pocket of her bottle-green corduroy jacket. She herself had been a volunteer here for several years because she loved the sounds the exhibits made, she said, and the strangeness by which they could make them, and did I really not want to hear the Wurlitzer?

I shook my head.

She said, yes, she *and* her husband Lawrence, who had died only eighteen months ago, were both volunteers. Lawrence was a City & Guilds practising electrician, she said, in his seventy-sixth year and more or less retired. All his life, said Dorothy, he had yearned to be a musician in one of those wonderful brass bands like the Black Dyke or the Grimethorpe Colliery. He learned the cornet from an early age and was actually quite a virtuoso by his teens, but when he told his father, who was also an electrician — for a while they worked together — when he told him that he wanted to dedicate his life to playing the cornet and eventually rising to become the conductor of one of the great brass bands of Britain, that that was what he wanted in life, his father said, No, son, finish apprenticeship. You can always have, he said in his Skipton accent — I remember it well, you see, because you could spread it with a knife like margarine, his accent … Dorothy adopted a deep voice from the north: You can always have troompet, lad, aside your pillow.

Even when I first met Lawrence he loved the pit bands, even more than he loved me, in a way. And he used to tell me that one day he'd be good enough — because of his excellent cornet-playing — to be taken on by the Grimethorpe or the Black Dyke, and he'd become one day their conductor, out the front waving his baton — he'd bought one already — and they'd play, under his direction, *All in the April Evening*. You must know it, said Dorothy, know the words, perhaps the most beautiful hymn in the English language. Know the tune, and the words, you must, which are quite slow … All in the April evening, she began, reciting, April airs were abroad. I saw the sheep with their lambs, and thought on the lamb of God.

In recent years Lawrence discovered the internet and — I don't know where he found them — he'd watch one after another those little films by choirs and bands performing *All in the April Evening*, even the famous Grimethorpe, and the tears would roll down his cheeks for as long as he was watching. He couldn't stop sobbing, he found the music so moving. He knew every note, every word. He had so much wanted to conduct it.

Dorothy paused. As people, she said, we are mostly very close, the volunteers, more or less friends, and like to help each other when we can, and when Lawrence heard that Dr Richmond, who lives in a nice house in Richmond just up the river, was having trouble with his orchestrion, a German instrument made in 1910 in Leipzig, he went around to see if he could fix it. In some of the old instruments the wiring is not so rigorously safe as it is nowadays, and the insulation, which is mostly a kind of thick plaited fabric enveloping the wires, is often frayed. Imagining the wear and tear of decades was probably the last thing on the minds of those who put the instruments together, she said. Rats can eat the insulation, too, and it may also in some cases disintegrate all by itself, if you've ever seen old wiring.

So Lawrence went around this particular night to see if he could fix Dr Richmond's orchestrion, and the doctor had loaded it with a roll ready to play. It was *All in the April Evening*, so you can imagine how keen Lawrence was to hear the machine work. Perhaps Dr Richmond knew that Lawrence just adored the tune, and Lawrence would have told him anyway. Lawrence and Dr Richmond turned the power off and on to try to make the orchestrion play before Lawrence removed the machine's back panels and began to investigate the wiring, which was original, its insulation crumbling. Electricians are used to getting shocked in their line of work — electrically shocked, I mean — and most of them are so very careful these days and know how to mitigate any damage the electricity might cause them. You might not know that they sometimes test for the live wire, the blue or the brown, by tapping it against the backs of their hands. They get a jab, but no harm is done. Sometimes electricians can get careless, though, even City & Guilds men, and who knows what happened on this particular night? Lawrence was testing electrical connections inside the orchestrion, and I suppose he was *very* keen to make it play *All in the April Evening*. He was getting Dr Richmond to switch the power on and off at his call when suddenly the instrument burst into life and for a second or two it played the first few bars of Sir Hugh Roberton's sublime tune. Dorothy broke off to hum them, but stopped when her lips began to quiver. Slowly, she ran her fingers along the fur of the pipe-cleaner before sliding it into her pocket with the others. At the same time, she went on, Dr Richmond heard a thumping, a kind of commotion, as he later told the coroner, coming from the back of the machine, and Lawrence fell out of the orchestrion dead. And the music stopped. Well, you know, said Dorothy, Dr Richmond was a skin specialist and I don't think he had kept up his first aid, but he did what he could, believing that Lawrence was probably dead anyway, he told the coroner, even before he fell backwards — Dorothy gestured — onto the Axminster. The coroner decided accidental death, of course, absolving Dr Richmond of any blame, which was a correct judgement, in my view, even though Lawrence was my husband. But I've often hoped that he heard at least a fraction of the tune, the tiniest phrase, before he died. In summing up, the coroner said that Lawrence's arms, which had been outstretched as if he were directing the Grimethorpe Colliery band, say — the coroner actually named it — had been unwitting but perfect conductors of the electricity inside the orchestrion. And therefore of the music itself, said Dorothy, sighing. He had also been a perfect husband, she added.

RETRACING my steps back to the apartment, I recalled Madame Pic's crypt and wondered if the last music, the last organised sounds made by humans, might come from barrel organs cranked by hand in the depths of cellars and basements and caves. Presumably an annihilation of the human race would involve the obliteration of its power supplies, its wind turbines, solar, hydroelectric and nuclear facilities, probably in infernos, and this would mean the end even to digital devices of all sorts once their batteries had gone flat. Diesel-powered generators might provide electricity for a while, but they too would eventually exhaust their fuel. As human beings died out, there would be fewer pianists and violinists, flautists and guitar-pickers, and you would eventually be very lucky indeed to be among a group of survivors comprising anyone who could hold a tune or blow a mouth organ. Soon they too would be gone, exhausted, and the last men and women, the very last in some lucky places, might have a hand-cranked barrel organ or pedal-powered player piano with which to make melodies. Would they do it? Would it be something they *needed* to do? Freud maintained that we made music to ward off paranoia, and there can be no doubt that one of its major purposes is to soothe. But just when it would appear that the human race, or what was left of it, needed soothing most, total silence would descend. And of the punched rolls left for the cranked instruments there might be little choice, only the most popular tunes of their days being available, songs such as *Amour sous la lune*, and *Wo ist der Leiermann?* in Europe, and *Piano Roll Blues*, *Boots & Saddles*, *Jolly Darkies*, *Make That Engine Stop at Memphis*, and *Dizzy Fingers*, say, in the United States. Perhaps Percy Grainger's *Country Gardens*, a roll the composer himself cut, might be available in Australian bunkers.

And eventually, when the survivors are too tired to sing themselves to death, to emit even the most feeble notes, they would turn to cranking organs, one might suppose. And soon the hands that cranked the handles would weaken, and the last man-made sounds on Earth, his last reedy notes, would wheeze from the pipes, handles slowing, the notes bending and drooping, to give way finally and inevitably to silence. Complete and utter silence.

ONCE I HAD deposited my belongings in a locker — no cameras, no pens, but you may take your spectacles and a notebook, said the stern woman behind the counter of the West Sussex Record Office — I entered a brightly illuminated reading room, a big contemporary space lined paradoxically with dilapidated historical journals, books of all sorts, some of them with broken spines, and old broadsheet newspapers bound in leather, their covers dry and cracking. At large tables laminated in white, snowy heads were down, busy with ancestors. I asked for copies of the *West Sussex Gazette & South of England Advertiser* published after Tuesday the 27th of May 1958, when the New Zealand pianist Richard Farrell was killed in a car accident on a well-known major road only a few miles east of here.

A chatty librarian brought a single heavy broadsheet volume almost immediately and dumped it — somewhat indelicately, I thought — in the V of a solid black rest of hard foam rubber. I sharpened a pencil and turned the weekly's fragile, tobacco-coloured, pages, finding no report of the accident in the 29th of May edition but a ten-centimetre item at the top of the first column of news on page two of the 5th of June edition. (The *Gazette*'s front page was occupied by advertisements, and the second might easily have been the major news page in those days.)

Headed *Fairmile Bottom Crash Inquest*, it reported the opening of an inquest at Littlehampton by district coroner Mr F. F. Haddock into the deaths of Mr Richard Bradshaw of Rowhook Farm, Rowhook, near Horsham, his wife Margaret, and Richard Farrell in a badly damaged car in the early hours of the 27th of May. About 4.35am, PC A. E. Robbins went to a spot, said the report, about a thousand yards south of Whiteways Lodge and saw a badly damaged Ford Zephyr and three bodies lying nearby on the road and the grass verge. Identified by a friend, Farrell was said to have lived at Wilberforce House, Clapham Common, and Mr Bradshaw was a company director and friend of the pianist. The brief report ended with a kind of afterthought — Mr Farrell's body had been flown to New Zealand.

With hasty care, I turned the big fragile pages to a fortnight later and struck gold, finding a report on the inquest, which had reopened on the 11th of June. In fine print under a heading *Three Killed in Night Crash: Inquest Story*, the copy ran in small type almost the length of an entire column, amounting perhaps to seven or eight hundred words. A coroner's jury, it began, had decided that the trio's deaths had been accidental after the car that Mrs Bradshaw had been driving left the road on a right-hand bend and was wrecked against a tree, as the report put it. Dr J. Ford of Chiltington told the inquest that Mr Bradshaw and Mr Farrell had died from fractured skulls and that Mrs Bradshaw had died from a fractured skull *and* a broken neck.

On the eve of the accident, the trio had dined with Donald Frederick Goodhew of Yapton, a former naval officer, shipmate of Bradshaw and the holder of a Distinguished Service Cross. The report is unclear about who submitted to the court that Mrs Bradshaw drank two gins and tonics, as it was put, before dinner and a glass of wine — the type and quantity unspecified — during it. Mr Haddock asked Mr Goodhew if there had been any quarrels or unusual events during the meal and received the reply, No. Mr Bradshaw in fact spent most of the night trying to fix a gramophone so that the company could hear some of

Mr Farrell's recent recordings. On leaving Goodhew's at about two in the morning, no one complained of feeling unwell, there was no reason to hurry, and Mrs Bradshaw had driven the road many times before.

Lorry driver Peter Alfred Johnson of Siddlesham came across the wreckage and the bodies at about 3.30am. No other cars were about, but he had noticed several mist patches above the tarmac. PC Nicholls of Petworth attended the scene, seeing a completely destroyed, as he put it, soft-top Ford Zephyr convertible upside down, and clothing and bits of car scattered over a wide area. A large tree nearby had bark torn off it to a height of ten feet, and pieces of bark were adhering to the Zephyr's front bumper. A tyre impression on the grass verge ran for 396 feet (more than 120 metres) and to its left was a four-foot drop to woodland. Other tyre impressions showed that the car had travelled crabwise, as PC Nicholls put it, to the centre of the road then left the verge and hit the tree *without touching the ground*. Its nose had collided with the base of the trunk, he told the jury, and the rear must have risen and hit higher up. The road was dry, the surface and camber good, and PC Nicholls could find no evidence of faulty steering, brakes and tyres. The Zephyr must have been travelling at some speed, however, because the chassis was cracked on both sides and the transmission was bent, he said.

In summing up, Mr Haddock said that he wondered why the accident had happened at all. Mrs Bradshaw might have dozed off or perhaps the windscreen had misted up. A combination of many things might have caused the tragedy, he said, or it might have been over-familiarity with the road and that the car *was travelling too fast.*

Immediately above the *Gazette*'s report of the inquest, a short item noted that the mayor and mayoress of the nearby town of Arundel had entertained three hundred at tea, and, below it, a report that the Arundel Football Club had had a celebratory dinner for winning the Sussex County League Championship Cup.

It appeared certain that the piano and any anxiety it might have caused Richard Farrell had played no part in his death. There seemed to be no other conclusion, shredding my thesis and hopes. But, I thought, perhaps Farrell had had a recording session in a day or two and he had urged Mrs Bradshaw to accelerate, to get him home faster. Perhaps he was desperate to rest before a concert. Perhaps he had been in the front passenger seat, had begun to sing a Beethoven sonata and she had swooned. Desperate ideas, I realised. Silly.

FAIRMILE BOTTOM runs for a little over three kilometres in a north-east direction between the miniscule village of Slindon and a vast roundabout where the road joins the A284 and the B2139. Like so many English highways, it has retained at least one of its archaic names. Why Fairmile Bottom? Who knows? It seems, indeed, to be a landscape of no special allure even if the gentle climb away from Slindon is fair, in the sense of an easy and scenic drive, and you take without the slightest concern the five slight curves to the top of the rise and a roundabout, where a small café with an enormous car park from which you may set off for walks in the high and rolling South Downs serves arguably the worst coffee ever prepared by man. Perhaps the carriageway these days is a little wider than it was in 1958, but it remains a two-lane road with an excellent surface, cambers and alignments, providing not a single challenge to a competent driver.

The A29, as Fairmile Bottom is better known, though, is the way back to London, and its traffic is constant, a diametric difference from what its congestion must have been at two o'clock of a Tuesday morning almost six decades ago. Because of the vehicles, I could not dawdle, but as I drove I enjoyed patches of late-autumnal yellows and russets on the Downs to the east, and was surprised by the narrowness of the grassy verge on the left and the fairly unvarying thickets of woodland on either side of the road made up of saplings of no more than an arm's thickness. I'm no good with European species, but I guessed that the trees might have been a mix of alders and ashes, beeches and birches, dogwoods, elms and oaks, and I wondered if among them were English yews, the tree that represents uncannily both death and eternity, of long life and fatal toxicity. Occasionally, I would observe a tree with a barrel trunk, but they were rare, and as I approached the last gentle right-hand bend where Farrell had died, I looked to the left and thought I glimpsed a sturdy specimen with a grey-green trunk. Vehicles behind me pressed, and there was nowhere to park, so I drove the final kilometre to the roundabout, circled it, and returned down Fairmile Bottom, discovering a few hundred metres nearer the bend a patch of dirt and stones in which I could leave the car in some safety and begin walking towards the accident site.

A country road, Fairmile Bottom has no footpaths, of course, and the verge was not only less than a metre wide, cars whooshing by me quite close, but its grass was long, the earth beneath it soggy from recent rain, so much so that I began to feel as if I was walking on a foam-rubber mattress. Most of the trees had already lost their leaves, but I had gone no more than fifty metres when the bough of an oak that had retained much of its dark-green foliage bent in front of me as if to bar my way. No point in pressing on, it said. Nothing to see here, mate. But I ducked under it, and soon my socks were sodden, my shoes squelching, making the going even harder.

The grass seemed to get longer, patches of it up to my knees, the traffic constant. I began to think I was wading through treacle, and I feared that I might collapse or lose my balance and topple on to the road in front of a Sainsbury's delivery truck. Drivers must have wondered with what madness I had been struck, this staggering man, but perhaps in Britain, which is renowned for its odd souls, a lone figure wading along the narrow verge of a busy country road might have seemed run-of-the mill.

The bend still perhaps three hundred metres distant, I took two or three photographs, watched an approaching lorry negotiate it with grace, and returned to the car. What would I have seen there anyway? Would I have found the tree, six decades stronger, the one I thought I had seen from the car, the one that had killed Richard Farrell? I would have needed to cross the road, too, a tricky manoeuvre. Would I have jumped down off the verge into the bog in which the woodlands flourish? How deeply would I have sunk into it? Would I have put *myself* in danger? Would I have sunk into it, finding it impossible to extricate myself, sinking lower and lower until it eventually suffocated me, disappearing under the ooze for the sake of a manic quest? I had satisfied my curiosity up to a point, I believed, and I headed back to London.

THE DRIVE was not without incident. Between Coldwaltham and Pulborough, two birds landed on the road in front of me. The first was a pheasant, its body fat, speckled plumage magnificent, its blue and turquoise neck garland opalescent, its wattles of such a glaring scarlet that I was forced to blink and brake hard, giving the bird time to take off in a slow and ungainly ascent, appearing so heavy that it would have amounted to a hearty dinner for several, I thought. I hoped that the driver of the car behind me was attentive enough to avoid an accident. He or she was — and did.

Much more canny, and less than a minute farther on, a raptor of some sort, speckled again in pale brown and white or black and white settled on the tarmac and, without my needing to slow down, took off about its business in half a second, off on the hunt, no doubt. (The ether later told me that only sparrow hawks and kestrels are reasonably common in the area, so it might have been one of them — I am no twitcher.)

And I was tempted to remember Farrell's dream, to link my sighting of a bird of prey of some sort to his nightmare about the boy and the fox and the falcon. I had seen no live foxes on my drive, but I had noticed several patches of gorgeous russet fur by the roadside attached to smeared carcasses. I was suddenly tempted to link it all to some psychic or physical cause-and-effect, some peculiar and special danger of driving in Sussex? Behind the wheel, had Mrs Bradshaw been surprised by a fox crossing the road in front of the Zephyr or a barn owl swooping at the windshield? More importantly, what would it say about my mental condition if I could resist embroidering the truth for the purposes of my own peace of mind? My notion that pianos kill pianists was unravelling, it seemed, and perhaps I was seeing sense, but it hurt me to give in. And perhaps, it crossed my mind as the place names passed by, signs to Coneyhurst and Coolham, Billingshurt and Barns Green, that the accident that caused my sister to lose her fingers then her life might have been my unwitting or perhaps even unconscious attempt to save her from the nightmare of trying to conquer the big black Steinway waiting to bully her centre-stage, save her from the agony of trying to achieve perfection when she knew that it was impossible, remove her from the general terror that accompanies playing the piano at elite levels.

TURNING LEFT out of Notting Hill Gate Underground station, I took another left and walked south down Farmer Street to arrive a hundred or so metres later at a T-intersection with

Hillgate Place, a stronghold these days of upper-middle-class wealth and privilege.

A pretty, narrow street, it's lined on both sides with rows of nineteenth-century double-storey terrace houses painted in the palest shades of blues and greens and greys, sugared-almond colours, you might say, a stronger hue such as ochre or mid-blue occasionally interrupting. Spear points topped the glossy black pickets of their fences, which separated the pavement from the area steps to the basements, and each house had a walk-up of three or four steps to bevelled front doors.

I used both the knocker and the buzzer at No. X. Within a few seconds, an elegant woman half-opened the door. She wore dark-blue tailored trousers and high heels, a ballooning cream blouse that might have been made of silk, and a necklace of what

appeared to be heavy ceramics in strange shapes and various shades of violet. Her blond hair appeared to have been only recently and expertly coiffed, and her make-up was fastidious.

I was unsure how to begin, unsure even about why I should be harassing her. In the back of my mind, I had the impertinent idea of perhaps cajoling whoever answered the door into letting me see the front room where Mewton-Wood had committed suicide. The woman who stood in front of me was unlikely, I knew instantly, to offer me such a privilege.

I was a writer from Australia, I said, and did she know that a famous Australian pianist, Noel Mewton-Wood, had once lived in her house?

No, she said.

I was writing about him, I said, and could not resist knocking on the door.

She was mute.

I apologised, asking if she had lived there for long.

Five or six years, she said, a suspicious expression on her face beginning to hint at uneasy thoughts about this strange man without *bona fides* coming to her home and asking her about an unknown musician — an *Australian*, what was more — who had once owned her house.

It was long ago, I said, and I might have mentioned the 1950s.

She said nothing.

Did she know the previous owners of the house? I asked, attempting to peer past her into the front room, an elegant, pastel-painted space in brilliant yellow in which there appeared to be a fireplace, an ornately framed mirror above it, and a bowl of flowers, gladioli perhaps, on the mantelpiece.

Yes, she said, she had known them.

And did they ever mention Mewton-Wood?

No, she said, grimacing, and adding quickly, Look I'm actually quite busy. I'm working, you see, and I really don't have time to chat.

Fine, I said, thanking her and searching for leave-taking words, which became a mumble about just wanting to let her know that a great pianist had once lived in her house. Just wanted to let you know, I repeated, and she closed the door.

THREE HOUSES up, a young black photographer was taking pictures of one of the most beautiful young women I have ever seen, her dark eyes enormous, her face triangular, riveting, the shape of faces that Hollywood likes to give to the digital heroines in sci-fi epics. Or the face-shape of a praying mantis. I found myself trying not to stare at her. The photographer and I compared cameras, his interest in my inferior device genuine. I was intrigued not only by his latest-model, super-duper Nikon, as he put it, but the foot-square light high up on a kind of tripod and pole that softly lit the model's face, supplementing the low, weak sun that shone on to this side of the street as she posed in an assortment of fur caps, ear muffs and winter stoles.

He made his income mostly from wedding photography, he said, but he also sent pictures to fashion magazines, hoping to break into the freelance market. I could tell him about freelancing, I said, adding that mowing lawns and walking dogs for money were much more lucrative. He laughed. He already knew that, he said.

The pair was fascinated by Mewton-Wood's story, and within a minute or two of my rambling précis of the pianist's life, the photographer asked an obvious question: Did you tell the woman, he said, gesturing up the street, that he had committed suicide in her front room? We all laughed as I shook my head, and the model said in a very soft, sweet voice inflected perhaps with Middle Eastern overtones, Ooooh, ghosts!

LATER THAT day, I tried to Skype Dr K. I wanted to tell him that I had become used to being a rat on an exercise wheel and hadn't, not once, been tempted to let go of my dead man's handle. In short, I was confident that *doing* things had diverted me from miserable thoughts. I was feeling upbeat, as they say.

Her hair pulled back in a grey ponytail, an elderly woman came up on my laptop. She was the receptionist, she said, and no Dr K had ever worked at St Sebastian House in her memory, which stretched back seventeen years. Who did I mean? she asked.

Dr K, I insisted. This is his Skype address, I said. I know it's correct, I added.

She shook her head and frowned. No Dr K had ever worked here *clinically*, she said, and she could think of only Dr Knopfel, who was a psychologist and a board member at St Sebastian in the 1960s as well as a professor and well-known critic of the Soviet scourge, as he used to call it. Around his university he was known as Dr K. He had come out from Czechoslovakia, and was renowned for his stern rhetoric, she said, and he sat on the convocation only until other members voted overwhelmingly to ask him to leave because of what they perceived as his radical rants in lectures and on the radio, pontifications that were delivered in a slow and heavily-glottal-stopped eastern-European baritone.

They gave St Sebastian a bad name. Publicly and privately he condemned the polity behind the Iron Curtain and its ultimate quest to step across Europe to the very doors of the French people themselves, many of whom colluded. The English would be next to fall, the poison of Communism eventually destroying the whole of the civilised world. It had already eviscerated his home town Prague, he used to say, and the world's peoples would become trapped in its terrifying, totalitarian vice if we were not extremely careful. (I'm not sure that she put it in so few words.) But to my knowledge, she said, Dr K had never made clinical observations, did no rounds of the wards. Was this the Dr K you wanted? Because he is long dead. I thanked her and closed the connection.

JL, WHOM I had not heard from for many months, which was strange, had also emailed me. He had been pre-occupied with a personal tragedy, he wrote, and he was sorry that he had not had the time to get in touch. He hoped that my project was progressing successfully.

He himself, he said, had recently lost a first cousin, Terry H, the son of his mother's brother, to whom he was especially fond, the head of English at a secondary college in Gippsland, a husband, father and new grandfather. They met fairly often — JL would drive down to the coastal village of Port Albert or his cousin would drive up the Calder freeway — so that they could argue in a good-natured way about the latest novels, writers in general and grammar and punctuation. Terry could see no point in *not* splitting infinitives if it made reading and writing and communicating easier, for instance, whereas I, JL wrote, am a stickler and can't abide to boldly go. I once phoned him, he wrote, to say that I'd found a split infinitive — to ever hear — on page 73 of *Nostromo*, Conrad's greatest story. Conrad, the Pole who had become an English stickler! Terry liked John Banville's books and I didn't, and I tried to get him to read W. G. Sebald and Thomas Bernhard and even one or two of the novellas of Patrick Modiano, who seems very perceptive and is a literal wanderer in the great tradition of walking-writers who take in what surrounds them. I especially like a quote from the latter's book *Pour que tu ne te perdes pas dans le quartier*, he wrote, shunting his email up a siding. It's *Le present et le passé se confondent, et cela semble naturel puisqu'ils n'étaient séparés que par une paroi de cellophane. Il suffisait d'une piqûre d'insecte pour crever la cellophane,* in other words, the present and the past merge, and that seems natural because they're separated by only a sheet of Cellophane, which may be burst by an insect sting. My translation, he added. It reminded him, he wrote, that most of us should strive to insulate ourselves against worrying about time and be vigilantly dubious, the words he used, about the notion of the future, a concept that, in truth, was a mirage. Moreover, we should try to understand that the past envelops the present — and vice versa — to such a degree that our focus should be only on the now and how it transpires. We cannot break our contract with the present, he wrote, and we should use it wisely.

My wife and Terry's wife were also close, JL continued, and the four of us often met for dinner. But early last year Terry had begun to rant unusually over his soup — his rhetoric odd because he was liberal in the best sense — about such things as the length of girl students' skirts, which he felt should be compulsorily knee-low not thigh-high, as he put it. He dismissed the lack of a future for the workers at Gippsland's coal-fired power stations once they were closed — he had no sympathy for them, repeating, Them's the breaks, them's the breaks — and the demonising of sharks along the Australian coast in the wake of several fatal attacks and many sightings: he wanted government support for search-and-destroy missions. He had never, never been an unthinking man, and this radical about-face in his opinions suggested to me that some kind of chemical imbalance or electrical misfiring had overwhelmed certain critical neural pathways in his brain. We know a vast amount and almost nothing about the brain, JL wrote, and each organ is a universe whose workings we have no hope ever of understanding entirely. We would be better off investing funds in research into how brains work, he wrote, his words echoing for a sentence or two the rhetoric of his earlier emails, than rocketing off to Mars.

Terry had several times told me that he was depressed, JL wrote. He was sicker than we realised, he said, more ill than even his wife knew, and the empty, frightened look in his eyes told me that he was being utterly sincere about a mental condition whose full effects only he could feel. He was incapable of understanding them, he said.

And then he had a stroke, and in an instant he lost his ability to read, his favourite pastime, and write. He still had ideas, he told me, but he couldn't express them, couldn't get them from his brain out into the air. They would evaporate somewhere between his mind and his mouth, and he would end several seconds of trying to articulate a thought with total capitulation and the words, Yeah, yeah, meaning, Take what you can from my hopeless attempts to communicate. He said that losing his mind was worse than becoming blind, which is what most people might think is the second worst affliction after death. A blind man can use braille, he said, and if he were blind he might be able to feel at least *some* of the books he loved. A weakness on his right side also worried him. He could still walk, even if he limped slightly, and he could grasp the table knife in his right hand, he said, demonstrating above a slice of roast chicken. But he could no longer feel the knife-handle in the palm of his hand. He lost his job, of course, and the whole rigmarole of applying for a disability pension distressed him.

Three months after the stroke, he decided that he would never again be able to read, never be able to regain the skill he most loved exercising, despite one of his therapists having said that he could recommence learning English, reinforcing initially the vowels and consonants and their sounds and roles in language. Very soon after he would progress, she said, to *John & Betty* — you know, John can run, Betty can jump. And he told me standing on the back lawn of his former fisherman's cottage with its smoking tent for mullet one Sunday afternoon after lunch, wrote JL, that he could think of no reason to persist. The *frustration* — the word he most used about his condition — was unbearable, he said.

My wife and I returned home, said JL, and the following morning his wife Janice rang us distraught. Overnight, while she had slept, Terry had disappeared. She went to the beach, where she discovered that his small aluminium dinghy, the beloved tinny from which he used to fish for whiting — mullet were a by-catch — in the seagrass reserves around Scrubby Island and even farther out to sea near Clonmel Island and Sunday Island, was gone, the padlock that secured it to a star picket laying open on the sand, key still in the lock. She returned to the cottage to discover that the portable outboard motor that powered the dinghy was also gone, and she called the police.

You might have read about the search; it was in the news, helicopters scanning the sea, volunteers scrub-bashing through thick tea tree around the coast. Then, three days later on its nightly crossing to Devonport, the Spirit of Tasmania car ferry almost ran down the dinghy in those notoriously rough seas halfway across Bass Strait. In the light of a full moon, a deckhand saw the little boat, and the ship slowed to take it on board. The police later asked Janice if the dinghy usually had an anchor and she said yes and they reported that the tinny was lacking it. No sign of life vests, either, which were found a week later washed up on Woodside Beach. The outboard's fuel tank was empty.

Terry's disappearance reminded me, wrote JL, of the novelist Virginia Woolf, who, before filling her overcoat pockets with stones and walking into the Ouse river near her home in Sussex, a county of tragedy, one might add, wrote that exquisitely painful and beautiful letter to her husband Leonard, saying that she felt sure that she was going mad again and that she could no longer go through those terrible times, as she put it. She stressed how happy they had been, how much joy he had given her, but that she couldn't keep on spoiling *his* life and that she could no longer fight her disease.

And then, halfway through the text, the lines slanting upwards, which graphologists say usually denotes optimism, she pens three agonising words — I can't read — echoing precisely, exactly, the sentiments that Terry had expressed to me several times, including on the eve of his disappearance. So I have been a little pre-occupied with these matters, JL wrote, and we are helping Janice and her family come to terms with the tragedy and will probably be involved in that task for an indeterminate period. To be perfectly frank, I haven't been pondering your project and its problems and opportunities for some time, he added, and I expect that that situation will not change. He finished by saying that no remnants of Terry had been found.

JL's email shocked me not only because of his cousin's apparent suicide. I was, it seemed, on my own, Dr K having also disappeared, and JL, who had provided several valuable leads, now intent, and rightly so, on more important matters. It meant that I would have to try to come to terms with my own demons without their guidance, which I had hugely valued.

Might this force me to reassess my notion that pianos kill pianists? Start again? Pause the project to see where it had taken me and assess its worth? The idea that pianos were dangerous was so dear to me that I was loath to let go. Was I any better? Was I well enough to persist? Was my grip on the dead man's handle secure? I had certainly made progress, and the work I had done to try to prove my thesis had pleased me immensely. It surprised me that *doing something* had made a difference. *Do something! Do something!* I was reminded of R. D. Laing's exhortation to his anguished patients to *do something!* Walk around the block. Whistle a Crosby hit. Knit a scarf. Darn a sock. Peel an orange. Pat the dog. *Do something!* There was something in *doing something*, I decided.

NOT LONG before she died, Virginia Woolf turned down a request to resume teaching at Morley College, which since 1884 had provided evening classes to London's working men and women of south-east London and was by the 1940s an eminent institution specialising in adult education. Its principal Miss Sheepshanks, after all, had recruited the young and beautiful Miss Stephen to teach composition, history and literature between 1905 and 1907, several years before her marriage to Leonard. Perhaps she got more from her teaching than her students, Quentin Bell, one of her biographers suggests. She wanted to get to know them, get them to write about themselves, and she discovered that they were intelligent folk despite their lack of education. She called her English composition class the most useless in the college, but what could she do? Among her students is an old Socialist, she writes, who thinks he must bring aristocrats into an essay about autumn, a Dutchman who believes at the end of the class that I have been teaching him arithmetic, and anaemic shop girls who say they would write more but that they get only an hour for lunch. One of her working men is an Italian who reads English as though it were medieval Latin, and another is a degenerate poet who rants and blushes and almost seizes my hand when we happen to like the same lines. The first sentence of one of her lectures begins, The poet Keats died when he was twenty-five, and he wrote all his work before that. She was, after all, only in her twenties.

Perhaps the most surprising thing about Morley was that two of its directors of music, Gustav Holst and Michael Tippett, remain among the most eminent of English composers. The college was intellectually and vocationally energetic, inclusive, and diverse in its offerings. By the 1920s, the music department was only one of many, a total of almost two thousand five hundred students learning English literature and art, history and economics, French, German, Italian and Spanish, gymnastics and folk dancing, sight-singing, harmony, first-century music, violin, home nursing and dressmaking, botany, mathematics, physics, electricity, physiology, and Man and his world. If only there were more Morley Colleges, one on every street corner, one is tempted to think, the world might change for the better. On the 15th of October 1940, two aerial torpedoes, as an official report calls them, scored a direct hit on the older part of the brick campus, killing fifty-seven victims of earlier German attacks who were sheltering in the refreshment room and gymnasium. There were no casualties among staff and students. The wounded, said an official notice, received all possible attention, and classes resumed almost immediately.

As did the concerts for which Morley was famous. London's finest musicians, including Noel Mewton-Wood, played at Morley, and the Australian probably performed for the last time in public in the Holst Room, which I wanted to see. I could do no more than glimpse the small whitewashed space through a door opened only a few centimetres, said my guide, Morley's senior librarian. We should not disturb what appeared to be a class in jazz trumpet that was in full swing. A plain space, the Holst seemed to be at basement level, shallow windows barely high enough to reach the fading evening light outside. Across the back of a low platform behind a black trumpeter, who was alternating between lecturing and trumpeting, was the room's only feature of note, a strange floor-to-ceiling curved rear wall of splendidly polished marquetry. Its shape reminded me of a Cinerama screen. And at 7.30pm on Sunday the 18th of October, 1953, fewer than seven weeks before his suicide, Mewton-Wood played here Schubert's four impromptus opus 90, which were composed two years before the composer's death in 1828 at thirty-one, the accursed age. Weber's A-flat sonata opus 39 and Busoni's *Fantasia Contrappuntistica* were also on the program. I could find no reviews of the concert, and I wondered what went through Mewton-Wood's mind as he played. His partner Bill Fedrick or Federick or Frederick was probably in the audience and had not yet started to complain about the pains in the abdomen that presaged his death. But had police been threatening the Australian, had someone been blackmailing him over his alleged trawling for rent-boys? Was a former lover about to talk to the Press? The mirth provoked among his students when the trumpeter-teacher pulled out a large white handkerchief, flourished it, mopped his brow and bald skull, beamed a smile and burst into the first few bars of *Mack the Knife* in a gravelly bass offered no answers, of course.

IN THE British Library's small archive on Mewton-Wood I discovered John Amis's notes on the pianist, which were presumably drafted for his book. Written in a decisive black cursive script on both sides of four rectangles of white cardboard around which new shirts had once been carefully folded for sale, their top edges tapered to make shoulders, they added only a little to what was published in *Amiscellany*. The scarcity of deletions suggest that they were penned quickly, truthfully, and with great affection and a little piquancy. Amis notes, for instance, that several homosexuals had committed suicide after their partners had died, presumably not long before Mewton-Wood's death, positing that the act was some kind of romantic response — *almost fashionable*, he writes. It had never occurred to him that the Australian was queer, but these days — the notes are undated — if there are no girls around and a bloke seems to be having no sex then he is queer. The Australian's playing was alive, considered, illuminating and could be beautiful. Omitted entirely from *Amiscellany* was how the pianist got the cyanide, but Amis's shirt-notes say that Noel had managed to persuade a chemist in a Cambridge laboratory to provide it, ostensibly for killing rats.

Mewton-Wood could be a bit of a show-off, but never an offensive one, and he enjoyed farting resonantly, as Amis puts it, once misjudging his flatulence, soiling himself, and being forced to change his trousers. The notes throw a little more light on the astonishing incident when Amis played the orchestral introduction to the Busoni piano concerto in the empty front room of No. X Hillgate Place and a string broke. Until that moment, Amis writes, he had never believed in ghosts. But the incident surely amounted to Noel's communicating, coming in on cue. Amis falls into hysterics — after he has got over the fright — and Dulcie arrives and says, For God's sake, what are you laughing for? His notes say he told her that Noel had been in touch, a shocking but friendly gesture from the other side in the very room where he had ended his life. Or am I being silly? he asks himself. Mewton-Wood played concerts throughout Britain and the wider world, say the notes, and at one in Turkey he was upstaged for some moments by an enormous black cat that wandered on to the stage.

ISLA BARING had no cats, black or otherwise, in the crowded top-floor flat in south-west inner-London that she had shared with Amis until his death in 2013. She could really add nothing to what I already knew, she said, showing me a shallow pile of memorabilia that failed to provide more clues about the possible motives for the pianist's death. And in discussing Mewton-Wood with her and other Londoners who were interested in his life, I was getting no closer to understanding what was going through his mind as he swallowed the poison. Isla was more concerned about an upright piano that John had inherited, a second piano. Where was it? While the concert grand dominated her small living room, making it an expedition to get to a sofa and arm-chairs, the upright had disappeared altogether. Never got to the flat, as far as she could tell.

And over a fine lunch of salmon and a little composed salad, which contained tomatoes and artichokes, excellent foodstuffs for foiling disease and omens, I began to feel that the causes for all effects *must* be concrete and discoverable, and that to specu-late about the psychological consequences of playing the piano at elite levels, to theorise that such an activity can, *in extremis*, kill, might be a totally worthless idea. Mind you, this also told me that I remained confused, a man who still believed that extreme anxiety could bring on all sorts of actions, whose mind was a whirlpool of turmoil when it came to understanding the day he removed his sister's fingers.

FOR SOME months I had been making enquiries about the Mewton-Wood archive at The Britten Pears Foundation in Aldeburgh, Suffolk, home of the composer's music festival. It had sent me scans of letters between Dulcie and Britten and Pears, and one or two between Noel and the musicians that were of lesser interest — they are about concert dates and practical matters. Deeply melancholic were Dulcie's letters after Noel's death; she referred to her son as my dear Noel, our Noel, and even my dear, dear Noel, in a firm, forward-slanting hand, large writing in blue ink. She reported difficulties in settling back into Australia, calling it a crude place where stimulating discussions and exchanges of opinions are non-existent — in Australia, one doesn't criticise — and that it had been a heart-rending return *in patria*. She sends Britten her darling Noel's coffee cups, hoping he will use them, with grateful thanks for all you propose to do in memory of our Noel — I say our Noel because he loved you too. The burden of the respectful and sympathetic return mail from Britten and Pears was that Noel was in their thoughts.

Then, out of the blue, an email arrived from the foundation's archives department, a certain Holly Patel the signatory, saying that they had overlooked a suicide note Mewton-Wood had written to Patrick Trevor-Roper. It was in their keeping, and would I like to see it? They also had photographs of Mewton-Wood and several concert programs from the Aldeburgh Festival confirming that the Australian was a frequent performer. I replied immediately, asking for scans, and they arrived six hours later.

The black-and-white images showed Mewton-Wood with Britten and, presumably, Bill Fedrick or Federick or Frederick, who holds a black homburg, wears a bulky pale overcoat, his plain oval face straining to look natural for the lens, his hairline in significant recession. But it was to what the foundation had called the suicide note that I paid most attention. Scrawled in blue ink and undated, it was difficult at first to decipher. Indeed, I read some of its words several times before determining what they said. The note begins, Pat darling, You will be very angry with me for what I have done. Please forgive me. But I can't go on without my darling Bill. It says that the pianist's whole life hinged onto his, it has now collapsed completely, and I don't feel is worth repairing. He writes that he knows that everyone thinks he is so lively and — the next word is poorly drafted but might be energetico — but it's only because Bill was there with me. Now that poor old darling Billy has gone —

At that point, Mewton-Wood starts a new paragraph, the dash after the word gone especially poignant, I felt. He asks Trevor-Roper to apologise to his friends, and he thanks the eye surgeon for the enormous kindness you have shown and the trouble you have taken. I feel it is more than anyone has a right to expect from friends. Love Noel.

What the note failed to tell me, of course, was if it had been written before Mewton-Wood's first attempt to end his life or later, just before the successful one in the front room at Hillgate Place. What it undoubtedly demonstrated, though, was the pianist's deep love for his partner and the role losing him must have played in his decision to end his life. I remained unconvinced, though, that other factors — especially pianos — were irrelevant. In fact, in a curious paradox, the note goaded me to increase my efforts to prove or disprove that keyboards can kill.

I KNOW GUILT, as you are aware, and after I had lunched on an appalling burger from a greasy spoon just before the railway viaduct on the South Circular its talons tore into me. I suspected that the grey meat patty was really a disc of meat substitute of doubtful composition, a product from the days of post-war British food coupons and a cousin of the egg substitute I was once served in the United States. Who knows what was in it? To analyse it completely would have been a challenge for any laboratory. And fresh food from a Tesco was only a hundred metres from my front door.

I belched loudly several times while moving my table and laptop closer to the bay window. I wanted better light to take

notes on what the experts thought about the terrors of elite pianism. In earlier sorties online I had discovered that many researchers' conclusions, the findings of people who know, had agreed with mine about the villainy of pianos. In the mood I was in, I needed reassuring. The shift also allowed me to see passenger aircraft coming in to land at Heathrow. You could set your watch by them. It seemed that every sixty seconds precisely an aircraft appeared in my window on its final approach, swallowing a minute under the airport's new time-separation — rather than distance — scheme. The strategy looked as precise as an eighteenth-century Harrison sea clock, examples of which I had seen at the Royal Observatory in Greenwich

soon after I had arrived in London. The jets reminded me of Modiano's contention about the past and the present and the sheet of Cellophane separating them. I imagined that the planes' noses were enhanced with stings, that the aircraft had become a line of giant flying insects with deadly proboscises, which were constantly bursting films that propelled successive minutes into the past.

In the digital ether, more learned articles and books than I could have ever imagined discussed what they called performance anxiety — stage fright. Supported by graphs and boxes and tables, their conclusions were similar. Researchers and scholars decided that for some professionals, performances were characterised by fear and dread. Dianna Kenny cited Chopin, Maria Callas, Enrico Caruso, Horowitz, Casals, Pavarotti, Arthur Rubinstein and even Rachmaninoff as sufferers. She quotes Chopin's saying that audiences intimidated him, that he felt choked by their breath, paralysed by their glances, and struck dumb by their unfamiliar faces. The relationship between performer and audience is personal, she writes, quoting Louis Armstrong, who just wanted to put on a good show, and Mozart, who revelled in altering his playing during performances to manipulate his listeners' emotions, adjusting the present according to how his audience had reacted in the immediate past. (Perhaps he'd read Modiano.) She cites a relatively unknown but highly competent Canadian pianist for whom the past and the future fail to exist; that there is only the present, his focus being on trying to broadcast instantaneously his musical imagination.

She quotes former Australian prime minister Paul Keating's breathtaking eulogy of Geoffrey Tozer, a phenomenal artist, who died young of liver disease. I recalled that, in one of his emails, JL had mentioned that he had interviewed Tozer before he played the thirty-two Beethoven sonatas — JL attended every concert over several nights — in the Assembly Hall in Melbourne. His playing was uniformly excellent, said JL, but he was ambivalent about the man. Sitting in Tozer's mother's living room in a middle-class suburb of Melbourne, he had asked the pianist how he remembered the tens of thousands of notes in the Beethoven sonatas and the pianist had more or less harrumphed and dismissed the question out of hand. He *ridiculed* it, was the way JL had put it. He said you *don't*, of course, remember *all* the notes, but it is because of familiarity with a whole piece after many, many hours of work that you can play it. Muscle memory and the like. But while Tozer made them a cup of tea, JL had gone to the pianist's piano and played the first few bars of the slow movement of the Pathétique, opus 13, which was open on the music stand, an egregious act, under the circumstances. And when the pianist re-appeared holding a tea tray he smiled a little patronisingly and said that it was the first time a journalist had played for him. It should be the other way around.

Tozer had plump, white, baker's hands, wrote JL, perfect for the music he kneaded, a figure of speech that failed in my view. His performances of the Beethoven sonatas were uniformly superlative, even if for a few of the thirty-two he had propped a mini-score on the Steinway's stand. But, as Keating said at the pianist's funeral, Tozer had lost the spiritual sustenance that acclamation brings, and he went on to accuse, in St Patrick's Cathedral, the Sydney and Melbourne symphony orchestras of treating the musician with contempt and malevolence, the words he used. He was a massive loss to Australian musical culture, said Keating.

Tozer turned to other things to sustain him — mainly alcohol — and he declined vertiginously, ending up turning pages for lesser musicians for fifty dollars a concert, living in dilapidated rooming houses when he could afford to but under a bridge when he couldn't, preferring to spend what handouts he scavenged on booze rather than food, and dying at fifty-four.

Kenny remarks that artists such as Tozer and Callas — who died of a heart attack, lonely and broken, at fifty-three — fail to *persist*, and awful things follow. Music-performance anxiety is more complex than other types of angst, she writes, involving — and she cites many other researchers to support her contention — personality, brain-based skills, physiological arousal, task complexity and mastery, situational factors and memory capacity, if I transcribe her correctly. She talks about focus, motor skills and posterior-cingulate activation. And it's not always true that consistently fine performers handle anxiety well. Musicians who perform at peak levels are self-confident and *expect* to do well.

They are relaxed yet full of energy, feel in control, can concentrate intensively, focus on the task, are positive about what they are doing and stay committed and determined to the end of a piece. A medium level of arousal is essential for peak performance. Too much or too little can be destructive.

The pages rolled by, and Dr Kenny, professor of psychology and music at the University of Sydney, as she was billed, piled complexity after complexity on to the demands of being an elite pianist, introducing distraction and reversal theories as well as what she called the catastrophe model.

Much less digestible than her theorising, however, was the appalling burger I had eaten, it reminded me. I began to get severe acid reflux, a malady that led to the gullet cancer that killed my father at an early age. Visiting Las Vegas because I'd never been there, I once thought I'd die there. Crossing the lobby of my hotel, I experienced acute chest pain and imagined that my heart was faltering because of the cacophony produced by hundreds of slot machines and their bells and whistles that seemed to rise to a nauseating crescendo as I approached the lift lobby. In my room, which seemed several hundreds of metres above the ground, I folded my arms over my chest as a dying man should, making it easier, I thought at the time, for those who would take away the corpse. I took a last look at the vastness of the mauve-tinted sky above a silhouette of distant hills, closed my eyes and expected never to reopen them. But after about twenty minutes the pain went away, and, back in Melbourne a few weeks later, I was diagnosed with heartburn.

Glenn D. Wilson and David Roland largely corroborated Dr Kenny's research, stating that stage fright was a common problem best understood as a social phobia, fear of being humiliated. Their long chapter in an anthology on the science and performance of music identified its causes and problems and concluded with brief assessments of treatments. Drugs was the first sub-heading, and while alcohol and Valium might get a musician through a concert, they create dependence and fine edges are lost, Wilson and Roland opined. Beta-adrenergic blockers, which many musicians take regularly, they add, are more promising, but drugs in general are inferior to psychological procedures that are aimed at restoring a performer's self-control. The best of the behavioural therapies involves systematic desensitisation. A pianist begins by imagining he is performing an easy piece for a few relatives on a friendly family occasion. Once he is happy with that, he moves on to performing for a few strangers, then a few more and so on until he can imagine being in Carnegie Hall playing the devilishly difficult *Diabelli Variations*, say, in front of almost three thousand total strangers. Desensitisation can work, the researchers say, but we should remember that many musicians perform for years without conquering their fears.

The authors cite a study of several pianists who were given two fifty-minute hypnotherapy sessions against a control group who got none. Those hypnotised showed significant reductions in performance anxiety straight after the treatment and even greater gains six months later. A poll in the 1980s found that more than half of British orchestral musicians used some form of complementary medicine, as Wilson and Roland call it, the most popular being the Alexander Technique, named after an Australian actor called Fred Alexander, who identified harmful postures and gaits and worked out ways to improve relaxation and reduce stress by teaching people to move and sit and stand in more comfortable and natural ways. Musicians needed regular sleep, exercise, and should eat healthily, say Wilson and Roland, and they should aim, if at all possible, to experience *flow* when they perform — what other studies called, I noted, *being in the zone*.

More aircraft had glided diagonally down my window pane by the time I had read these lines — perhaps another thirty or so — and, although the findings had confused me a little and I had stopped belching, my chest pain diminishing, an Omeprazole tablet kicking in, I got up from my laptop adamant about a single implication: it seemed certain that, depending on the individual, performing on a piano at elite levels was among the most terrifying of occupations and for many it remained that way irrespective of how often they willed themselves on to a concert stage. Moreover, Kenny and Wilson and Roland and the others had failed to address in any detail long-term effects of performance anxiety, whether it was a cumulative affliction that eventually opposed the will to live, inevitably resulting in a crisis, an explosion, a will *not* to press on but the opposite, a commitment to evade persisting, as Freud said, of finding oneself, like JL's cousin, no longer possessing the desire to fight. *Je n'en peux plus*, said Madame Pic, and I shuddered at the memory of her crypts. And nothing I read dealt with the conjuring required of elite musicians, the creation of magic night after night from outlandish contraptions of metal and wood and gut, be they grand pianos, clarinets, violins or trumpets. Art *must* live, and the musician does it through the miracle of bringing the deadest of dead materials — think centuries-old violins — to life.

In communal bookshelves downstairs I found *Science & Music*, by Sir James Jeans, among potboilers, including Dan Brown stories, old copies of *Woman & Home* and *The Lady*, and a catalogue of British trees. A much-admired classic on tones and tuning-forks, vibrations, harmony and discord, Jeans's book was revered when it was first published in 1943. It derides speculation on the mysticism of music-making, claiming drily that instrumentalists make tones and harmonics in various ways and the result of their efforts is called music. After all, who could deny the views of such an esteemed physicist and mathematician as Sir James. He writes, a little sneeringly, I thought, that many pianists are firmly convinced that they can put a vast amount of expression, the whole gamut of emotions, into the striking of a single note. The *untemperamental* scientist points out, he writes, that the pianist has only a single variable at his disposal: how hard he hits the ivory or ebony. Then, defeating his own argument, he goes on to point out that differences in what he calls the strength of striking also produce differences in the proportions in which various harmonics sound, altering a note's emotional quality. Nonetheless, says Sir James — I saw him mounting a soapbox — the greatest virtuoso who strikes a single note has no wider range of effects at her disposal than the child strumming at five-finger exercises. I wondered if Sir James, in his relatively long life, had ever been to a recital by a fine pianist, ever really listened to the magic great performers extract from dead timber and cold iron and steel and copper. He fails to deal with the effects that sounds in succession have, too, ignoring completely how music is made.

And what of the anxiety caused by having to be a consummate

magician concert after concert, knowing, even if you have never set eyes on Sir James's book, that your wand sags and your rabbits have a habit of leaping from the hat before they're supposed to? And sometimes bolt off the stage.

Nearing five o'clock, the sun was gone, pale light dying in the west, and I watched the insects minute by minute piercing Cellophane, their lights winking, sliding on their single perfect identical angle across my window. From where I sat, their paths never varied by more than a centimetre, I judged. But each of the aircraft had disappeared from my view as it slid beyond the window frame, and I suddenly had the terrifying thought that the airliners had evaporated, simply been vaporised if I could no longer see them. And although the aircraft had demonstrated an intimacy with the relationship between past and present, their disappearances suggested a discontinuance of time, as if they had not only dispensed with minutes one by one but could lean back against them, eventually arresting their progress altogether, stopping the hours and destroying the optimism the future implies, a dubious notion at any level.

I leapt out of my chair to crane my neck so that I could watch the next carrier — I recognised the Cathay Pacific logo — disappear among rooftops to the west, low enough now, I thought, to imagine its making a confident landing, continuing the seconds, minutes, hours and days that enslave us.

But the thought that aircraft could somehow disappear if I could not see them indicated a setback, the eruption of a latent psychological disarray. Perhaps it was brought on by reading the research, which confirmed that being a fine pianist was terrifying. And I rehearsed again, in agony, beginning to sweat and feeling so faint that I had to sit down, that dreadful morning when Anna helped me rough-saw some Huon pine. I had a chest of drawers in mind. I asked her to help me, I admit, but don't know why. She had done it once or twice before, and she was keen to repeat the dose. Unusually so.

I gave her safety goggles, but should I have stressed how carefully she should hold the wood? Told her to mind her fingers? She needed, I should have told her, to concentrate less on the pencil line my saw-blade was following — even rough cuts should be more or less precise — and more on where her fingers were? She would have known it anyway, of course. And if that was true, perhaps she did place them in the way of the blade, to be severed on purpose, an idea that both torments and reassures me. There is a chance that she wouldn't have sacrificed her career like that, bearing in mind how quickly she fell apart once she was unable to play. Which left the possibility that I had hurried the blade along the line to remove her fingers on purpose. Vengeance? My answer to her getting all the luck and me none? An unimaginable idea. But when I consider it, I instantly recall that most of us fail to understand ourselves.

As night invaded the room, the vile questions that had constantly arisen since her death now bedevilled me, answers unforthcoming. I lay on my bed, tossing and turning, comforting myself with the notion that pianos punish certain pianists in certain circumstances. The research had shown it. That was all. But I felt more confused than ever about my role in Anna's release from the keyboard and her eventual plunge from Mt Buffalo Gorge, an abyss that she and I both loved. I needed the expert advice I was hoping to get in the Czech Republic, even if my confidence that anything might help me was waning, my grip on the dead man's handle slackening. With no great conviction, I boarded a plane for Prague next day.

WHILE THE flight was short — a little over two hours — yesterday's anxiety and a sleepless night had taken their toll, and somewhere over Belgium, perhaps, I fell into a troubled slumber. During it, the terror of performing returned. The audience behind me had grown, filling grandstands like those at the Melbourne Cricket Ground, which can accommodate a hundred thousand spectators. People shook their fists at me and jeered. Seated at a black Steinway on a vast and otherwise empty stage, the music remained upside-down. When I tried to turn it right way up it reversed itself. This amused me, and I began to giggle. Right side up … reverse. Right side up … reverse. I thought of trying to play it as it appeared, upside down, wondering what it would sound like. The crowd booed, yet I felt a weird confidence that I would be able to perform well. I turned to the spectators and smiled and waved. I remembered that I hadn't rehearsed at all and that I wasn't even sure what the music was, let alone whether I could play it. It looked like Beethoven, but was it the simple and short number twenty in G major (there seemed too many notes) or the much harder number thirty? They were my best guesses, and I took a pencil from my pocket and began to scribble the music as it might appear right-way-up, trying to invert the notes by hand. The jeering increased, and in this crescendo Anna appeared and sat on the music stool alongside me, smiling sympathetically. I'll fix it, she said, or words to that effect, and she reached up to the music with her right hand. Of course, the hand lacked fingers, and she couldn't grasp the pages, even though she was trying to. And at that instant a voice woke me to say that we were preparing to land at Václav Havel Airport.

I DECIDED to walk from my hotel on Olšanská to Kafka's museum. I hurried, actually, in the cold and slatey air with the strange expectation that I would meet someone there without knowing whom he or she might be. I didn't want to miss the meeting, failing to be tempted by the bratwurst-in-a-roll stand at the top of Václaveské, striding into the much narrower cobbled Melantrichova, taking even narrower alleys to the vast Old Town Square, Staroměstské náměstí, admiring, as always, the astonishing simulation of the past that its cobbles and ornate buildings provide, its baroque and Gothic churches of St Nicholas and Our Lady of Týn, which clashed with the modernity of the lumpen statue of Jan Hus, the Protestant precursor who was burned at the stake for daring to criticise Catholic orthodoxy. I took Karlova west, a narrow lane that twisted and turned past shops whose windows glittered in the gloom with Czech crystal, ancient and modern, suites of six glasses in all shapes and sizes and cuts, crystal birds in contemporary curves and colours, and many small bells decorated with golden garlands and tiny ceramic violets. Karlova narrowed, the cobbles becoming smaller and harder, their tops more rounded and more ruinous to my ankles as I walked. The farther I went the more I felt that the stones across which I tramped were trying to restrain me, as if something or someone had commandeered them and was attempting to prevent my reaching the museum. A stream of tourists accompanied me, all heading in the same direction towards the Charles Bridge, not stopping for even a glimpse inside St Clement's Cathedral, intent on their destination.

The closer I got to my goal, the stronger I felt that someone — or perhaps two people — were following me, making sure that I reached my destination and met whoever was expecting me. I glanced several times over my shoulder, seeing no one sinister in a crowd mainly consisting of Asians. For all that, invisible hands seemed to propel me forward.

Charles Bridge — Karlův most — is these days dedicated to pedestrians and must be among the most photographed structures in Europe. Today, though, and probably every day, those who were on and around it held metre-long sticks and were taking photographs of themselves and, as a background, the bridge and its grey-drenched history, the route Joseph K. took in the last chapter of his novel. The grey stones and the castle on the hill behind them were merely a backdrop, a décor feature, a flat before which they were playing out a highlight of their lives.

At its western end, on the other side of the Vltava River, the lesser-town side, the crowds dissipated, and I walked fewer than two hundred metres and slightly downhill, taking U Lužického semináře and Cihelná, which are set back from the western bank, to arrive in the museum's forecourt, where two bronze men urinate into a pond in which they stand. And while tour guides holding aloft a fake tulip or a car aerial with a small Czech flag, say, lead their groups to the statue of the urinators, few people seem to enter the museum.

A long low cream-painted building with a mansard roof and dormer windows tiled in rust-red, a former brickworks, in fact, these days it holds many treasures from Kafka's life, or,

as the website puts it, an exhibition that is divided into an existential space and an imaginary topography. The museum is in the attic, and I could discern neither blatant existentialism nor imagination — perhaps because of the darkness — after I had mounted the pine treads illuminated in a red the colour of arterial blood. The museum's gloom was so profound, in fact, that its clear purpose was to obscure everything but the historical documents and images, which were only slightly more brightly lit behind glass in cases, filing cabinets, on thin iron bars that stuck out of a pile of what looked like coking coal, projected on to veils of gauze hanging from the rafters and, in one case, projected from above onto something like a small canvas trampoline. Once my eyes got used to the lack of light, I made out heavy exposed timber beams and struts and was careful to avoid them. For quite some time — it was early in the day — I was alone with Kafka.

The museum's ambience was as bleak as the blackness. A soundtrack on a loop played monotonously — a jackdaw called, a nice allusion to a possible translation from the Czech of *kafka*, a single low note perhaps produced electronically reverberated,

and occasionally a string quartet played a doleful and repetitious morsel of about a minute long, reminding me of the music of Philip Glass. He might have indeed written it, I thought. A spiral staircase behind glass or Perspex climbed towards the roof, ending abruptly before it arrived.

There was much to learn. A cage searches for a bird, said the museum's first panel. Franz Kafka was born into a myth called Prague, it added. His home was laid siege to by dead brothers, distant sisters, cold governesses, and a caustic cook. His world was seen through a veil of fear and guilt, and the boy's father loomed, leaving no space for his son. In a glass case nearby were pages from the writer's famous letter to his father, which his mother never delivered, an incomplete plea, Franz writes, that begins by saying how afraid he is of Hermann and goes on to detail in widely-spaced and beautifully penned lines, art in themselves, I thought, the emotional abuse he has suffered at his father's hands, the inferior nature of his father's Judaism — Franz would strive to find a more acceptable, deeper form of it — and a challenge to Hermann to accept that if he thinks he is blameless in the breakdown of their relationship, then his father ought to accept that he, too, Franz, is also blameless. They are both too old to start again, he writes, but what if they could negotiate a *kind of peace*, as Kafka puts it, a diminution in your unceasing reproaches?

More examples of Kafka's exquisite penmanship glow in the dark as well as a letter absolving him from studying law at Prague's German University, a list of philosophy courses in which he enrolled in the summer semester of 1902 at the Karl-Ferdinand University, and photos of the writer as child, dandy,

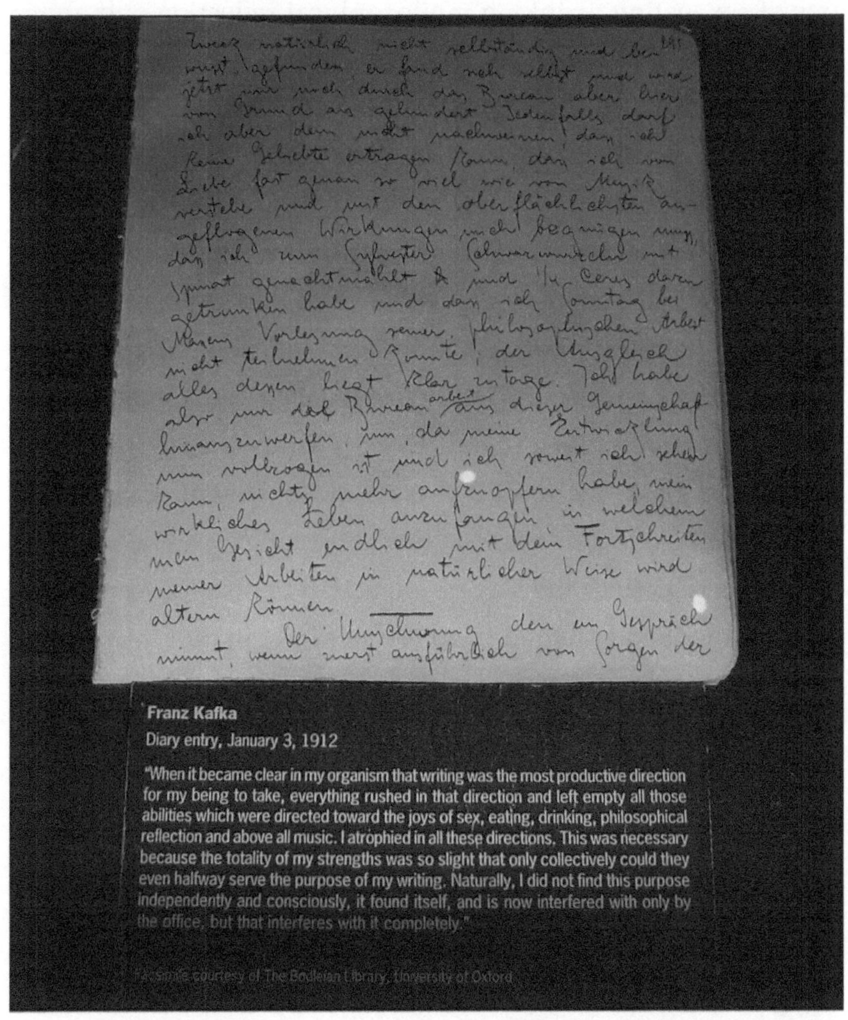

Franz Kafka

Diary entry, January 3, 1912

"When it became clear in my organism that writing was the most productive direction for my being to take, everything rushed in that direction and left empty all those abilities which were directed toward the joys of sex, eating, drinking, philosophical reflection and above all music. I atrophied in all these directions. This was necessary because the totality of my strengths was so slight that only collectively could they even halfway serve the purpose of my writing. Naturally, I did not find this purpose independently and consciously, it found itself, and is now interfered with only by the office, but that interferes with it completely."

Facsimile courtesy of The Bodleian Library, University of Oxford student, lover, bureaucrat and so on. Both a lawyer in the Austro-Hungarian bureaucracy and a creator of literature, Kafka was riven with anguish over his double life, says a panel.

Then followed a particularly revealing diary entry, I thought. Dr K, who signed his letters Dr K, writes that when it became clear in my organism that writing was the most productive direction for my being to take, everything rushed in that direction and left empty all those abilities which were directed to the joys of sex, eating, drinking, philosophical reflection and above all music. I atrophied in all these directions, he writes. A few of his cartoons are on display, lanky black figures with dislocated joints, their small heads cradled in an elbow or fallen on to a table top in despair.

Notes and commentaries summarise the importance of several stories, and I was especially drawn to the only model in the museum, thankfully not a working one, of the killing machine from *In the Penal Settlement*, sometimes called *In the Penal Colony*, a story I had recently re-read. Even if I pushed my face hard against the glass, the replica was so dimly lit that details were hard to make out. But the machine's workings were all there at perhaps a twentieth the size of the actual battery-powered contraption that had emerged from Kafka's imagination — the Bed, on which the condemned man is laid face-down, the Designer, which was supported by four brass rods about two metres above the bed, and the glass Harrow, its sharp needles writing increasingly deeply on the condemned man's body over twelve hours the rule he has disobeyed. I saw a miniscule version of the electrically heated basin of rice-pap that the condemned man — once his felt gag is removed — may lap at during the first six hours of his sentence. After that, he is no longer in any mood to eat, the story goes. And I noticed the ferocious steel spike that, at the end, drives through the condemned man's skull to finish him off.

In the story, page after page of gruesome description of the death machine is partly balanced by the views of a witness to the execution whom Kafka calls the explorer. The latter labels it inhumane and unjust. But no other Kafka tale is so bloodthirsty, revealing the extent, I believe, of the writer's mental turmoil, an indication of the depth of his own regrets and incapacities and a special kind of guilt — probably unconscious — he felt for having to legitimise despair and the grotesque in the service of his art.

And what does the story's denouement mean? The officer who is demonstrating the killing machine to the explorer, a prisoner already strapped under the Harrow, decides to make the machine *more convincing*, as he tells the explorer, by taking the condemned man's place, replacing HONOUR THY SUPERIORS! with BE JUST!, which the needles will engrave on him. Does truth need the ultimate sacrifice? Is that what Kafka is saying? Must we die for it, die for our art? After all, great pianists must forsake all to perform at a standard that is acceptable to them. And Kafka himself sacrificed a normal life, as his diary notes confirm, to express the truth as he saw it. Died so that his messages could live. How many non-pianists like Jan Hus and Dr K, I asked myself, were prepared to do that these days?

A panel says that for Kafka's only public reading outside Prague — in Berlin — he chose *In the Penal Colony*. It perplexed intellectuals attending the event, says the notice, and three women fainted. Kafka was labelled a dilettante of horror who had caused an excess of nervous tension. He himself said the reading was a failure. The panel says that he was having nightmares about a machine that was subjecting him to interminable torture when he wrote the tale, and its writing coincided with the resumption of his engagement to Felice Bauer, whom Hermann thought, if I'm not wrong, was not good enough for him. Kafka wanted to publish the story with *Metamorphosis* and *The Judgement* in a volume called *Punishments*. His editor rejected the idea, but he was determined to get it into print, and it appeared five years later in a collector's edition. Another panel says the tale anticipated the naturalisation of bureaucratic murder, the beginnings of modern justice, and I doubted that any other object anywhere could be as deeply distressing as the model of Kafka's killing machine. It discombobulated me to such an extent that, in the near-dark, I saw a row of empty directors' chairs and slumped for several minutes on to one.

A narrow corridor of floor-to-ceiling filing cabinets in what appeared to be a glossy navy-blue — it was too dark for me to be more precise — some drawers open to reveal more documents about the writer and his works, led me to the museum's only brightly lit space. Opposing mirrored walls perhaps three or four metres apart funnelled towards a screen, a white sheet perhaps two metres square, on which were projected more cartoons, one of them a jaunty bowler-hatted dandy larger than life, Dr K himself, striding across Charles Bridge. I could not understand the space's relevance, what it was supposed to be saying, but when I stood between the mirrors, I saw myself disappearing into infinity, my image heading for the abyss, as the French say.

And although I stood absolutely still, I began to notice movement in the farthest reflections. It appeared as if someone were striding towards me, an image at a time, out of the chasm, each iteration engulfing the precedent. It was not until he stopped perhaps three metres from me that I realised that it was my Dr K, his lab coat scorching white, the black stubble of his skull still uniform in height, his beard neatly tonsured, his skin ghostly. Neither of us moved, and I was tempted, at first, to ask him why I had been unable to get him on Skype.

So your project appears to be at an end, he said.

His presence instantly terrified me, but I managed to stammer what I thought was an appropriate response.

Why do you say that? I said.

You are here, a place that celebrates the impossibility of closure, as the saying goes, where more questions are posed than answers provided.

Can't humans hope for satisfaction? I said, seeking a kind of intellectual truce with my interlocutor. For the sake of *peace*, I added. The real Dr K had wished for it.

An infinite amount of hope fills the universe, he said. But not for us.

Because of mistakes? Accidents?

We bumble along, adrift, repeating errors that we hope to correct one day, unable to escape. We go around in endless circles, causing trouble for ourselves and others. Sometimes we save ourselves — opt out, really — by the act of suicide, or what might be called suicide by accumulation, a slow excavation of our beings, which ultimately results in death.

I began to sweat and feel faint. But this man, who knew too much, deserved rebuffing. I had to challenge him.

Is that what Kafka tells us? I said. That humans are beyond hope?

He says that we have no idea what we are doing and no way of doing it any differently. We experience a living death, like the hunter Gracchus, and only drastic measures can rid ourselves of it. You have been in the museum some time. You must have understood all of this, the simplest of propositions.

I nodded, perhaps unconvincingly.

So, *are* you at the end of your quest? he asked. Have you found enough pianists who were killed by their instruments? Have you reached any conclusions? Assuaged your guilt about your sister's accident, perhaps? Transferred it to a dumb instrument?

His allegation shocked me, and I felt the onset of vertigo. But at that instant a visitor, an elderly gentleman holding a Chinese fan and wearing a purple anorak, a tartan trilby, and a Burberry scarf, copious white hair protruding from under his hat, the first person I had noticed in an hour, joined me between the mirrors. He looked English. I pulled myself together before realizing that Dr K's presence would embarrass both of us, causing a scene, even if it failed to embarrass Dr K, whom I turned to look for in the glass.

He had gone, and the visitor peered at his own receding images, smiled at the cartoon, fanned his brow and left.

Are you? demanded Dr K, who re-appeared.

Am I what?

Have you successfully transferred blame, or is your coin ready for Charon?

My knees began to give, and I thought I might fall. Dr K was no longer an ally but a tyrant, someone whose views I no longer wanted to hear, whose frankness cut me to the bone, as the saying goes. To stop myself from falling I placed a hand on the mirror, knowing that it would leave a smudge. Someone would have to wipe it clean.

Not entirely, I stammered.

Surprising myself, I confronted him, saying that I was coming around to thinking that I had been right all along, that pianos were indeed deadly — deadly, I spat — although I had had, at times, some doubts.

They can kill, I told Dr K. I have no doubt that pianos can kill.

Who? he said.

Pianists, of course, I shouted, hoping that no one was near enough to hear and that the man in the purple anorak had moved a good distance away.

Pianists! I shouted again.

Dr K shrugged, and our eyes met in a long and ungracious stare.

Determining the truth of anything is always difficult, he said. Impossible, actually. We make up the truths that suit us. Get your coin ready, at any rate, to pay the ferryman. He is waiting for you on the banks of the Styx.

Trying to regain my composure, I said that I had a last visit to make. People to see. I needed expert corroboration, I said.

Make your visit, he said, preening his beard. But keep an open mind. He smiled. I am pleased with your progress. It could go either way.

At that, he turned and began stepping into his own images,

smaller ones successively engulfing bigger, so to speak, which took him farther away, out of my reach, diminishing him by the second, until he disappeared altogether.

I was relieved. It was as if I had challenged and perhaps obliterated the only part of me that could question my ideas, my actions. No one could reproach me for whatever happened next.

I DROVE THE fifty or so kilometres south-east of Prague to the village of Divišov, enjoying the excellent freeway, light traffic, and a low sun that illuminated a frosty morning, casting a pale translucent veil over gentle hills, open fields, and occasional villages, some with onion-domed churches. I was heading there for two reasons. The first was to ask a piano-maker if something was built into pianos, something in their morphology, that endangered those who tried to play them. The second was to try to discover whether pianos had maimed Vladimir Sofronitsky, one of the greatest keyboard artists of the twentieth century and a man of enormous sensitivity.

The E50 gradually ascends, in fact, and as I reached a kind of low summit, some kind of pass between hills, what I thought had been ice on the grass and saplings beside the road thickened and deepened and was, in fact, several centimetres of snow. And by the time I turned off to take the narrow road two kilometres to Divišov, to Paul McNulty's fortepiano workshop beside the village church, there were snowdrifts of a third of a metre or so encroaching on the tarmac, leaden clouds not only descending but deepening and darkening.

A thousand souls in total, Divišov was cream-coloured and more modest and plainer than a factory wall, more ordinary in appearance than I had imagined from images I had seen on Google. Even its church was unremarkable, and the only colours I could make out in the gloom came from the bright lights and promotional placards of a small supermarket, which was also in the centre of town. Two-storeyed houses appeared to be painted the colour of egg shells, and red-tiled roofs predominated. At ten-thirty on a mid-week morning on the cusp of winter, nothing moved, and I recalled that paradoxes not only intrigue and amuse us but are too numerous to mention. That machines as full of life, as glossy and intricate, as gorgeous in appearance and as perfect in sound and mechanicals as McNulty fortepianos — some say the world's best — could be crafted and shipped worldwide from as modest a place as Divišov, a village known for the small motorcycle factory on its outskirts and a nearby castle of middling fame, astonished me.

The McNulty campus — home as well as workshop — is right on the cobbled street, a former two-storey, seventeenth-century manor house that had burned down in its early years and was rebuilt to become a doctor's surgery, then a blacksmith's, then an ironmongery that made hinges for the castle doors, and now a workshop that produced musical instruments. (It was never to be called a fortepiano *factory*, Paul's partner, the pianist Viviana Sofronitsky, daughter of Vladimir, once told me bluntly in an email, implying that more craft, more attention to perfection and detail happened inside *this* workshop than occurred in any big piano factory.) A huge grey timber door, graven and splintered in places, suggesting that it might have begun to swing many centuries ago, gave entry, and I rang the bell beside its man-sized hatch.

Paul and I had been email correspondents for several years. I had attended a complete cycle of Haydn's keyboard sonatas presented by Geoffrey Lancaster in the Melbourne Recital Centre, and Geoffrey had put me in touch. Paul's emails showed him to be, in turn, intense, funny and puzzlingly cryptic, a Texan who had become padlocked to his craft, the key lost, and who loved it so much that it was all he did, and who, despite speaking only rough Czech, was obsessed with producing perfection and passing on his skills to the ten or so apprentices in their twenties and thirties whom he employed. I was curious to see what he looked like, of course — excited to meet him — and the hatch opened on a man of medium height, neither slim nor plump, his Beatles-style haircut salt-and-peppered, his beard and moustache greyer than his unruly thatch, his John Lennon glasses perfectly round, his smile

enormous. He wore scarlet bib-and brace overalls over a heavy-duty, long-sleeved black t-shirt, and his shoes, obviously his workshop shoes, which might once have been worn on long walks in the nearby forests, were now broken, the seams bursting, revealing black socks. (I imagined the shoes' sliding about erratically, around and under his immaculate instruments like injured moles.)

The colour of the overalls suggested that he was ready to attend an emergency — any emergency — a fire, say, or a road accident, and I felt for several minutes a sense of unease, that I was intruding, and that he might at any minute need to be called away on life-or-death business. But no accident disturbed our first hour together — or any other, for that matter. At first, we talked about everything and anything but music and pianos — even the recently elected Donald Trump — and drank hot coffee and an even hotter Czech soup of ground pork and vegetables made by one of several part-time house-helps Paul and Viviana employ. That the cook was also the mayor of a nearby village could not be detected in the flavour of the broth, I thought, which was, at any rate, profound. Divišov, Paul said, was at five hundred metres, and that was real snow outside. There was even more in the courtyard before the main workshop, he said, and more was expected tonight.

Two delivery vans under snow were parked on concrete cobbles, and near them were remnants of dying autumn lawn. Near a cherry tree and a pear tree bare of their leaves, branches heavy with ice, several corrugated-roofs sheltered timber planks of many thicknesses cut from several species. A terrifyingly big bandsaw that cut logs horizontally was nearby. Crusts of snow clung to the ends of many planks, and if you half-closed your eyes, they appeared to jiggle in the sombre light, as if affected by

Brownian motion, as if they couldn't wait to be brought to life in a McNulty instrument.

In two large rooms attached to the house, paint and plaster on their walls peeling, Paul showed me more planks and sheets of timber, including spruce soundboards that were maturing in controlled atmospheres. He adjusted the climates using the kinds of humidifiers and heaters you can buy in any small-town retailer, one of them strapped up with gaffer tape, I noticed.

In faded black letters the single word STROJIRNA, meaning machine-works, in modernist block capitals loomed above the entrance to the dull-grey cement-rendered, two-storeyed

workshop, and, once inside and out of the cold, it was easy to see that mechanical saws and planers of enormous bulk and precision did a lot of the gross tasks that preceded the more exacting handiwork of humans. And it occurred to me that before powered bandsaws and planers existed, *all* the work in a piano factory had to have been done by hand. Yet even then instruments were produced at an astonishing rate, Paul told me. One of his young craftsmen — there are several women — slipped a damper jack of pear wood three millimetres thick, twelve-and-a-half wide and a hundred and twenty-five long through a massive, rumbling electric planer time and again so that it would eventually slide perfectly between rectangular holes in two rungs of rails. He had a pile of them to hone. Paul said that each pass through the machine shaved about a tenth of a millimetre from the tawny-coloured hardwood, whose grain was so tight that I searched but failed to find it, even with my loupe. After each pass, the apprentice tested the precision of its fit, how well it lifted and fell in the rails. It seemed fine to me after perhaps four or five passes, but he shaved and shaved until he was completely satisfied.

McNulty fortepianos were made of spruce, maple, beech, pear, ebony, linden and alder woods, Paul said. The white keys these days were of bone not ivory, but many of his models were — apart from the strings — devoid of metal, held taut by the classic woodworking joints, mortice and tenon, and dovetail. Pegs that take the tension of the strings are plugged into maple both ends, and frames as well as soundboards are spruce, which also plays a part in the workings of the keys. The shanks of the hammers are of pear wood, and the hammer heads — tear-shaped and less than a centimetre wide — are of linden.

Everywhere, fortepianos in varying stages of construction — one or two with sides simply blocked out, some still without keyboards and strings, their veneered cases revealing exquisite high-gloss grains — stood about in no particular pattern, and I watched how patient and unerring, in cluttered surroundings, was the work that went into them, the walls hung with chisels, saws, and knives, some in *ad hoc* cabinets. At one point, I felt that there might be enough planks of varieties of wood standing about for them to speak in unison, a timber choir, you might call it — tenor, soprano, contralto and bass — that might give a view on what Paul was doing to them, how he was making trees sing. How the slabs and planks and veneers felt about his shaping them. That he was an excellent conductor.

In an upstairs room I watched a young woman shellac ornate legs that would soon support McNulty pianos, wondering how many female lac bugs from the forests of India and Thailand had contributed their resin to a single brushstroke. A young man, a Russian whom Paul told me later had enormous promise, hammered into a maple bridge tiny brass guides that would maintain the tension and separation of strings. They had to be perfectly placed, Paul told me, and if any part of any of his pianos was ever imperfect, the part — not the whole piano — would be thrown away and a new one made. He did perfect, and that was that.

He showed me to a large table in an upstairs room where he had been experimenting with hammers, which swing on a wooden arm about half the length of a chopstick to hit the strings, making the sound. Geoffrey Lancaster had asked him to make a keyboard with wooden hammers, without the usual felt or leather surfacings. He would persist until he had succeeded in producing a sound that was *interesting*, he said. His pianos, he reminded me, were mostly copies of those of the best makers of the eighteenth and nineteenth centuries, before the advent of the modern grand piano in around 1870. The bigger, noisier animal was more difficult to tame. It was designed to produce sound that filled the increasingly large concert halls that were being built across the world. Lately, he had produced exact replicas of favourite pianos of composers such as Brahms and Liszt. The earliest fortepianos, the ones for which Haydn and Mozart and Beethoven and Schubert had written their music, were delicate and responsive, he said, their keyboards and keys a little narrower and shorter, their soundboards and mechanics designed to produce intimate tones in the salons and drawing rooms of aristocrats.

The modern piano did have a tendency to terrify pianists, Paul agreed, bass strings crossing over the others to make the soundboard resonate with more bombast, and iron frames allowing enormous tension to be applied to all the strings, meaning more strings and more sound and bigger forces at work all around, even for the player, who needed to be a heavy hitter. Fortepianos mostly had timber frames, and in many only a single string was used to make the note. In a contemporary piano, three was the norm.

It seemed the right moment to ask him why he enjoyed recreating instruments that had been superseded, why he remade the past. His only hope *was* the past, he said, and his fortepianos gave anyone who was interested the chance to play music in a way that was of the day, performances that would have been recognisable to the composer. Big piano manufacturers produced thousands of instruments a year and quite a few were duds. His workshop could produce at most a dozen. The Kawai that had been taken to the Sydney International Piano Competition had been accompanied by a gaggle of technicians but still couldn't measure up. (Piano-makers were no less prone to gossip than the rest of us, I noticed.) The Fazioli in Sydney that the finalists used was a special favourite of Paolo Fazioli, however, a very dear instrument, and that might have been why the young pianists selected it, he said. No pianos were ever culled from his workshop because of a lack of craftsmanship. They never got that far. I asked him why perfection obsessed him. He said he declined to call it that; for him it was just workmanship.

He made fortepianos because it was the only thing he knew how to do, he said. He was born in Houston and grew up in Dallas, and like many children of the sixties and seventies played the guitar. I was a dying rock-and-roll guitarist, he said, who gave it up to go to Baltimore to learn how to play properly, classically. But in my penultimate year in college, my teacher took me aside and told me I wasn't going to make it. So I took a job as a night attendant at a parking garage, which was my ideal employment because it gave me time to read. I had forfeited ambition, you might say. And one night, my eyes propped open with toothpicks, I was reading a book by Studs Terkel, the oral historian, who had interviewed people about their work. In fact, I think the book was called *Working*, but I might be wrong. And, you know, there was only one guy in the whole hundreds of pages who was happy with his job, and he was a piano tuner. And at four in the morning a light went off in my head — my road to Damascus — and I walked up the hill first thing to the music school and asked someone where I had to go to become a piano-tuner and he said Boston, so I went.

Massachusetts's capital had a harpsichord-building clique in those days, and my teacher, who was in this whole scene, had built his own instrument and got me interested. I listened to a lot of lectures on piano history, and in one of the Boston workshops a guy had machinery and plans for eighteenth-century pianos, and after two years of study I graduated as a piano technician and worked for a dollar an hour building harpsichords. I became a member of the starvation school of piano-building. You build an instrument a year and never have enough money. (Since then, I might add, said Paul, I have made two-hundred-and-ten instruments and up to fourteen in a single year.) So I made my first fortepiano, but was offered an excellent opportunity to maintain another for John Gibbons, a very fine player, on a European tour with the Orchestra of the 18th Century, Frans Brüggen's famous band. I took one look at John's piano, and it was terrible. The strings had a habit of breaking, and the case was falling apart, and John and Frans asked me if I knew where they could get a replacement. My piano, my first and only one, had been sold to the Norwegian Academy of Music in Oslo, and I said, well, there's mine up in Oslo, and Frans said he wanted it, and the academy shipped it down to Amsterdam the very next day.

When Brüggen heard it, he wanted one of mine to keep, and one of the cellists in his orchestra paid up-front cash for it. Overnight, I became a piano-maker. With the money, I rented a small workshop in Amsterdam and began reading a book, Bruce Hoadley's *Understanding Wood*. I read it over and over again while I waited for wood for my pianos to dry. Soon, orders arrived, including one from Paul Badura-Skoda who had a recording contract to honour. But his record deal fell through, and he said he didn't need the piano anymore, so Trevor Pinnock, the harpsichordist and another of the real champions of playing music on instruments for which it is written, heard mine and said he'd take over the contract. And it kind of just mushroomed from there.

I spent eight years in Amsterdam, Paul said, then moved to Prague, sharing a workshop with a harpsichord maker, then this place became available and I bought it and I've been here for twenty years. I met Viviana several years ago because she wanted one of my pianos. He smiled.

I wanted Paul's views on whether pianos could maim and, in some cases, kill. No one knew pianos better. Could malice be built into them somehow? Were they inherently dangerous? Did tragedy and pianos go hand in hand? You'd better ask Viviana about that, he said, because she performs and her father, you know, was justly famous for his sensitivity. But what do *you* think? I insisted.

The modern Steinway was an outdoor instrument, he said, and you had to wrestle with it to play it. The concert pianist is striving, Paul said, for Olympic-level performance every time he or she sets foot on the stage … at least nine-point-nine out of ten. We are talking about perfection. Every time. *Every* time. A modern piano is bigger and more static in its sound — harder to get nuances out of and therefore harder to produce differences, individual interpretations and so on. You have to work harder, and that must be nerve-racking. Mozart, Haydn, Beethoven and Schubert had almost no experience of this sort of thing — the stress — because they composed and played at an intimate level for perhaps a couple of score people in a noble's salon. There is a fierceness of engagement with modern pianos, he continued, the words he used, and Viviana will show you her father's practice Bechstein with the inside of the lid chewed out above middle C and a couple of handspans either side of it. His fingers did it. Not by scratching the varnish with fingernails, but just by the hours and hours of practice he had to put in and the repeated blows the tips of his fingers, the soft bits, delivered to the opened lid as he played. You'll see it, he said, a huge sunrise of bare wood where

the varnish has been worn away. And have you seen pianists'
hands? he asked.

Yes, I said, it was the name of the book I was intending to write.

They're enormous, he said, and I am always shocked by
the hands of Ronald Brautigam, a friend of mine who has been
recording with my pianos for years. They're just raw cement-lay-
er's hands, the hands of a brickie. And Alfred Brendel's fingertips,
which he taped over each concert to stop them from splitting open.

And Richter's, I added, which looked as if they throttled pigs.

Every time she plays, the contemporary concert pianist
has to reach certain physical limits, said Paul, then try to push
beyond them. And because of that they are people who are very
protective of their sanity. Playing the grand piano in front of an
audience of thousands is never a comfortable place to be. There
is an eerie combativeness between player and piano, the words
he used. And as pianists hone their skills and protect their sanity
— at least some of the time they protect their sanity — they are
being constantly reminded of their fragility. There are bound to
be blow-ups.

And all *he* had to do, I said, was *make* them. He smiled. His life
was here, in Divišov, and it would end here, he said, and it pleased
him. He had been lucky enough to make a successful instrument
at his very first try. He and Viviana took no holidays, and when
they travelled it was only to demonstrate McNulty pianos at trade
shows and in concerts. His schedule, seven days a week, all year
around, saw him in the workshop for anything up to a dozen hours
in every twenty-four.

But we should see the finished instruments, he said, guiding me around corners and up a tight spiral staircase of narrow

timber treads — Watch your head! — to a brightly lit attic that so astonished me that I looked around for something to lean on.

Perhaps eight different pianos gleamed like new cars in a showroom, except that this showroom eschewed young men in snappy suits, suave women in stilettos, marble floors and spotless floor-to-ceiling windows. Here the illumination was by several rudimentary skylights, the floor was of plywood and the powder-white walls were interrupted occasionally by raw pieces of piano cases and a big shabby backcloth in what appeared to be cheap brushed nylon. (I was reminded of the backcloth at Kapell's last concert.) A piano dolly was in the middle of the room, nowhere near the pianos but watching them, it occurred to me, like a sheepdog its flock. McNulty instruments, with their brass inlays and curlicues — PAUL MCNULTY, PIANOFORTE FABRIKANT, DIVIŠOV, in three decks on an opened lid — exquisitely grained and polished veneers, gold-plated decorative

roses, the latter made, said Paul, by the local metalworker who had told him that this property was up for sale, and ornately fret-worked music stands, also made locally, contrasted so sharply with the showroom's practicality, that the thought came to me that, just perhaps, Divišov pianos were the pinnacle of what man could craft from wood, among man's greatest creations in timber, and I regretted that *Australian Woodworkers' Monthly* had folded and I had no other outlet for an article about being here.

Viviana appeared from nowhere in black trousers, a black roll-neck sweater whose collar she tugged at with both hands like a pensive heroine from an early Jean-Luc Godard movie, her ginger hair thick, short and wild, a stern look on her face. She sat at an instrument and began to play then stopped to tell us in a lightly glottal-stopped accent that we were talking too much. If she was to demonstrate the pianos, we would have to remain silent, she said. She continued, moving from one instrument to another and play-ing beautifully bits of Haydn and Scarlatti, Beethoven's *Moonlight* sonata, the first few bars of the *Waldstein* sonata and Schubert's *Wanderer* fantasy, switching repertoire depending on whether she was sitting at the keyboard of the Stein copy from 1788, the Walter from 1792, the Boisselot from 1846, or Brahms's preferred piano, the ornate and lovely 1868 Streicher.

Viviana hushed us several times — I was unable to con-tain my joy at hearing these instruments and told Paul, asking him questions. She noticed. At one point she leapt up from the keyboard, beckoned me, grabbed a nearby chair, positioned it two-thirds of the way along the Walter, I think it was, and bid me to sit so that I could hear best its special harmonics. And proba-bly separate me from Paul.

The range of tones and nuances the pianos produced surprised me. Using knee levers under the keyboards and a thin push-pull steel rod above them that adjusted dampening, Viviana conjured timbres that would be impossible to reproduce on modern pianos. And although at times she pounced on the keyboard as her father must have done, producing huge volume, she made music that filled the space, which might have been similar to that of an eighteenth-century drawing room. These were pianos that looked immense fun to play, that helped you to create the sounds you were trying to produce, that didn't demand that you entered an octagon bare-knuckled, surrounded by chain-link fencing, ready to fight to the death. Their tones were elegant, pure and sweet — a little more stringy, you had to say, than modern pianos, but pure and sweet nonetheless.

Paul and I went to a corner of the attic — while Viviana concentrated on a Chopin nocturne — where he told me that his instruments were just lighter and more supple, a joy to make music on. I can see that, I said. And each piano, he said, had its own character. I could tell, I said. Viviana stopped and glared. We shut up, and she recommenced the Chopin *da capo* — from the top. The music she was playing, said Paul, fitted so well the instrument she was playing it on. That was the heart of the matter, he said, all there was to it really, and on my instruments no one needs to fear *not* performing as the composer would have wished.

Viviana finished her demonstration and said she had to fly, first to the accountant, then to make final arrangements for a short visit to Moscow. She left the day after tomorrow, but she could chat about her father tomorrow evening, she said, smiling for the first time.

AS SNOW FELL heavily, one of Paul's apprentices led me to a cream-painted residential block at the very edge of town where Paul and Viviana had found me a room for the night. An evening gloom as grey as a whale descended quickly, almost to darkness, and the apprentice handed me a bunch of keys, told me I was on the top floor, and drove off.

The building seemed to lack an entrance. Peering through glass on the ground floor, I made out in the quarter-light a kind of tea room, a kitchen and an open area with tables supporting upside-down chairs. Behind a kind of bar, shelves held bottles of dark-coloured liquors with brightly coloured labels. The bar and the tea room were devoid of life, and no one was about inside and out, no lights on in the windows above me. I trudged through the snow, circling the entire building until I found a tight, spiral stair-case in what appeared to be stainless steel, each tread drilled with many holes. I took it to the top floor, perhaps the fourth, where there was a door. I tried several keys before one worked, realising there was no chance of my freezing to death outside.

But for many minutes I stood on the perforated steel of the landing, unable to move. I had an elevated view over the road we had arrived by and its new houses. Beyond them were fields. Borders and fences were impossible to discern because of the depth of the snow, and one could make out only a few lights in houses in the far distance, which beckoned like the future. Otherwise, there was not a single sign of life, and in the breathless air snowflakes drifted, rendering the whole scene artificial, as if what I was witnessing lacked reality, had been contrived espe-cially for me. I wished I'd had my camera, but it was in the car downstairs. In the diminishing light, it probably could not have done justice to the panorama anyway. The almost-white of nearby snow at the base of the building turned to many shades of grey as I looked towards the horizon, pastures, meadows and small copses retreating into the distance as if they were theatrical flats, joining an intense grey of sky at the horizon. The softness of the greys amazed me, the galahs at JL's bounding into my thoughts. I tried to stand as still as the air, my shoes suddenly spiked and imbedded in planks. Silence overwhelmed. I have seen the fireflies of Borneo turning mangroves into Christmas trees and the vast sparkling heavens above central Australia. But what I was witnessing now was equally unworldly, even other-worldly.

I noticed a patina of ice on the railing, which led my eye to the spiral staircase and an immediate shock; it continued to rise even though I was on the top floor. Although curious to know how high it went — and why — I willed myself not to look up. Instead, I decided to imagine that it ascended forever into the gloom above me, rising, rising into another consciousness amid the leaden snow-bloated clouds, and if only I could gather myself together and mount the stairs, I might arrive at a place from which there was no turning back, as calm and as quiet as the landscape in which I was immersed, and my torment would at last be over.

VLADIMIR SOFRONITSKY was a pianistic giant, and if you read his website and watch his YouTube clips and a short Russian documentary about him archived in the ether you get the impression that he was not just mysterious, as the material asserts, but that his playing had a special magic, characterised by its emotional connection with those who heard it. It moved audiences. In the documentary, Viviana, his only daughter, a woman who must be one of Vladimir's last creations — he died in 1961 — says that her father had a connection with God when he played. His concerts in Paris in 1929 conquered the city, says the narrator of the documentary, but he was to leave the Soviet Union only once more. During the siege of Leningrad in 1941, the temperature in one concert hall was minus-three Celsius. He wore gloves, cutting out the fingertips. Afterwards, he was ecstatic, saying that the concert-goers, which the clip shows were wrapped in furs, had listened so well, and that it had been easy to play for them despite the cold. The following year he was evacuated to Moscow.

In the summer of 1945, he was woken in the middle of the night by a knock on the door of his apartment. Are you Sofronitsky, pianist, said men at door. Pack suitcase and come. Our general secretary asks for you to play at Potsdam, at conference of victorious leaders. And, at Stalin's personal bidding, he went. The film says that nature had endowed him with a passionate soul, deep intellect — his father was a physicist — and virtuosity. His sensitivity was equally big. He was completely devoid of ambition, constantly doubted himself, changed dates of concerts, delayed his appearance on the platform, at times went home at intermission or cancelled performances altogether. Mounted police were needed to control the crowds trying to get into one of his concerts, and, after another, a fan gave him a goldfish, which died soon after. Some days later, a student came to the door for her first lesson with the great Sofronitsky. The pianist opened it grief-stricken. He could not take her today because the goldfish had died, and Viviana says in the documentary that he mourned it for three days. His soul had no skin, she adds. He couldn't go into shops or use public transport because of a fear that people disliked him.

The recordings and the clip make a strong case for the argument that every one of his performances was different, that they were like life itself, a succession of unique events, and that each was an attempt to interpret music only for those who were listening. He made several recordings, but referred to them as his corpses; they were done, finished things, no longer alive. He won a Stalin prize, the Order of Lenin, and despite his dislike of the Soviet system travelled with it. He loved and respected other pianists, from Glenn Gould the mad Canadian, to Van Cliburn the Texan, to his compatriots Emil Gilels and Sviatoslav Richter. Gilels thought he was the world's best. There is a lovely story about Richter: Sofronitsky once said to him that he was a genius. Richter replied to Sofronitsky: But you are a god.

His last concert was at the Moscow Conservatory in January 1961, and he died from cancer seven months later. Viviana, the daughter of Sofronitsky's second marriage to Valentina Dushinova, one of his students, has memories of neither her father nor mother, who died when she was a toddler. But she sustains his legacy, a kind of marshal of what is written and said and thought about him.

AN ATTRACTIVE woman, she made Russian tea and sat opposite me at the kitchen table the following evening. In a cluttered living room behind us was her father's Bechstein, a cello resting on top. Even from metres away the half-moon of abrasions caused by countless hours of soft collisions that Paul mentioned was clear and startling.

In the documentary on your father, I said, the narrator calls him a *mysterious* musician. Why?

She apologised for her English and said that he was a pianist who focused on eternity, connecting direct with God, a very mysterious phenomenon. His gift, she said, was supernatural, and every performance was a new one depending on the instrument he was playing, its powers, and who was listening. One night it might work, and we all go to stars, she said, and another night it does not work at all. She said that he could make channels to the audience and God.

Was she religious? I asked.

She laughed. Not at all. It's a spiritual thing. And on some nights my father would look even from the wings of the concert hall at the audience and feel nothing, and he would go home and leave a note that the concert is cancelled.

But did he cancel because he doubted himself? Because he was frightened of the instrument on the stage?

Not at all, said Viviana. If he felt somehow that he was unable to make channels with an audience, if they could not help him create magic that night, he would cancel. She has felt it herself, she added, playing in Vienna not long ago, when the more honest thing would have been to get up and leave. But these days we have a program, she said, and you can't do that.

What you say seems to suggest, I said, that Sofronitsky was an unstable performer.

She agreed.

Was he ever frightened of the piano?

Never, she said. It's the same if a piece is long and loud and fast or if it's simple like the *Moonlight* sonata. One time it will be just boring playing and another time the audience will remember it their entire lives. She stressed, gesturing emphatically, main thing is if you have channel or you don't have channel. I wasn't entirely convinced, and asked her an obvious next question.

So your father was afraid of failing to make channels?

She wanted to explain, she said. Right now sex is very popular, she said, and there is sex when you unite with each other, and sex which is very nice and pleasant. But there is a big difference. And Viviana burst into a huge smile then peals of laughter.

Was she serious? I asked.

Yes, she said. It was not a question of technique, she added, but actually the main important thing is you make a channel.

How do you dig them? I asked.

In Russia there are two important things, she said. Love and — Paul has given me the word — *vocation*, your work. But love for work comes from *you* — she pointed abruptly, and I leant back to avoid being poked by a fingertip that was half a meter away — and it is very seldom, and you are very lucky if you have this thing in your life. So you need to soul-search to find the thing you love doing, and this you can get.

How did your father acquire his channel-digging expertise? I repeated, probably rudely.

I don't know, she said.

Our conversation seemed to be heading towards the aims and ambitions of civil engineers, so I changed direction, asking Viviana why her father was never interested in playing in the West.

If you are real artist, she said, it doesn't matter where you play. If he was ever interested in following his compatriots to the West like Richter and Gilels it was really secondary. It is much less important than being conscious of a spiritual relationship with art.

And he was okay with the Soviet government? I asked. (One source says that he suffered a lot from the hopeless stupidity, as the source describes it, of Russian officialdom.)

He was not okay with the government but it doesn't matter. Not important, because he was above it and dealing with higher matters. Governments will come and go but what you do stays. Jesus Christ says what belongs to Caesar give to Caesar and what belongs to God give to God. I am not religious, but he is a wise man. We should develop what talents God has given us, she said. Even the worst person has tiny, tiny good, and if I am successful and play for him in prison and help him connect to God, I make this channel, and it will be a plus. She smiled.

We compared hands and spans, pressing together our palms. Her span was immense compared with mine. Her little fingers almost made right angles with the palms.

I have better stretch, she said, because I am born in Moscow.

Nonsense, I said, and she threw back her head and shook with laughter.

If you go to Moscow Conservatory from the age of six then you have better span, she said.

I said that from my listening to your father's playing he was able to pick out melodic lines better than almost any other pianist I had heard. He was also unafraid to play a piece more slowly or faster than the speeds that composers mandated.

She waved a hand. What is correct tempo? What is correct pedal? This is all unimportant. He was building channels. (Here we go again, I thought.)

Classical music has become dull, she said, of no interest to most people because there is said to be only one way of playing a piece, one perfect performance, one ideal. If someone plays differently it is wrong. It's like a perfect hamburger. And as soon as a perfect performance is recognised, she added, it will be frozen there. But there is another performance, and you take the music and put it through you — she pointed at me again; I drew back — a *live creature*, and you make life. If Gould and Rachmaninoff play in world piano competitions like Sydney these days they would not make the second round. (I thought of Kenneth Broberg and instantly agreed.) This is clear. The good thing about McNulty pianos is they come from a time of playing differently and you hear absolutely differently the same piece in the same room. It was vital that people got back their creativity, she said. God created us, so we should be creative in return.

Are you sure you're not religious? I asked.

Not at all, not at all, she said, beginning to laugh again.

She lived and worked in the United States and Canada before she met Paul, she said, and in 1994 took Canadian citizenship. It was so important for people to do art, she said. Technique was not important. Creation was everything. She was at a church wedding in Canada and a black woman sang *Amazing Grace*. She had *horrible* voice, but it's best I ever heard because she had channel. Viviana wasn't laughing. Not even smiling. Just nodding her head.

It was past five o'clock, coal-black outside, and she still had loose ends to tie up for her trip. We had, at any rate, I said, found an excellent place to stop, and I got up, turned and looked with longing at Sofronitsky's piano. Could I try it? I asked, instantly regretting my request. A catastrophic replay loomed.

Of course, she said, gesturing at the keyboard. I sat on the piano stool, several emotions mounting. What a fool I was, I thought, recollecting the Spivakovsky effect. My fingers would turn to jelly, begin to shake all over the notes, make a cacophony, perhaps get stuck between the keys, as the joke goes. No music was on the stand, and I felt more vulnerable than ever. The worn arch of bare wood, a signifier of great work by a great player, humbled me, then, suddenly, from nowhere, I was overwhelmed with relief and I relaxed. For no apparent reason, an enormous contentment superseded my initial terror. I wondered if the great Russian had sat upon the stool I was sitting on, perhaps a ridiculous thought, and I realised that I was perhaps living a fleeting moment of the present infused with the past, an instant in which I could afford to cast off inhibitions, as they say, place my hands on the keys and just see what happened.

So I did, playing short bites of things I knew by heart — the aria from the *Goldberg Variations*, the first few bars of Beethoven's third and fourth piano concertos, and the piano's debut in Mozart's sublime and mysterious C-minor concerto, perhaps the greatest composition ever written for piano and orchestra.

To my ear, I had never played them more confidently, and, as my fingers wandered by themselves over the keys, Viviana left and came back with her camera and took photographs of me at the keyboard. I could have wept with joy, feeling it was the greatest compliment anyone could have paid me.

Could she Facebook them? she asked. I nodded enthusiastically.

Perhaps she was right about the channels. Maybe spectral vestiges of them had remained — important, invisible musico-archeological sluices in and around the Bechstein that Vladimir had painstakingly dug with his big bare hands, his conduits. They were still there, it seemed, irrigating the link between player and listener, player and music, between Viviana and me. I was as non-believing as she was, and I doubted that it had anything to do with God. Spirits — in a general sense — were another matter.

IN THE TARMAC black of the evening, I walked back to the workshop, flurries of snow falling, the last two or three of Paul's team rugged up and heading home in the other direction. My chat with Viviana and playing her father's Bechstein had thrilled me beyond measure. I was jubilant, in fact, joy effervescing inside me, dispelling the melancholia and uncertainty I had felt in the Kafka museum.

The brightly lit main room was empty and silent, no one working at three partly-built instruments, and I imagined that Paul was upstairs, wondering why, to start with, piano hammers needed felt or leather over their points of impact with the strings, and whether he should try a timber other than linden for the heads themselves. I debated whether to annoy him, but I was distracted by the hand tools hanging around the walls, a row of a dozen chisels here — many of them clearly old, their shafts worn down by constant sharpening — open cabinets of wrenches and screwdrivers there.

Paul had told me that sharpening chisels was twenty per cent of making pianos, taking one to a razor edge in front of me earlier in the day. Rough outlines drawn in red and black marker-pen declared the absence of spokeshaves of various sizes. Planes and grips were racked in open cabinets, and fine-toothed Japanese handsaws, handles long, blades of curious trapezoidal shapes, some appearing to have had chunks bitten out of them, hung.

They must all have specific purposes, I thought. And I looked at the backs of my own poor hands, their criss-crossed scars, the quaver with its flag on my forearm, which people sometimes see but never mention, of course.

Making them with sharp instruments had given me a kind of satisfaction in the past, and I thought back over more than a year of investigations, deciding that I could draw no *definitive* conclusions about the harm pianos could inflict, even if I was convinced that they had terrified many of the greatest pianists and even today had the capacity to damage those who were brave enough to try to master them.

Curiously, for amateur and professional pianists alike, however, playing a piano was also to come home, I decided, to take refuge in relief and contentment, an act that paradoxically imprisoned them, making painful demands once they were there. I reflected on the two occasions when JL was able to leave the stool altogether and watch himself play, floating above the keyboard, surprised at what he could do, astounded by the sounds he was making, free of the piano yet controlling it. And I also thought of Dr K's visitation in the Kafka museum and his contention that we were all confused and inept, going around in circles, and that I was transferring blame to pianos for the accident that had maimed my dear sister.

Was I more stable, though? Had the past year made any difference? Was I thinking more clearly? Was I better? Did I need to keep the wheel spinning, grip the dead man's handle so tightly? The awful thing was that I couldn't tell, couldn't be sure. Anna's subsequent decision to kill herself because she could no longer play, while destroying her, had also irredeemably diminished me, of course, and it appeared almost certain now that I would never again become a whole self, a self completely worthy of an enjoyable life. *Do something*? I'd done what I could. Everything I could. Almost everything, I thought, surrounded by sharp blades.

Fomite

More novels from Fomite...

Joshua Amses — *During This, Our Nadir*
Joshua Amses — *Ghatsr*
Joshua Amses — *Raven or Crow*
Joshua Amses — *The Moment Before an Injury*
Charles Bell — *The Married Land*
Charles Bell — *The Half Gods*
Jaysinh Birjepatel — *Nothing Beside Remains*
Jaysinh Birjepatel — *The Good Muslim of Jackson Heights*
David Brizer — *Victor Rand*
L. M Brown — *Hinterland*
Paula Closson Buck — *Summer on the Cold War Planet*
Dan Chodorkoff — *Loisaida*
Dan Chodorkoff — *Sugaring Down*
David Adams Cleveland — *Time's Betrayal*
Paul Cody— *Sphyxia*
Jaimee Wriston Colbert — *Vanishing Acts*
Roger Coleman — *Skywreck Afternoons*
Marc Estrin — *Hyde*
Marc Estrin — *Kafka's Roach*
Marc Estrin — *Speckled Vanities*
Marc Estrin — *The Annotated Nose*
Zdravka Evtimova — *In the Town of Joy and Peace*
Zdravka Evtimova — *Sinfonia Bulgarica*
Zdravka Evtimova — *You Can Smile on Wednesdays*
Daniel Forbes — *Derail This Train Wreck*
Peter Fortunato — *Carnevale*
Greg Guma — *Dons of Time*
Richard Hawley — *The Three Lives of Jonathan Force*
Lamar Herrin — *Father Figure*
Michael Horner — *Damage Control*
Ron Jacobs — *All the Sinners Saints*
Ron Jacobs — *Short Order Frame Up*
Ron Jacobs — *The Co-conspirator's Tale*
Scott Archer Jones — *And Throw Away the Skins*
Scott Archer Jones — *A Rising Tide of People Swept Away*
Julie Justicz — *Degrees of Difficulty*
Maggie Kast — *A Free Unsullied Land*
Darrell Kastin — *Shadowboxing with Bukowski*
Coleen Kearon — *#triggerwarning*
Coleen Kearon — *Feminist on Fire*
Jan English Leary — *Thicker Than Blood*
Diane Lefer — *Confessions of a Carnivore*
Diane Lefer — *Out of Place*

www.ingramcontent.com/pod-product-compliance
Lightning Source LLC
Chambersburg PA
CBHW021304190726
48288CB00003B/680